Aviary

For Shelley —
 With my very best —
Thank you _____
        Deirdre

Aviary

A Novel

DEIRDRE MCNAMER

MILKWEED EDITIONS

© 2021, Text by Deirdre McNamer
All rights reserved. Except for brief quotations in critical articles or reviews, no part of this book may be reproduced in any manner without prior written permission from the publisher:
Milkweed Editions, 1011 Washington Avenue South, Suite 300, Minneapolis, Minnesota 55415.
(800) 520-6455
milkweed.org

First paperback edition, published 2022 by Milkweed Editions
Printed in Canada
Cover design by Mary Austin Speaker
Cover art by Allegra Lockstadt

22 23 24 25 26   5 4 3 2 1

First Edition

978-1-57131-142-9

Library of Congress Cataloging-in-Publication Data

Names: McNamer, Deirdre, author.
Title: Aviary / Deirdre McNamer.
Description: First edition. | Minneapolis, Minnesota : Milkweed Editions, 2021. | Summary: "Aviary explores the rich and hidden facets of human character, as illuminated by the mysterious connections among the residents of a senior residence in Montana"-- Provided by publisher.
Identifiers: LCCN 2020051026 (print) | LCCN 2020051027 (ebook) | ISBN 9781571311382 (hardback) | ISBN 9781571317384 (ebook)
Classification: LCC PS3563.C38838 A95 2021 (print) | LCC PS3563.C38838
    (ebook) | DDC 813/.54--dc23
LC record available at https://lccn.loc.gov/2020051026
LC ebook record available at https://lccn.loc.gov/2020051027

Milkweed Editions is committed to ecological stewardship. We strive to align our book production practices with this principle, and to reduce the impact of our operations in the environment. We are a member of the Green Press Initiative, a nonprofit coalition of publishers, manufacturers, and authors working to protect the world's endangered forests and conserve natural resources. *Aviary* was printed on acid-free 100% postconsumer-waste paper by Friesens Corporation.

For my luminous sisters, Megan and Kate
And again, and always, for Bryan

IT'S LIKE A LION
AT THE DOOR

1

While they slept, the sun lifted itself above the mountain surround to spread light on the little city below. Inside that city, urban deer glided across frozen November lawns to return to their hollows under backyard pines. Feline huntresses licked the blood off their paws and went home for kibbles and stomach rubs. A tied-up, shivering dog made three tight circles in the dirt and began to bark. Two joggers with lights on their shoes panted grimly and stepped up their pace. An old Falcon moved slowly, ejecting rolled newspapers onto front steps. And then a roseate calm prevailed, and the mountains moved in closer.

While they slept, in their boxes inside the bigger box of their four-story building, street sounds began: the buses, the early workers. The river moved with low-water deliberation through the center of town, carrying oblong shards of ice beneath one bridge and then another. A muttering man with crazy hair dragged a lumpy sleeping bag from a stand of tall bushes and resettled himself beneath the second bridge, up under the trusses, a few yards from the coffee place on the ground floor of the new bank.

They slept not far from the river in a neighborhood thickly planted with maples and tall old homes, in a twenty-four-unit residence for seniors called Pheasant Run.

In a normal autumn, the maples put on showy displays, fanning high into the sky, then shattering into slow red waterfalls until the branches were lattices, not crowns, and the sky was twice as large. This year, the leaves have refused to drop. They have clung, ash-colored, to the branches, inspiring general unease and several letters to the newspaper, which invited a certified arborist to weigh in. He explained that the normal separation process between leaf and twig produces a membrane that seals off the leaf and enables it to fall. Extreme cold at the wrong time, like the shocking, subzero stretch of days that happened in October, can derail that process, he said. The tree "basically clutches," and the leaves stay attached. They were strange, those gray leaves, abiding in the wrong place at the wrong time. They turned the trees to sepia-toned photographs, or remembered trees, or witnesses to some sapless aftermath.

They slept at Pheasant Run, and then they woke and prepared to move into a day with nothing, yet, about it to suggest the small and large shocks to come.

Faint, predictable smells trickled into the hallways: oatmeal, burned toast. Some televisions were turned on for talk shows or weather, and a few were loud enough, because of their owners' hearing difficulties, that the adjacent tenants began another day feeling cranky and contemplating notes of complaint.

The morning noises tended not to include conversation, as most of the residents lived alone or with an ailing, late-sleeping spouse.

At six thirty, Cassie McMackin in #412, an early riser by habit, drank her coffee and counted the pills she had accumulated during her late husband's long decline. There were relaxants that had unsuccessfully addressed his night roaming, plus several versions of painkillers, prescribed after two falls and some broken ribs, and so dizzy-making for Neil that he started giving them wary, sidelong looks whenever she urged one on him, and it soon became clear that nothing was better than something.

Now she had a couple of fistfuls in the narcotic and soporific categories, and this evening she would take them all, with antinausea medication and as much wine as she could get down. It was time. She had become tired of the world. Her blood didn't want to go anywhere anymore, and had it not been for the instructions of her bossy and indefatigable heart, it wouldn't. She didn't want to occupy some interminable waiting room where nothing was wrong and nothing was right, her motions mechanical, eyes on the tyrant clock. It was time.

At eighty-seven, she was fine-boned and straight-backed, and she tended to wear interesting clothes, like the silk robe she'd thrown on over her nightgown, a shimmering gold-toned garment with bat-wing sleeves. Her silver hair framed her face in a short pageboy. The red lipstick and frank black eyebrows of her earlier days had muted to softer shades, but it was a face that echoed unusual beauty, still.

Right this moment, what she missed was the prospect of a second cup of coffee with her friend, John Quant, who had moved, a year ago, into an apartment on the third floor of the building, directly beneath her own. Soon after they met, they had progressed from polite greetings to longer conversations, to morning coffee, to dinner in Cassie's apartment every week or so, with candles and maybe a TV movie with dessert. She had felt in his company as if she was emerging from years of emotional and physical hibernation. Her happiness shocked her.

She liked his looks—tall and sharp-shouldered, his eyes an inquiring blue—and she liked his wit, his laughter, and his combination of irreverence and courtliness. Eventually, she had felt between them a tacit acknowledgment of an alliance that could only be called romantic, in the sense that it fanned outward into whatever futures they would be granted, and it shimmered with excitement in that space.

And then, four weeks ago, there had been a sharp knock on her door, and he told her he was moving back to the little town up north where he had been a boy. For the first time since she'd known him he seemed evasive; he said only that Pheasant Run was not a good fit for him anymore, that he didn't like the feel of the place, and he particularly didn't like the new on-site manager, Herbie Bonebright. He told her he didn't feel he had a choice. He wouldn't look at her straight on. He had closed and locked the door to himself.

And he was gone, in a blink. She'd heard not another word from him, and knew she wouldn't. All she could do was add him to her list of those who'd left. John Quant, and before him her only child. And her husband of six decades. They'd flown away, leaving her craning her head skyward, aghast, as they became pinpricks and disappeared. She couldn't fully believe it, still. The flights. This final aloneness.

Down the hall in #406, Viola Six breathed out the blue vapors of a receding dream. *It is near*, the walls whispered. *It is nearly at the door.* In the dream, a man in a suit had approached her from a distance, requesting payment in full, yanking off his face to reveal something that looked exactly the same. The terror of it had shocked her awake.

Rising shakily, she gathered herself to make a cup of tea, then padded to the living room window to wait for full, dispelling daylight to arrive. A long-legged cat jumped from a tree branch to the roof of a tall house across the street. It climbed the steep slope and perched near the chimney, inky and totemic against the silvering sky. *Who do you think you are?* Viola asked it, and caught a glimpse of her young self dancing wildly with a stranger at a roadhouse near the lumber mill. Her fiancé, Ollie, leaned against the bar and looked at his shoes.

Increasingly, Viola's interrogations of her surroundings were rebounding as memories that accused or threatened her. The phenomenon gave her the panicky feeling that she lived in a sealed cavern that was nothing but Viola enclosing Viola. She was the walls; she was the interior; ongoing human life was somewhere outside. The feeling increased when she was particularly anxious about her financial circumstances, as she was today. If Captain, the man she took up with in her sixties, hadn't convinced her to buy into a scam that depleted every penny of her savings, she wouldn't be living now on minimal Social Security and a small widow's pension from Ollie, three-fourths of her income going to her rent and food. The other fourth she allocated down to the penny, and if there were unforeseen expenses, as there had been this month, she had to live for a few days or a week on dry cereal and powdered milk, plus some canned goods from the food bank. She knew, in her worst moments, that she was just a few small reversals away from homelessness, that it waited for her, patient and dead-eyed, just out of her sight.

To distract herself, she sat down at her typewriter to work on her memoirs, hoping she could complete a section she'd begun a week earlier that concerned her temporary escape from Ollie in the late sixties and her subsequent month in Europe, traveling alone on meager savings accumulated over many years, ecstatic with possibility. She held her curved old fingers over the typewriter keys, but she couldn't seem to type and finally let her hands fall to her sides.

Next to her typewriter, she'd propped the photo that a flower vendor had taken of her as she leaned, insouciant, against a carved white pillar in Rome. Her long hair shone, and her face was full and smooth. She wore a wicked grin, the one she sometimes tried to recreate in the bathroom mirror as an antidote to the wrinkled mouth, the shrunken, docile eyes that met her gaze. Today, though, it was too much; the gap between her and that person in Rome was too wide. She turned the photo facedown on the desk and closed her eyes against a brief and terrible vision of herself, curled on the sidewalk under a large piece of cardboard.

"Not me," she whispered. "Not that."

In the basement of Pheasant Run, inside one of the slat-doored storage units, a boy named Clayton Spooner roused briefly from a long sleep, then sank back helplessly into the dusty quilt that held him safe. He shook off the residue of a long dream filled with sirens and flame-breathing birds that swooped down to pluck enemies from skyscraper roofs and drop them into a yellow, snake-filled lake on the next planet over.

His neck felt twisted, crooked, and sore. He had slept with a shallow cardboard box for a pillow, and he reached around in the gloom for something kinder. Powdery light sifted through the slats of the door, cutting everything inside with pale bars. One bar bent itself across something that looked like bunched material, a sloppily folded curtain perhaps, and he reached over and pulled it to him. He adjusted it under his neck and stared at the spaces between the slats and tried to think about everything that had brought him, so young, to his prison of a life. Bullied, drugged by doctors, enraged; stationed on the outside of everything calm and consolatory, peering in, until the end of time.

Most days, nothing much happened at Pheasant Run until midmorning, when the mailman arrived. They had their Facebook and their email, most of the residents, but a real letter was another thing altogether. And most still wanted any income—a pension, their Social Security—to

arrive as checks, though it meant mailing them to the
bank with deposit slips, or making the sometimes complicated trip downtown.

Around ten o'clock, the elevator came alive to ferry
its cargo. In the lobby, a polite and faintly excited milling
occurred while the mail was dropped behind the small
brass doors banked on the wall. And then keys were retrieved and their owners discovered something, or nothing, or something in between, ridiculous and empty, like
a flyer for a hemp festival or a brochure for oxygen sys-
tems tailored to individual lifestyles.

Anyone who got an actual, identifiable personal letter studied the envelope, studied it again, smiled in a
way that was particular to the occasion because most of
the recipients were all too aware that most of the people
shutting the brass doors of the boxes had gotten nothing.
Mostly nothing. And it was perhaps because of that fact
that the mailman tended to talk in soft, respectful tones,
as if he were at a memorial.

It had been the same man for several years now. He
was lean and lined from the elements, and he wore log-
ger boots through every season. He was patient with the
not-infrequent requests that he take another look in his
bag for an expected piece of mail. He touched the women
lightly on the tops of their hands and offered the men a
gruff shoulder thump from time to time. He seemed to be
aware of his role as the personification of both possibility and disappointment and walked the distance between
those points in a careful and deft manner.

When he was gone, the lobby felt irrelevant and somehow too bright, and so the lone elevator was summoned, and

it clicked and sighed and fell and climbed again, and eventually everyone was back in his or her separate space and day.

A week ago, the mailman had come and gone as usual, but the elevator button had produced no movement, and the residents could hear, a floor or two up the shaft, the sounds of vehement banging.

It was the new manager, Herbie, once again trying to fix something he knew nothing about. The elevator had jammed shut on the second floor, trapping two residents inside, and he had arrived to hit the door's bottom with a wrench, at length, before he gave up and called the repair company, which took an hour to arrive. Herbie's theory, he said afterward, was that the door was slightly misaligned with the groove on that floor, and might be restored without recourse to expensive outsiders.

The building's residents didn't know what exactly the repair company had done, but the remedy was clearly temporary because the elevator had now acquired an ominous ticking sound. And since this potentially malfunctioning elevator was the only one in a building whose occupants had reached various stages of physical impairment—more than a few dreaded the prospect of navigating several flights of stairs—traveling in it had become a quiet terror. Think about a medical emergency. Think about fire, about howling dogs and the blocked opening of the cave.

There existed, then, a recent wariness among the residents of Pheasant Run, about the building itself and about the manager, who had been installed on the premises by the property management company that the building's condominium owners had hired recently to replace a predecessor.

Longleap Enterprises had come forward to offer its services at a much lower cost, one that seemed remarkably sensitive to the fixed incomes of the building's residents, the quiet distempers of the building itself, the erratic condominium market, and a long period of deferred maintenance. The company moved Herbie into a recently vacated second-floor apartment owned by a businessman who lived out of state.

Within days of his occupancy, several residents raised complaints about him: that he was lazy, that he lacked the barest handyman skills, that he frequently disappeared for hours at a time, that his manner could be brusque, and that the spelling on the notes he left around the building was a baboon's. (The building's water would be turned off soon for several hours of repair to the boiler, said his most recent note in the elevator. "If not fixed now, we will be playing catsup.") Worst of all, he had, within a week of moving in, caused a small grease fire in his kitchen that set off the alarms and put everyone in the building severely on edge. Though he had extinguished it in a matter of minutes, the odor of ash lingered for days.

There was also the matter of the renters moving out. Most of the condominium owners in the building also owned an apartment or two that they rented. In the six weeks since Herbie had arrived, three renters had departed abruptly, and their apartments remained vacant. Herbie, some were saying, had bullied them into leaving. But why?

His work uniform was a Hawaiian shirt, Bermuda shorts, and flip-flops. On colder days, he replaced the flip-flops with plastic clogs and added a fleece vest. On his big bald head, he wore a Steelers cap with a long brim that shaded rimless glasses embedded in a pudgy, forgettable face. The lenses looked like something a crow would want to pick up.

His impassive face, combined with his habit of wearing tropical clothes at all times, conferred upon him a kind of ethereal remove, as if Pheasant Run and its residents were a mosquito dream he was having as he lolled in a hammock a wide world away from them all.

At seven this morning, Herbie descended to the lobby in the ticking elevator. His habit was to walk three blocks to a sports bar that served a cheap breakfast. He always left on the dot, having informed the residents that, for the next hour, he was off the grid, absolutely—no phone, no iPad—and any nonemergency problems were their own.

Today, he left the building, but he didn't go to the sports bar. Instead, he walked around the neighborhood for a while, then turned down the alley behind Pheasant Run and pulled on a rusty door that opened on stairs to the basement parking garage. He drove his car out of the garage and parked it in the alley in a spot that couldn't be seen from the building or the street. Upon reentering the basement area, he summoned the elevator.

Huffing slightly, he dry-swallowed an oblong white pill and prepared himself for the unusual demands of the day ahead. He had messages to convey in no uncertain terms. He had responses to imagine and missteps to avoid. He had, perhaps—this realization came to him in a toxic rush—his own life to keep safe. Unbelievably, it had come to this. They might already have him partly erased.

2

The fourth floor, this early morning, was strangely quiet. Most days, Cassie McMackin woke to the presence of Viola Six's manual typewriter clattering away at the other end of the hall, and it gave her a small boost. She'd think about how the sharp taps, the pauses, the ping of the carriage return had not a whiff of the casual or offhand. Typewriter typing always sounded like a speech. And the way a person had to sit at a typewriter—confrontational, alert—reinforced the intensity of the effort.

By contrast, the postures assumed by those composing messages on their smartphones or iPads were furtive, whispery. Their arms, their bodies, did not seem central, or even important, to the effort. The body made a cave around the device, and the digits tapped and scuffed somewhere in the interior. Watching her fellow humans' involvement with their communication tools, Cassie had the growing sense that bodies, as bodies, were becoming vestigial on a mass scale. More and more people clearly conducted their social lives, their travel, their shopping, their entertainment, and their learning in a realm that had almost nothing to do with moving their corporeal selves through space. They existed mostly in the big brain, the forest of pixels.

She felt an overwhelming tenderness at times for the younger denizens of this brave-or-not new world. They'd lived their entire lives in a glittering roar of data, images, gossip, greetings, stunts, games, polls, exhortations, lists, porn, mayhem, and ads—all of it arriving and leaving so rapidly that it couldn't form abiding constellations of persuasion or experience. How, then, could they feel assured that they had a hand in creating themselves, by selecting and evaluating what to pay attention to?

Not that she wanted to be a Luddite. She didn't. She could appreciate the liquid beauty of the new technologies and webbings, everything so small and instant. And it was undeniably innovation on a stupendous, species-altering scale. Also, at the personal level, it was sometimes comforting to her to know that bodies were becoming somewhat irrelevant to experience. Socialization had become unlinked from physical movement or physical effort. Being old, in physical decline, unable to move very far or very fast, didn't matter so much inside the communal brain.

Maybe that, the hive, was what would be shipped to another planet when this one became physically uninhabitable. Maybe bodies wouldn't even come along. And for that matter, what about vampires? Why the fixation in popular culture with vampires, bloodsuckers, exsanguinators, those emptiers of the bodily life force? Could it be an intuitive recognition on the part of the species that the individual, autonomous body was being displaced, was going away? Could visions of vampires be a way to inoculate en masse against the oncoming rupture?

Oh, stop! Cassie shook her head hard. These were the musings of either prescience or senility, and she didn't have the energy to make the distinction. They were also, she knew, her mind trying to run from itself, from the memories that could bring her to her knees and the knowledge that she was about to leave it all behind.

The pills resided inside an old printer that she'd stashed, minus its depleted cartridge, at the back of a closet. Her daughter Marian had bought the printer and a desktop computer for her, and she'd tried for some months to use them, but that was years ago. She finally got so irritated—the computer was constantly asking her if she wanted to update this or that, constantly framing her emails with ads, like an adrenalized huckster barging into a private conversation—that she reverted to longhand and stamps but kept the computer and printer on the faint chance that she'd someday change her mind. Marian had mildly reminded her that a letter took a week to reach her in Beirut, where she worked as a senior wire service reporter, but she hadn't nagged. Cassie's last letter to her, the frankest and most loving she ever wrote, arrived three days after a bomb in a vegetable market blew Marian off the face of the earth. Five years now she had been gone, outlasted only a few months by her father Neil.

Cassie never told Neil about Marian. He was in the hospital when the word came, struggling with a respiratory infection, and had reached the point, mentally, where he had trouble retrieving Cassie's name. He knew something was wrong that day—he kept searching her face for clues—but she said only that she had been very worried about him and nothing else was upsetting her. She couldn't bear to tell him that his daughter had been annihilated, that he would never see her again. It would have been like loading bricks on the back of a child. It would have told him that nothing about this life came out the way it was supposed to. And so she didn't. And three months later, he had moved on, or out, or over, to inhabit the same absence his daughter did.

Oh my allies, my loves, she thought. *My lost ones who, at the very end, have left me now so lost.*

She had a recorder she had bought at a yard sale. It was the kind that had been innovatively small when it came out. Now it was laughably out of date, but it worked, and it had come with a small box filled with empty micro-cassettes. They were exactly like the microcassettes she'd used in her first telephone answering machine. She still had those because she never erased the messages but simply replaced each cassette when it was full. In the bottom drawer of her dresser was a shoebox filled with voices leaving her messages. "Call me," they said. "Would you like me to pick you up?" they said. And because most of them were from people long dead, she had listened to them only when she could, and sometimes, listening to them, she had wept.

For the past few months, Cassie had talked into her tape recorder from time to time, saying whatever came into her mind. At times she pretended she talked to a sympathetic, imaginative human, one eager to hear anything she wanted to say, happy to listen to her talk as long as she liked. Other times she viewed the dispatches as auditory Post-it Notes. Mark this. It might be some odd snippet she'd found in the newspaper, or read on a sign, or overheard on a walk. It didn't have to be portentous. It just had to confer a delicate quiver of disruption or irony.

Her first idea was to explore what her life had added up to, what seemed worth remembering. Why had she chosen what she'd chosen? Why had she suffered in the ways she had? What had enlivened her? What would she do differently?

Smaller, odder questions then began to surface. What is most strange about the experience of life on this earth? How do our fellow creatures behave? What are the smallest components of joy? Caught enigmas. She'd heard the phrase somewhere and it seemed to apply.

On this last day, she would play back her recordings and then decide whether to destroy them or not. Who would care, really? After John Quant, the only person she considered a friend, if not a particularly close one, was Viola Six. And Viola was, quite possibly, losing her mind.

She hoped Viola's silent typewriter didn't mean she was getting ready to pay an early-morning visit and expand upon the television program she'd seen about scheming real estate developers in Spain who terrorized old people out of their apartments so they could obtain the properties cheap. Granny rattlers, the smart-alecky reporter had called them.

"One group of poor women actually sued a group of the rattlers and won," Viola had told her. "Aging Davids against corporate Goliaths. And it's not just Spain. The

UN is investigating far and wide." Her eyes, as she told the story, widened with excited fear.

This conversation had taken place yesterday in the lobby, near the mailboxes. Others were present, of course, and Cassie found herself wishing Viola would speak more softly, or at least forge some kind of context for her report.

"The point being," Viola said, "it could easily happen here." She fixed a dark look on the assembled as the mailman strode through the front door. "It's safe to say that Spain has no monopoly on granny rattlers."

Viola also had fervent theories about Herbie Bonebright and had promised to share them with Cassie very soon. Was she taking medication that made her so paranoid and voluble? And what was she writing so doggedly at her typewriter? Letters, perhaps. But to whom? She seemed basically alone, except for her son Rod, a seedy sort who came and went infrequently. *Alone, but fiercely self-contained*, Cassie thought. Her demise would be a shock to Viola, but not a lot more than that.

Viola's agitation made Cassie deeply uneasy. They had too much in common for her to be able to place Viola in some category that didn't actually or potentially include herself. They were both in their mid-eighties, both living alone. They both read books—real ones—and kept up with the real news. They both were living out their days, a few doors from each other, in a condominium building, their "fair house built upon another man's ground." The line came to her from the Shakespeare series on *Masterpiece Theater*—she couldn't remember which play it was from—and it accurately summarized a feeling she knew Viola shared: that in old age, one's presence was no longer anchored to earthly life in any reliable way. A hovering had begun, above a world that now belonged, in all substantive senses, to others.

It was a fearful thought, and fear was such a meaty, breathing thing. What was that creepy old poem, maybe a nursery rhyme?

It's like a lion at the door;
And when the door begins to crack,
It's like a stick across your back;
And when your back begins to smart,
It's like a penknife in your heart;
And when your heart begins to bleed,
You're dead, and dead, and dead indeed.

To banish it, she put on her birdsong CD and did her stretching exercises. She imagined herself as a tangerine-colored finch, stretching her wings to move swiftly through canopies of glittering leaves. Move now. Enter this last day.

"I needed someone," she said aloud. "And I had hoped for just one more person to need me."

She took some deep breaths and opened the living room curtain. Apart from the strange, furred trees, everything looked mostly as it usually did, this early-winter dawn: the pink sky, the encircling mountains, the dark cat that navigated the gambreled roof of the tallest house. All of it seemed, in some way, a map. Why, she wondered, had she never found a way to read it?

3

Viola Six's only child, Roderick, had borrowed her rent payment to go to Jackpot, Nevada, promising to repay her before it was due on the tenth. He'd told her the trip was to investigate the possibility of opening a Jack in the Box franchise, but she'd received no money and no word, and she had to assume that her $700 resided now in a casino vault.

Nothing, then, to pay her landlord, Rydell Clovis, a retired university professor who lived down the long hall in #410, one of two units in the building that he owned. She would simply have to go to him and explain. The thought made her face burn, as he was an imperious, smooth-voiced man whose manner called up a phrase from her grandmother's Psalms: *His words were softer than oil, yet they were drawn swords.*

On her desk, under the facedown photo of herself, was a letter from Mavis Krepps, the president of the condominium association, which had been distributed to both owners and renters a week ago. It was so long and complicated that Viola knew she would have to read it several more times before she understood it fully. The gist, however, was clear: condo values at Pheasant Run had steeply declined over a period of years, ever since revised borrowing regulations had drastically reduced the pool of potential buyers; renters in the building were now inexplicably moving out, which further affected those who owned the units; the owners were reluctant to raise rents because they were well aware that the financial burden would be untenable for some; deferred maintenance loomed; and there was the possibility that the association might decide to sell the entire building to an unnamed party.

If that happened, Viola and the building's other renters would have just a month before they had to vacate. "As always," Mrs. Krepps had added unnecessarily, "if a tenant is evicted for cause (felonious damage, harboring a pet, nonpayment of rent, etc.), the premises must be vacated within the week."

Mavis Krepps had long ago been a classics instructor at a small college somewhere in the Midwest and she liked to salt her communications with references to antiquity. She finished her letter with a plea for Olympian calm amid the uncertainty.

"Rumors abound, most of them without substance. Please remember that nothing regarding a potential buyout has been written in stone, or is even close to the stone-writing phase. In addition, it is simply not true that the no-pet rule applies to goldfish or small caged birds, as several renters say they have been told. In closing, I will leave you with a thought from Hesiod circa 700 BC: 'Gossip is mischievous, light and easy to raise, but grievous to bear and hard to get rid of. No gossip ever dies away entirely, if many people voice it: it too is a kind of divinity.' A thought to live by! Have a lovely weekend!"

Viola clenched her eyes. *Cast me not off in the time of old age; forsake me not when my strength faileth.* The words came to her and made her wish she weren't an atheist. What a comfort it would be to say them and believe, as her grandmother had, that they made their way to a gargantuan, sympathetic Ear.

Heavy on her mind was the documentary she had seen recently about real estate developers in Spain who were intimidating old people into moving out of their rent-controlled apartments so the properties could be renovated and sold for astronomical sums. They stopped at nothing: burglary, threats, maintenance neglect, even installing criminal elements on the premises.

And now—could it be coincidence?—Pheasant Run had this new on-site property manager, Herbie, and there was nothing about him that didn't seem suspect.

The man could put on an amiable face and talk pleasantly about lawn mowing and garbage pickup when the spirit moved him, but Viola sensed strongly that he was a gangster, essentially, and not impossibly an ex-con. Those two eyeteeth weren't missing for nothing.

At least three other tenants—all of them renters—had confided to her that Herbie had come to them with bizarre threats and accusations. He would say he smelled a dog on the premises and that the tenant's days were numbered. He would refuse to fix a wonky stove burner or a bathroom leak and tell the tenant the problem was in his or her head. He refused requests to test smoke alarms, and, pressed by courtly Leo Uberti in #402 to do so without further delay, had called him a mental case to his face.

To the building's condominium owners, on the other hand, he presented a dim but helpful face and scurried around as if he lived to be of assistance. Who was he, anyway? What was his plan? What were his orders?

She tried, now, to blink herself crisply and confidently into the day. She had to banish the specter of herself under a piece of cardboard, or in a Medicaid nursing home that breathed urine and utter exhaustion. She had to trust that her landlord, Clovis, was a reasonable man and would exhibit a degree of flexibility. And perhaps, too, the sale of the entire building was only wishful thinking on the owners' part and would never happen. There was no reason to anticipate disaster.

Perhaps Roderick would even come through with the money he owed her. She tried to banish the image of her aging only child driving off to Jackpot in his old Impala with the drooping tailpipe, again so misguided about the course of his life that it made her light-headed. Every initiative Rod undertook—the bogus marriage to the Slovakian teenager, selling special vitamins for guard dogs, the parrot-breeding enterprise—had been idiotic and a disaster. On top of that, she didn't really like him. Never had.

She wobbled a bit as she stood. Her toes hurt more than they usually did, and her muscles, as usual, seemed to be taking a nap. How long had it been since she had been able to move with alacrity, or even with a kind of stately aged smoothness? Not since the botched knee replacement and then the procedure that was said to have unbotched it but had actually left her with so little strength that her balance was thrown off and she took a few falls, including the big one that landed her for a month in bed.

"Another crash like that, and life as you know it will be over!" said Rod, who had never been successful at masking his darkest wishes with a veneer of concern.

It had been a week of difficult letters. Two days ago, she had finished an important one to her neighbor Cassie McMackin, whom she trusted instinctively, though she wondered at her seeming unconcern about a building sale. The unsent letter was Viola's insurance against simply evaporating from the zeitgeist, in case she had to depart the building suddenly and without explanation as a result of a letter she had sent a day earlier to Longleap Enterprises. In it, she had voiced her opinion that Longleap was a front for real estate developers trying to force out the building's occupants, mostly through the efforts of the new on-site manager, Herbie Bonebright. She had a good idea what his real job was: to scare renters into leaving, which would push the condo association in the direction of selling. "Please be aware that some of us are onto you, and we ask you to cease and desist or we will alert the proper authorities," she had finished.

As soon as the note disappeared down the mail chute, she realized what she had done. She had made herself a rabbit in their headlights. All they had to do now was mow her down in some fashion and make it look like an accident.

This had made an escape plan necessary. After writing her letter to Cassie, she had put it, her phone, fifty dollars in cash, and her emergency credit card in the zippered pocket of her pink ski jacket. This afternoon, she decided now, she would take the city bus to the downtown terminal, get the next bus to the airport, and buy a one-way ticket to Los Angeles. There she would post the letter, pay cash for a bus to Santa Barbara, and begin her new life.

Rod had given her the phone in return for the Jack in the Box loan, and even taken the time to show her some of its more extravagant features before he left. She suspected he'd stolen it, and that as soon as she used it, her whereabouts would be signaled to the police and she'd be arrested for some kind of fraud. That was the sort of thing that could happen when Rod gave you a gift. So she would leave the phone, wrapped in a newspaper, on a bench at the downtown bus terminal. She liked the thought of it resting there, sending out its tiny futile signals while she boarded a long silver jet and rode it through the clouds to the Pacific.

She made another cup of tea and drank it slowly, then decided that since she was up and around, she might as well take the elevator to the basement and retrieve her gun and her Thanksgiving decorations from her storage unit. She liked to tack her crepe-paper turkey with the ruffled tail to her door at least two weeks before the holiday because November was such a grim, dark month and anything vivid and celebratory could only help. She would do that today, so no one would suspect anything was out of the usual with her. Her gun, a .22 pistol given to her by Ollie many decades ago when he was working night shift at the mill, belonged right now in her apartment, so she could use it if she had to. Though there might not be bullets. She would have to see.

It was only 7:20, and no one was likely to be up and about except Herbie, who would have left for breakfast, so she didn't change from her pajamas and bed jacket. When the elevator door opened, she was startled and embarrassed to see Leo Uberti, her neighbor down the hall. He looked just as surprised as she felt. He was breathing rapidly, as if he had a heart condition he'd kept under wraps.

Uberti was a retired insurance agent who had given himself in his golden years to his first love, oil painting. Sometime in the past few months, he had grown a thin goatee that was only slightly paler than his skin, and he had a new-looking stocking cap pulled low. He smelled faintly of turpentine, as he always did. His eyes were large and kind. Viola didn't know him well, but had always felt, in his presence, a certain calm. Maybe it had something to do with her sense that he seemed to live almost entirely in his imagination and therefore had no stake in making trouble for anyone in the flesh.

"Mrs. Six," he said, tipping his fingers to the rim of an imaginary fedora. "I was just going to tap on your door to see if a fellow early bird could spare some coffee."

"Anything wrong?" she asked, holding the door open.

"It's nothing," he said quickly, patting his sternum. "Got moving too fast." He looked at her a little more closely. "And we are arrayed in the raiment of evening, I see," he said gently.

"I'm sneaking down to get some things from my storage unit," Viola said. "I had no idea anyone would be running around yet."

"'Running' is putting it very kindly," Uberti said. He took a deep breath.

"Come get the coffee in ten minutes," she said.

"I think I'll probably lie down for a while," he said. "This day already feels a little strange on the edges, wouldn't you say?" He took a long, shaky breath and tipped his absent hat.

In the basement, Viola stared at the dim hallway of the wooden-slatted storage units. Something was wrong with hers. The padlock was gone, the hasp swung loose, and the door was fastened shut with twine. She stood frozen, a few feet away. There was a smell. It was greasy clothes and dirty hair, with an overtone of something yeasty and sweaty. There was a sound behind the door. It was small and conical, air sipped in, air blown out. It paused and something shifted. An involuntary squeak came from her throat, and she slid her slippered feet backward until she could make her body turn toward the elevator door. She battered the call button, another squeak leaping from her. How long would it take her to get up the stairs, if she managed to get up them at all? There was a click and a whir and the door opened.

Inside her apartment, she swept her gaze around the little rooms. Tears of violation and rage began to seep down her face. Someone was in her storage unit, breathing deeply in the dark, waiting his chance to sneak up the stairs and do whatever kind of unmentionable harm he could. She tried to think about what she should do.

She grabbed the blue canister that was supposed to make everything smell like linens on a clothesline by the sea and gave the room a thorough spray, then she made herself a very small gin and tonic for her nerves and tried to imagine it as an elixir, a poultice. She took deep breaths and imagined the potion making its way to her inner recesses, where her saddest thoughts beat their heads against the walls of dimly lit rooms, stunned by the world's iniquity and willingness to betray.

Here she was, living the last shard of her life, and she kept expecting a reprise of that experience she'd had two decades ago when that wealthy charlatan had convinced Captain to invest all her savings in a company that would fail—that had been *set up* to fail, for the shadowy financial advantages the con man and his cronies would enjoy. In good faith, she and others had handed over their hopes, their small insulations. As always, the memory made her light-headed and full of dread. And today, that feeling was combined with a peculiar alertness. Something was repeating. Something rapacious was on the move.

She retrieved the letter from Mavis Krepps, then put it down without reading it. She had to stop blowing embers into flames, as that way lay insanity. This she knew. She stared at the china shepherdess on her knickknack shelf and tried to envision sun and sheep and blue sashes. Her heart began to thud in her ears.

"Go!" she whispered. "Go, Viola—get out! It's time."

She walked as rapidly as she could to her bedroom, where she pawed among her clothes for something to wear. She thought of calling Cassie, but there wasn't time. She needed to move fast and she needed to move alone. She kicked off her slippers and grabbed a pair of slacks and a sweater. The inbound bus stopped on the half hour a block away. She had eight minutes. She swooped up her pills from the bathroom and sat on the bed to remove her pajamas.

Someone knocked hard on her hallway door and she twitched so violently the pill bottles flew from her hands. Someone fiddled with the knob, and inserted a key, because of course he had a key, and there it was, in the next room, her name in Herbie Bonebright's sullen tones.

4

From his hiding place in the storage unit, Clayton Spooner consulted his phone and saw that he'd now been there for more than fifteen hours.

Almost 7:35. His mom was going to discover pretty soon that he hadn't stayed at Steiner's last night, as he'd texted her he planned to, and that he wasn't at school. The principal's office always contacted parents about no-shows by the end of the first class, so she'd have a panic attack then and call Steiner and so on. He texted her. *No worries if school calls, mamacita. Will be in 2nd class. Xplain later.* He thought about adding a grinning emoji. Thought better of it. She wasn't going to be smiling at emojis today. *Things r fine*, he signed off. He hoped that calling her *mamacita*, rather than Carla, as he usually did, would help.

He thought about the day outside, the humans churning into motion, and put his hands over his ears.

He thought about yesterday and fought a horrible urge to weep. His teeth began to chatter and he couldn't make them stop. His hands trembled and he pressed them to his mouth, then jerked them away, disgusted at the new pimples above his lip.

First there was the battle with Carla about the pills, when he'd refused, again, to take them, and she'd completely lost it and thrown them in his face, to rattle and skitter all over the kitchen floor.

"Don't, then!" she'd shrieked. "Don't focus on anything worthwhile, God knows. Your studies, your grades. Don't give in to any kind of ambition that's going to get you down the road. Don't pay attention to anything like *that*."

Her eyes squeezed shut, as though the enormity of her grievances had engulfed her. She was dressed for work in her black pantsuit, which had a bunch of white dog hairs on the back. How ambitious are dog hairs on your butt? Clayton wanted to say, just to watch her go further ballistic. But he didn't dare. She was too angry and she had the circles under her eyes that meant she'd stayed up until the early-morning chat shows, writing in her journal, pacing her room, maybe even calling Clayton's father, Frank, to hiss at him about his phony life and his phony values, all of it embodied in the twenty-two-year-old he'd shacked up with across town.

She did that sometimes, and then, come daylight, blue crescents under her eyes, she pulled herself together and went off to her job as a house stager. It was a profession she'd chosen just before Frank made his first break, the one in which he said he wanted only to be alone for a while so that he could reacquaint himself with himself and come back a better husband and father. The reacquainting took place in Costa Rica, and Carla hadn't spared her son the details: that it cost half their entire savings and that in addition to Frank's singed skin, he had returned with a stupid light in his eye and an STD, one of the easier to treat.

When she loudly wished for him a brain-eroding, terminal disease, he decided his options should include a fuller investment in his autonomy, and a week later he moved in with Jailbait, as Carla referred to her.

To Clayton, his father explained that it was a sorting-things-out time that would make them all stronger and that his new friend Kaycee was wise beyond her years and someone he felt he could learn a lot from, and he thought Clayton was having some respect issues when he responded to the moving-in news by blowing a mouthful of Cheerios back into his bowl.

Carla, laid off from her office manager's job in a downsizing at T&P Motorhomes the month before Frank went to Costa Rica, had looked around at the skittish housing market, then gone to every open house she could and realized that most homeowners had silly taste and a fetish for clutter that was likely to cost them a respectable sale. A house wasn't going to sell itself. The messiness of current lives had to be stripped away in order to entice the imagining of new ones.

She'd majored in art history during her two years of college and had worked, before T&P, at a high-end furniture store under the tutelage of their resident room designer, and, quite simply, she had an eye. This she mentioned to Clayton quite often. In fact, she talked about the details of her new profession to an extent that made him want to shout and flee.

Because her house-staging philosophy relied heavily on the techniques of serenity, a phrase she had coined herself, she headed off in the mornings nearly toppling under her arsenal of room soothers: wine country coffee-table books, skinny branches in a severe black vase, a small rock fountain that splashed and babbled when you plugged it in. Foster, their schnauzer, typically experienced a frenzy of separation anxiety as she left, and he raced, yipping, in circles around her ankles until Clayton pulled him away.

"Fuck, Foster!" she'd shriek. "Why don't you just kill me and be done with it!" And then she was gone and Foster began to calm down, and Clayton could begin to breathe.

What he hated most about the whole situation, the bust-up and impending divorce, was that he felt a terrible pity for both of his parents, mixed in with the red anger. The pity wouldn't ever go entirely away, and it weakened him, and he felt that the only way he could stay upright and even make it into the next month or so was to have very little to do with either of them.

The fact that Jailbait was the half sister of one of his main tormenters at school only made everything all the more insoluble and dangerous.

From the time he could remember, Clayton had felt assaulted by the noises of his life. His volatile, overenergized parents. Everything humming and beeping and barking and yelling, until he yearned to simply push himself down to the floor of a lake and lie in the watery silence, muffled in the cool blue, ungilled.

Only once had there been a reprieve, of about a year. Then, in middle school, he slept almost normal hours and ran track, laughed sometimes with his mysteriously calmer parents, camped in the mountains with a neighbor family, got respectable grades in school. All those ordinary, quiet things.

The agitation returned when he was thirteen, just before he started to play video games with his new best friends Mack and Steiner. It found him; it lurked around, shivered all the borders, made him want to shout.

But the games, with their predictable chosen chaos and noise, actually had a soothing effect. The three of them took up their positions on the worn and puffy couch in Steiner's basement, headsets on, the Xbox at the ready. For hours at a time, they moved through urban ruins or desert war zones, shooting, trapping, torching, looting, and dying. Swarmed by yellow-eyed Nazi zombies and near death, they called on each other to bring the reviving hypodermic, and if it was too late, the screen trembled and went red and your death was blared in white letters, and then you moved back a way in the game and respawned.

Clayton liked it best when the action was fast and bloody and the kill count was high and death was avoided by individual shooting, leaping, and torching skills, certainly, but also by calling on your comrades to move through bullets and packs of mutant creatures in order to save you.

In real life, Mack and Steiner were similarly shuffling and sleepy-eyed. But put them in the game and they, like Clayton, manipulated triggers, bumpers, and joysticks with the speed and finesse of fighter pilots. They were in training for a world of endless war, endless permutations of endless enemies. And they were fearless and loyal, risking death at every turn to come to each other's aid. Grunting and cackling and whooping, they annihilated with abandon and arrived at game's end depleted and reinforced.

A kind of euphoria began to be upon him at times, and his growing success on the battlefields—with guns, against monsters, on missions, out of traps, newly heavy with loot—made him want to coax more risk and drama out of his nonscreen life. So he took a dare from Steiner and rushed up behind a cop and tapped the top of his holstered gun, so lightly the cop felt not a thing. Ha!

He found a cache of Hawaiian shirts at a thrift store, and a straw fedora, and he wore them every day for most of a summer. He became infatuated with the idea of old-time journalism where the reporter actually sat down with people for a few hours and got their whole story into his neat black notebook. And so he bought a black notebook and approached a couple of strangers at the mall, wearing his wildest Hawaiian shirt and his old-time newsman hat, and pleaded with them to sit down with him at the Orange Julius and tell him their true stories, and begged them—hold on!—not to get up and walk away.

Steiner, capable of betrayal to an extent Clayton could never have imagined, reported these escapades to his mom, who reported them to Carla and Frank, and that was the first trip to the first shrink.

He doesn't like to think much about what happened next.

Another kid at school had bought both *Call of Duty: Modern Warfare Remastered* and the multiplayer *Halo Wars 2* and had invited Mack and Steiner to his basement to play. When Mack mentioned this too casually, Clayton felt more shot than he ever had, and he doubted that he would ever respawn.

On the same day, his dad announced that he was moving into an apartment with his friend Kaycee. After that, the sounds of daily life turned into a roar as his mom tried to create a sense of purpose and bustle and multitasking. More phone calls, louder TV, Foster running around utterly batshit.

Clayton retreated to his head, where he reviewed some of the best kills and rescues he'd experienced. He lined up the enemies—zombies, turbaned soldiers, shock troops, grunts, brutes, space aliens, and mutants. He reviewed his kill chains and hammer sprees and medals. On a day he'd told Carla he was too sick to go to school, he ate breakfast, slunk to the couch, and reimagined a particularly memorable episode in which a pack of mutant dogs had, as one, leaped for his throat. Steiner's avatar, Slade, zigzagged to the rescue across a minefield littered with burning cars and pocked with sniper fire as Clayton's man tried to throw off the dogs so they could be shot or grenaded. His head felt as if it would burst. The universe was filled with snarling and barking. He could smell their saliva.

And when his eyes flew open, Foster was yipping and cowering and trying to scrape across the floor to escape another kick. Carla flew in from the next room and gave her son a look he would never forget.

"Don't you move another inch," she hissed. She yanked the old afghan off the couch and wrapped the whimpering dog in it to take to the vet. When Clayton was a small child, she used to wrap him up in the same afghan and prop him between her and Frank while they ate popcorn and watched antique reruns of *Candid Camera*, Clayton laughing so hard his stomach hurt.

The Foster that Clayton kicked so hard bore no relation to an actual dog. That animal had come from a realm of mayhem, near-death, and his yearning for the real-life friends who were drifting so rapidly away. But the fact that it had happened—Foster turned out to have a cracked rib and never again spun circles of joy when Clayton came into the house—combined with the fact that his grades had taken a nosedive and he couldn't seem to make himself pay attention to anything his mother was saying, had prompted more trips to another shrink.

That was a year and two shrinks and a bunch of drugs ago, all of it underwritten by insurance or his guilt-ridden father. Now, at fifteen, he had taken Ritalin for attention deficit hyperactivity disorder, Zoloft for oppositional defiant disorder, Risperdal for anger, Depakote and Abilify and, finally, lithium to stabilize his moods. He'd gained fifteen pounds, and he had tremors, acne, and insomnia. The two drugs he was on now seemed to clash with each other and sometimes made him want to destroy everything, wipe the earth clean, even of himself. Especially of himself. He thought of running away. He took refuge in elaborately detailed visions of himself in some heroic role, in some heroic life. Jumping out of a plane to fight a forest fire. Delivering piles of money and supplies, in his own silver yacht, to earthquake victims on an impoverished island. He wanted to instigate relief on a massive scale.

But he was just a pale, tremulous, pimpled, pudgy teenager whose old friends, Mack and Steiner, now occupied a social pod that excluded him, whose mother was an agitated, exhausted mess, whose father was in some kind of adamant trance.

His only consolation was his love for Raven Felska, the pale girl with black-rimmed eyes and tattooed sentences on her arms and hands. They sat next to each other in Spanish. She smelled faintly of tobacco and something else, maybe incense. They smoked together in the alley after school and rarely spoke, but Clayton didn't question their deep affinity, their shared sense of waiting, together, to be free from their ridiculous lives. She told him the inky words that snaked across her hands and lower arms were poem fragments. Sometimes he tried to read them when she didn't notice, and they meant nothing to him, which made him love her more.

Clayton's tormenter at school, Josh Anderson, had renamed himself Chaser and wanted everyone else to call him that. He was an angel-faced blond boy, a bit shorter than most of his friends, but fast and agile and mean as a viper. His ingratiating smile had put all the teachers in his pocket, and presumably his parents, too, if the car he drove, a new loaded Jeep, was any indication.

The only thing Clayton had ever done to Josh Anderson was to continue calling him by his given name, the name he'd known him by since grade school, no matter how upset Josh got. For his sin, Clayton had already been beaten up twice, once by Josh and once by Josh's right-hand guy, Troy. Josh had also discovered, through his half sister Kaycee, that Clayton was taking various medications. He began to go around telling anyone who would listen that Clayton was "special"—big quotation marks in the air—and should be going to a "special" school for retards. Yesterday morning he'd said it again, just as Raven passed them in the hall. Josh pointed at Clayton and lurched spastically, then turned to Raven.

"Hey," he said.

"Hey, Josh," she had murmured.

"Chaser," Josh said. "The name's Chaser."

"Hey, Chaser," she acquiesced.

Clayton felt as if she'd been captured, that she spoke from behind bars. The thought made him frantic with fury.

"Don't talk to him," he said to Raven, his voice ice.

"Josh!" he said, turning to him. "Why Chaser? Because it reminds you of someone who can run down anyone he wants? Who isn't a lame little midget with a lame little midget dick?"

And then three or four of them were on him, and when he saw an opening he hit Josh as hard as he could in the face and fled. Josh's friends bent over his prone and bloody form.

Clayton slammed through the heavy school door, almost knocking down two scrawny freshmen, and sprinted down the block. He heard shouts and veered into an alley behind the tall old people's building down the block, then realized they were probably coming at him from both directions and would engulf him at the alley's outlet. At that moment a large window opened on the ground floor and a tiny white-haired woman grabbed a rope that was attached to the lid of a big garbage bin. She stared at him.

"It's OK," he gasped. "No worries." He scrambled onto the bin and through the big sliding window so fast that the woman didn't have time to do more than step back and throw her hands up to her face. He ran down the carpeted hall, down a staircase. A door opened on a corridor of storage units the size of double closets. Most of them were padlocked, but the lock of the last one on the left had a hasp that hung at an odd angle. He jerked at it and the door swung open. Inside were boxes, blankets, lampshades, two old trunks, paint cans, turpentine, a saddle tipped on its horn. He grabbed a piece of twine from the floor and fastened the door shut behind him, then crawled behind the trunks and pulled a blanket over himself, and slept.

Fully awake now, he began to feel a kind of peace that he hadn't in a very long time. He was at the bottom of the lake, bobbing, closing his eyes, opening them to peer through the dark water. How long had it taken for him to drift to this place? What was it that had been done to him in that long sleep to leave him feeling so restored, so laser-like?

Once he heard footsteps. They weren't quick and brash like those of Josh and his friends, marching like mutants to drag him out by his hair. These were soft and deliberate. They stopped at the head of the storage room corridor and he heard light anxious breathing, and then they advanced toward him, a little slide to the feet like snakeskin, and he burrowed deeper under the blanket and tried to ignore his thumping heart. The steps stopped; the breathing grew louder. He squinted to see the vague form of a thin old lady in what looked like pajamas, and then she retreated. He was bathed in rancid sweat.

He shifted his position under the blanket and moved a box to stretch out his legs. It was a dark box, leather, with old-fashioned brass clasps, like the ones on his grandpa's ancient suitcase. As slowly and quietly as he could, he released the catches and lifted the lid. Inside, resting in indented old velvet, was a pistol. It had a dull gleam in the dim light and an eloquence that constricted Clayton's throat. Calm and beautiful and lethal, it seemed to have slid down a corridor of light from another age with the sole purpose of revealing itself to a worthy person who had suffered much and been wronged. He lifted it out and turned it this way and that, so that its intricacies of barrel and trigger and stock could show themselves to him. He rested it against his cheek.

After a while, he stood and stretched and used the blanket to wipe himself down. He was starving, he realized. Thirsty, too. He replaced the gun in its box and put the box in his backpack, then jumped back when an alarm went off somewhere above his head, as if the theft somehow had been detected. He heard running footsteps, some distant shouts and small cries. Another alarm joined the first.

Clayton hoisted his pack onto his back and scurried out of the storage unit toward the stairwell. On the first floor he ran toward the big sliding window above the garbage bin, smelling, now, a trickle of smoke. He vaulted himself out and over the bin and began to run.

Small sirens in the distance became rapidly deafening, and, in his confusion, he ran the wrong way down the alley and emerged near the front of the building, where several old people were huddled in their nightclothes. One pointed at him, and he pivoted in the other direction to run as he had never run before, the backpack hitting him hard between his shoulder blades. His breath came steadily, and he soon felt that he could run forever, that he could run forever toward Raven, in triumph, and that when he presented her with the gun, they would make their plan, together, to punish Josh and his posse into submission. Together they would do that. They would do whatever it took.

WHEN BEING HUMAN
IS FAR FROM ENOUGH

5

Across town, on the other side of the river, Chief Fire Inspector Lander Maki heard a humming sound coming from the living room. Rhonda was up early. He pulled on some sweats and running shoes, splashed cold water on his face, waved to her, and headed out for his early-morning slow run.

The sky was shedding its pink lights and firming up to a frank and cloudless blue, a November blue, with a desultory wafer of moon floating near the horizon. What had Rhonda told him about some Native names for the month of November? Beaver Moon, Goose Going Moon, Mad Moon. Why mad? Because a November day could seem to be caught, confused and blustering, between the falling gold of fall and the icy crawl of winter? Maybe, but not today. Today November was neither. It held the quietness of a pause. The feel of a something-before. A train whistle blew. A door slammed and a car revved up. Maki's breath smoked lightly before him.

He ran slowly through his neighborhood of small and aging houses, some with pin-neat yards, others benignly shambled. Turned-over trikes, clumped lawns, and rusty barbeques. There a tipsy pink flamingo, and over there an eave fringed with tattered prayer flags, another dangling dead flowers in a planter; a window with a Christian fish, another with a peace sign, another with a "Go Griz" banner. A neighborhood of cracked sidewalks, faded charming porches, kids, students, laborers, adjuncts, retirees, firefighters, do-gooders, DIY renovators—many of them up early with Maki, in their lighted kitchens, about to head into their days.

He rounded the last corner of his short run, slowed, then sprinted the last fifty yards toward the yellow glow from his own living room.

Inside, Rhonda was on her knees at the side of Siddhartha, their Great Dane, humming still and waving a glowing, braided stalk of sweetgrass over the dog's head. She looked up.

"Sid's exhausted from his criminal adventures," she said briskly. "It'll take a few minutes before he's clear."

The dog stretched on his huge sheepskin bed, the herby smoke moving in lazy wreaths above the odor that emanated from him. Over in the corner, their ancient turtle came out of its shell, stared around aghast, and disappeared again.

"I'm with you, pal," Maki murmured.

Sid had been missing for most of the day before, and when he finally showed up, he reeked of misadventure involving unfresh carcasses and some dairy thing that was worse. They'd managed to coax him into the shower with a piece of pizza and had tried to clean him up with Rhonda's cucumber body wash, but the smell lingered and she'd gone to bed claiming further steps were needed if the entire house wasn't going to take on a negative charge, making them all a little sad, once again.

Siddhartha had all the big-boned amiability and sensory acuity you would expect in his breed, plus an extra degree of alertness that stemmed from whatever circumstances had deposited him, thin and shaking, in a glass-sharded borrow pit on the edge of town, to be discovered and rehabilitated by Rhonda. He turned out to have, as well, another trait that seemed to go beyond his breeding and history, and could only be described as a certain large kindness. It was there in the way that he tipped his heavy head to fasten a liquid look of utter empathy on his humans, in the way he had risen from his sheepskin pallet on the few occasions when Maki and Rhonda argued and placed a paw on first one person's knee and then the other's, dissipating all unease or rancor in a matter of seconds.

Rhonda had been schooled as an actuary but worked now as a seasonal tax preparer and a volunteer at the Humane Society. She was also an aspiring animal communicator and had taken, by correspondence, a course called "When Being Human is Far from Enough." It coached the student in the most successful methods of establishing superhuman channels of communication with domestic animals. This pursuit complemented a tentative investigation into certain shamanic techniques and a new interest in the cosmology and spiritual practices of her Native American forebears on her mother's side.

She was a tiny, wiry woman with a huge mop of tight black curls and, Maki thought, one of the sweetest smiles on the planet. Only her crooked eyeteeth and a sandpaper laugh rescued her from forgettable perfection.

None of her woo-woo, as Maki sometimes called it to her face, made much sense to him, but he loved her enthusiasms and general largeheartedness because they were so at odds with his baseline temperament, which was gloom and a chronic expectation of the worst. She lifted him out of that murk for minutes, for hours at a time. More and more, too, he was coming to view her unconventional practices as ritualizations or codifications of an empathy so profound that it threatened, at times, to overwhelm her. Certainly it extended to the creature that was Lander Maki in a way he'd never experienced before. Not growing up. Not in his first marriage. Not ever.

"Make sure that sweetgrass is fully extinguished before you set it down anywhere," Maki said, waving away some smoke. "Run it under some water, actually."

Rhonda gave him an indulgent look. "Listen to him," she said to Sid. "He may be our beloved, but he is also the city's fire inspector, and if we do something careless and overheated, he will come and…inspect us."

"IN-spect," the mynah bird croaked.

Sid sat up and tipped his big Dane ears toward the bird, which had long ago left its cage for the day and perched now on a curtain rod, adjusting its scabrous claws to stay upright. The deaf cat sat on the window seat, pretending to meditate.

Rhonda had named the bird Flora the day they liberated it from PetSmart because she had felt, though it was an aged male, signals from it of a longing to cross genders. And why not? Were humans the sole possessors of cravings? Was it out of the realm of possibility that animals could make their needs known in some persuasive, if whispery, fashion? Rhonda thought not. Or said as much. Maki couldn't tell sometimes if she was making fun of herself.

Her exploration of telepathic communication between humans and animals, especially dogs who had behavior problems that were distressing their owners, seemed entirely sincere on its face. An actual meeting between practitioner and pet was not required or even desirable, she told him. A photo of the animal looking directly at the camera, plus a description of the salient trouble, was enough. And then, if you heightened your awareness through meditation to permeate the membrane that protects and limits humans from unbearable perception, a conversation could begin.

Her first case was a basset hound named Pepi who had a problem with rampant lawn digging. Pepi's human companion—Rhonda preferred the term to *owner*—was a friend from her Pilates class. She offered Rhonda some details about the digging and gave her a photo of Pepi. That evening, Rhonda sat down at her laptop, searched the dog's eyes, took in the dolorous jowls. She introduced herself and explained why she was talking to him. Her fingers flew over the computer keys as she posed questions and registered his answers, assembling a transcript that she later presented to Maki and emailed to Pepi's person. The gist of it was that the dog had been an alcoholic grave digger in a previous life and had never learned to deal appropriately with unpredictable funeral schedules and feelings of inadequacy and deprivation.

When Maki read that admission, he fell back on the couch and put the transcript over his face. She tapped on the printout, and he returned it to her, then buried his face in his hands to grin some more.

She was unfazed.

"I tried to remind him that alcohol blunted growth as well as pain, so it wasn't surprising that he had never moved beyond his repeating anxieties," she said with airy detachment. "They are the reason for the holes in the lawn. We're working on it."

She told Maki now that, while he was in bed and Sid was not yet getting the sweetgrass treatment, she had tried for the first time to connect with a truant animal whose photo and history had not been presented to her by its human. Could she summon contact out of an informational void? An image had come to her of her grandparents' old Bakelite radio, so she approached it and turned the big knob. First there was just static. Then she heard a doglike voice talking in low, wise tones that were just out of range, and then, louder, a voice that had a growly little purr on the edges and was identifying itself as belonging to a female Norwegian Forest cat, age two. She said she was sitting on the very top of a big house in the university district.

"Are you afraid you will fall from that tall place?" Rhonda had inquired. "Are you afraid you'll be hurt?" Her gaze grew distant.

"And she said…" Maki waited.

"She said, 'Lady, I'm a *cat*,'" said Rhonda. Then they were both laughing, and Rhonda was making passes of the sweetgrass over Sid's head in an antic and animated fashion. She stopped abruptly and stared gravely into the dog's eyes. She nodded.

"Sid wants you to make those eggs you made the other day. With extra for him."

Maki put together all the meals in the household because Rhonda was a disaster in the kitchen and because cooking calmed him. Lists, portions, methods, results—that was the ticket.

He didn't look like a person who needed calming, but how many do? In his late forties, he had a flat, rosy face and the almost lidless eyes of his Finnish ancestors. Even in suburban St. Paul, where he'd grown up and which was wall-to-wall Scandinavians, the occasional teacher or new acquaintance would be confused and ask if his name was Japanese. Maki, Skari, Talo—they were Finnish names and better sounding, Maki thought, than all those Olafsons and Offerdahls scraping their way across the endless snow. Clean clicky fish names, the Finns had, slippery and neat.

Maki spoke in low tones and moved slowly and alertly, as if his daily surroundings were as full of clues as the scenes of the mysterious fires he was so good at deciphering. In the kitchen he arranged his two cutting boards and his small glass bowl, his whisk and spices and skillet. He chopped the shiitakes he'd had soaking and sprinkled them with a little brandy, then sautéed them in walnut oil while he minced a handful of chives to add to the earthy stew. The eggs got a good whisk and a dollop of cream and were then folded into the mushrooms and chives while he turned the flame down very low. He wrapped a few pieces of thick peppered bacon in paper towels and cooked them in the microwave for six minutes while he stirred the eggs very slowly until they were coddled and creamy. When the English muffins were toasted and done, he buttered them, covered them with the crumbled bacon, added a sprinkle of malt vinegar (his special touch) and topped them with the eggs and a sprig of lemon basil. He left a sample of the eggs in the pan for Sid, who, of course, would have been just as happy with a bite of putrid rabbit skin.

Rhonda had moved from the floor to sit tailor-style on a faded velvet couch, their best estate-sale find. She'd extinguished the sweetgrass, but the smell of it lingered, and she sniffed the air as if the smoke were feeding her. Maki brought her the eggs and a strong cup of coffee on a lacquered tray.

"What a beast you are," she said. "Eggs, butter, coffee. So many sins on a single platter." She took a big bite and fell back against the sofa cushions. "I'm slain with pleasure," she whispered, impaling him with a stare.

Maki allowed himself a small smile. Because he was not an effusive or demonstrative person, he felt lucky that Rhonda supplied enough for them both, even though her growing-up years had been tempestuous and full of mistakes and terrible luck. There had been the crazy, controlling, charismatic first husband, several ill-advised friendships with out-and-out degenerates, a sporadic tequila problem, the trauma in the hypermall, all of it rife with strife and drama and tears—all of which Maki envied in a peculiar way, though he couldn't tell her that because it would seem to be discounting the pain that she felt had enhanced her talents for empathy and healing.

Six years earlier, just before they met, Rhonda was struggling through the dregs of a marriage to a man named Ridley who had begun as a set designer for a regional theater and morphed, via voracious networking and his sister's marriage to a billionaire, into a designer of hypermalls. They had moved from Seattle to Riverside, though even as she packed the last of their household goods, she knew she wasn't going to stay with Ridley, or live for any length of time in Southern California; knew with the kind of certainty that made her actions, she told Maki, seem those of a Siamese twin with entirely different priorities from her own.

But they took her as far as the new house with its whine of freeway traffic and air-conditioning always in the background, where she and Ridley ate takeout every night and she stared at all the boxes that sat around not wanting to be opened. And her Siamese shadow took her one day to the newly constructed hypermall that Ridley and the others on the design team had conceptualized and that was already drawing attention from developers with holdings all over the world, including, it would turn out, the consortium behind the construction of 1Borneo, the largest lifestyle hypermall in East Malaysia.

A prominent feature of the Riverside project was the Castle of Infinite Lavender Dreams, situated across an atrium from the Glade of Serenity, where behemoth screens displayed moving waterfalls and speakers mounted in the foliage made splashing water noises for tense and overextended shoppers who could take their ease on benches that had been molded to resemble ancient stone.

That's where Rhonda was sitting, waiting for Ridley to be done with a meeting, when a young man wearing white coveralls sat down beside her as if he were her brother and was sneaking a break. He smelled smoky. She scooted a few inches sideways to give him room—one of those ridiculous female deferences she'd been working her whole adult life to root out—and looked him in the face. It was a rather terrible face, because it talked but it was blank. Blank eyes and a blank mouth, somehow, despite his alarming words.

What he said, in a nutshell, was that he was going to march her up some back stairs to the top of the castle and hold her hostage at gunpoint until unspecified responders took him at his word and came up with a pile of money.

Rhonda had eyed the castle, seeing herself on the parapet with a gun at her back, seeing herself shot and falling—all of this in a span of seconds—and very slowly raised her arms in surrender. The man hissed, so she pretended to be adjusting her ponytail. A series of empty moments passed, a leaden, fated countdown. Rhonda kept her hands on her hair and closed her eyes. And then there were fast footsteps behind them and her companion on the bench was grabbed by two security cops who stood him up, frisked him efficiently to find what turned out to be a .22 pistol, and informed him that they had been watching him behave in an agitated manner, culminating in unmistakably threatening body language with Rhonda.

Rhonda calmly answered the questions of some other security people, gave her contact information, went straight home, wrote a brief note, bought a next-day air ticket to Montana because it was so empty and far away and she had some distant relatives there. And she never looked back.

Maki pitied her the experience, but also envied its utter outlandishness, its drama. Nothing remotely like that had ever happened to him. His childhood and young adult life, especially, had been bland and stupid to the point of idiocy. They had left him feeling, in his worst times, as if he lived in a sealed cavern of propriety and joylessness. He sometimes felt he might die from an absence of event.

There had been the inscrutable, taciturn parents, a slim, sandy-haired sister who became a stout school bus driver with no discernible relationships with anyone, and a little brother who'd grown into a gambling addict and then a sobered-up real estate salesman and then stopped calling or writing and, the last anyone had heard, was a facilitator at an upscale Christian wellness center in Costa Rica.

Their parents were now in an assisted-living facility called Forest Glen that his sister, Daphne, had found for them a few months ago near her apartment complex in a treeless commercial sprawl on the edge of St. Paul. It was owned by the behemoth ElderIntegrity chain, and Maki could only assume it was a dump, given his parents' modest resources, or that the facility's costs skyrocketed with each tick of decline in a resident's independence, and that the resident would be sent packing the minute the coffers were empty.

He tried not to think too much about the place, or about the fact that he had visited his parents only once a year since he left home.

"Bad son!" the mynah bird called, making Maki's fingertips jump.

"Matson," Rhonda mused. "There it is again. Maybe Flora once belonged to someone named Matson. Maybe he had financial reversals and had to give up everything extra, including poor Flora. Maybe he got bilked in a pyramid scheme or some kind of elder scam and had to move someplace that didn't take giant chatty birds."

"Bad son! Bad son!" the bird called.

Maki took a deep breath and released it in a purgative whoosh.

"Do you think we should cut out coffee?" he asked.

She gave it a few moments' thought. "No," she said. "That would be wrong."

She reached over and put a hand on Maki's knee, then went into their bedroom and returned with a small box, which she presented to him. Inside was a turquoise butterfly fashioned from metal and enamel that was suspended from a narrow strip of leather.

"You can figure out this situation," she said. "Right now, you can't make anything better for your parents because you feel too guilty. This will help you get past that. Wear this next to your body and it will help you feel like more things are possible. You won't feel tethered to the ground, where these people problems seem so big, so sad. You will see it all from the vantage point of something small and light, flying through the air."

Rhonda lifted it from the box and hung it around Maki's neck. While he waited to feel lighter, his phone rang, the first call of the day. He'd had the ringtone set on "Whistling Wizard" for a while, but the demented jauntiness of it was so at odds with the information he sometimes received that he'd switched it back to "Telephone."

The volume was set too high, and it sounded like something from an old detective movie.

"Eeep!" Rhonda said. "That's harsh. I don't like it. Sid doesn't, either." She touched the dog's adoring, upraised nose, and he barked happily. The cat left the realm of spirits and jumped down from the windowsill. The turtle's head emerged. The bird, Flora, made a creditable ringing sound, and Rhonda's gravelly laugh grew raucous.

I love this, Maki thought as he answered the call. *This sweet racket, I truly love.*

6

The dispatcher reported to Maki that a fire had broken out at the Pheasant Run senior residence over in the university district. The building had been evacuated, and the blaze was quickly extinguished. It had been limited, she said, to the second-floor apartment occupied by the building's on-site manager.

One resident fell on the stairs during the evacuation and had been transported to the ER. Another with heart problems had been treated on the scene for a slight case of smoke inhalation. A third resident, one Viola Six, had not been located, and the manager, a Mr. Bonebright, was also missing.

Maki had been called for the reason he always was: there were oddities. Though the blaze had originated and been confined to the kitchen, it didn't appear to be due to an untended stove. The firefighters thought they might have detected an accelerant. The smoke was maybe blacker than it should have been, and the burn marks suggested the kind of fast, hot fire that might have been set. There were also, notably, those two missing persons of interest.

Maki had recently bought a 1972 Volvo, cramped and army green with a wood-paneled dashboard, which he'd found on eBay for a price he still couldn't believe. Although Rhonda said it was like trying to drive an iron lung and refused to step inside it after a single trial run, Maki liked the car because it was so much more mechanical than it was helpful. It didn't worry about the driver being comfortable or about easing the efforts of window opening, brake releasing, seat adjusting, the way newer cars did. It treated you like a capable, physically competent adult.

Shortly after the dispatcher's call, Maki drove in his customary manner toward Pheasant Run, which meant that it took him quite a long time to cover the two miles. He liked to remind himself, as he drove, that the Volvo moved along the floor of an ancient lake, stupendously large, and that the mountains that began at the edge of the houses still bore the watermarks of that lake's levels during several glacial dramas that had drained and refilled the valley, time after time. Mountains as ancient shores. He found the idea oddly comforting.

Maki moved at a near-crawl because he felt that slowness, too, had become so rare as to seem almost extinct. By proceeding in a hushed and unhurried manner whenever he could, he felt like a scientist reintroducing a threatened species to its old habitat. The pace also helped him think, or rather it prepared him to think in the way that he knew he would have to in order to know what he was seeing at the fire site. Or not seeing. That was the essence of fire investigations: you had to put together a scenario from the presence of an absence. The art was in imagining what had been taken away, and how that might have happened.

Eyes half-closed, he saw everything via his inspector's antennae. There, an office building with a fire escape that looked as if it would blow away in the next wind. (He made a mental note to send a building inspector.) Over there, a handsome old house with a pair of dead cypresses that leaned against the desiccated wood of the roof. An errant bit of flame, a spark from a neighbor's grill, and the trees would ignite and torch the house in a matter of minutes. (The owners would be apprised of the danger.)

He rolled down the window and practiced his smelling. Rhonda liked to tell him that his exceptional olfactory gifts, his *hyperosmia*, made him almost a dog, and his twitching nostrils knew it to be true. Here were the cacophonous smells of a late-autumn morning in a Rocky Mountain valley populated by seventy thousand souls: evergreens, car exhaust, river water, just to record the top notes. It was several degrees warmer than normal, though the new normals made such comparisons increasingly irrelevant, and this November had the added strangeness of the leaves that had remained on the trees after that lacerating early-October freeze. Maki could smell them, too. They were crisp, but more vegetal than papery. They evoked a particular kind of dried mushroom, quite possibly enoki. There was also, in the air, the smell that was the absence of snow during what used to be snow season. It was a faint grave-like smell, chilled and dense.

He caught a whiff of something offbeat—a particular kind of smoke—and leaned out the window to inhale, almost rear-ending an elderly person driving as slowly as he was. Scolding himself, he refocused, but not before he registered the strength of the smell. Someone in the immediate area had burned very young wood the previous evening. This was woodsmoke from a sapling. Less than six months old, that sapling. And some pine cones had been added to the blaze.

His beyond-human smelling prowess was Maki's major natural advantage in his occupation. He could distinguish between fires that had been set with premium gasoline from those set with the lowest grade. He knew which smells were likely to be present in a cooking oil fire versus a blaze that had been helped along with even small amounts of a petroleum accelerant. Most rooms, to him, contained such a multitude of present and past human and animal presences, each entirely different from the others, that he sometimes became vertiginous from the sheer volume of the tracings and had to bury his face for a while in a small cotton pillow stuffed with pine needles that he kept in his briefcase.

To recall himself to his profession, he sometimes did a little mental drill in which he named as many kinds of smoke as he could and arranged them in order of personal attraction, most to least. Evergreen smoke was near the top because it was imaginary Christmases, the hearth, previous centuries, bonfires in snowy woods. Also, it was entirely uncomplicated. It was the smoke of wood, needles, and sap. Period. His next favorite was the smoke of good cannabis, and then that of burning tobacco. Powerful social, sexual, and meditative associations there, which he liked to review and think about. Down further was smoke that had a meat component—not bad if the meat was a salted rib eye grilled over a wood fire, a little worse if the grilling involved gas, or charcoal soaked with fire starter, so you got petroleum products added in. The really terrible smells involved burned fur or skin, as he knew from the aftermaths of several wretched house fires he'd investigated. And smoke that was made by burning plastics, rubber, or chemicals had its own lethality, man-made and unapologetic.

Down on the floor of the ghost lake, Maki's little city was a place where vivid bicyclists zoomed the streets, harrying winds were mostly absent, summer brought flourishing trees and flowers, independent bookstores thrived, and waitresses had master's degrees. Vigorous exercise and modest feats of physical daring were applauded. Hang gliders rose off the mountaintops and wafted like old music through the air.

Maki found himself appreciating, deeply, the salubrious qualities of the place and its surrounding physical grandeur—the encircling mountains, part forest, part scrub grass, and the way they rose into the broad sky like protectors and sentinels—but he also reminded himself to guard against enshrining it all, tempting though that was. After all, how perilously close the lively farmers' markets were to movie sets of idyllic overflowingness and goodwill! How monochromatic the handsome and tall young people! How full of misplaced zest the summer band laboring agriculturally in the river park! It was a place with such easeful surfaces that you had to work a little to see the warts, never mind the threats and the out-and-out griefs, the sort that had to play a part in the suicide rates, nearly the highest in the nation, of both the pretty valley and the grand, broad-shouldered state.

Well, there were always recumbent bicyclists as antidotes to the insistent pleasantness. A grim-faced man, in top-to-toe sweat-wicking garments in bright colors, pulled up beside the Volvo in a reclining position. These bicycles gave Maki the creeps. They were so joyless and passive-aggressive, the rider leaning back from the experience, watching his legs work. His tailbone ached just looking at the guy. The only time it ached more was when a recumbent bicyclist was attached to a baby carrier on wheels—rare, admittedly, but he'd seen it—and then the ache was combined with a certain quiet rage. There they were, adult and babe, moving two feet off the ground through tall herds of fast and heedless cars and trucks. It was the most witless embodiment of hippie-holiness and outright stupidity he'd ever seen. *No wonder I indulge modestly in pot*, Maki thought when he saw something like that. *It's the only thing that assures me I don't have to do anything. Those people just* are. However, conclusions like that were also the reason he was thinking of forgoing weed altogether. They just *are*. What a moronic rationale for bad behavior. It was the intellectual equivalent of predestination.

The sun had lifted fully over the valley, and the tawny parts of the mountainsides lit up like lions. Something about the light now made every glimpse of red take on an aspect of indelibility: the bandanna around that golden retriever's neck, its owner's hoodie, a scrim of maroon leaves on that Japanese maple, the fixed eternity of that stop sign. The redness also evoked flames, of course, and the case at hand.

Maki had a little vision, of the kind that usually came to him only in his first waking moments. Most of the time they didn't disturb him because he'd had them all his life, and they usually seemed less like missives than like helpful illuminations, as if he'd switched to the highest wattage on a three-way bulb. What he saw was something rocking like a pendulum. The moving object had no shape or color, but it had a powerful aspect of inevitability. Time was counting down, always counting down to a future still obscure. Maybe that was all it meant.

Pheasant Run, a classic sixties box construction, stood midway along a five-block corridor that ran from the high school to the campus of the university. Maki parked a block from the building, lit the first of the three cigarettes he allowed himself a day, leafed through his latest *Mother Jones* and finished reading an article in *The Nation*. His magazines relaxed him in a way that was necessary when he was about to wade into a fire scene because they identified patterns in destruction. They also confirmed that he wasn't as depressed for no reason as he sometimes thought he was. The problem wasn't necessarily his native Finn gloom; it was actual puffed-up, deal-making, happily lying, idealism-stomping operators and moguls and so-called statesmen like Little Boy at the helm, who were rapidly plunging the world into a kind of miasmic twilight lit only by the migraine shiver of dollar signs.

A group of young people walked toward the university. Others, younger still, headed toward the high school. The university-bound walkers included older sorts as well, as a number of faculty lived in the neighborhood. One of them held an unlit cigarette away from him as if offering it to invisible passersby. A man and woman with identically cut gray hair and matching briefcases and rounded shoulders looked as if they'd been lockstepping off to classes since they were five.

The high school students were uniformly underdressed, as always. And what they did wear seemed calculated to enhance their most unfortunate traits. Girls with baby-fat stomachs let them pouch and jiggle between tight T-shirts and low-rider jeans. Thin, apologetic boys, the kind who seemed to gain height as you watched them, extended their knobby knees through ripped denim. More than a few of both or multiple genders seemed to be wearing their pajamas. That one scuffed along in actual bedroom slippers. They hunched over their phones in masturbatory trances, thumbs flying.

The Pheasant Run occupants, many in nightclothes and jackets, milled uncertainly on the sidewalks. As usual, the firefighters had evacuated the entire building when such a move was entirely unnecessary. The fire had been put out quickly and thoroughly, and the smoke would have been confined to the lower floors. And still, everyone in the entire building had been rousted to make their way, the best they could, down to the lobby and out onto the sidewalk. They looked chilly and miserable and frightened.

Some were on walkers. A few firemen moved among the group answering questions.

A frigid, cantankerous breeze had come up, and it grabbed at the edges of the old people and rattled the clinging maple leaves. The sky had turned gray and clotted as some kind of new weather moved in.

Maki had a brief, mildly testy exchange with the lead firefighter, who finally agreed to move the residents back inside and reassure them that neither they nor the building was in danger. But before that was done, Maki used his phone to photograph the building's exterior and those standing outside it.

One of the residents, a lanky, silver-haired man in a tracksuit, approached him and introduced himself in a lecturer's voice as Professor Rydell Clovis, the wielder of the fire extinguisher. The hero of the day. Maki told him he'd want to talk with him at some length but needed some private time on the scene first. Clovis, excited and impatient, began to reenact his precise movements at every point after he heard the fire alarm. He sounded whipped up enough that Maki made a mental note to do a very thorough interview with the guy, and he sent him on his way. How many times had it turned out that the most enthusiastic witness to a fire had set a few of his own?

Not that this was necessarily an arson. He was going to jeopardize his own observations if he decided anything along those lines at this point.

He introduced himself to several other residents—a birdlike woman swaddled in a down coat, a bald man with an oxygen tank and a steady small cough, a stout and hearty-looking couple demanding to know how long they were to wait outside—and tried to convey a combination of reassurance and rigor. They could all expect at least a brief interview, he told them. He photographed them individually, for the record.

A stout woman with red hair in a topknot approached him and introduced herself as Mavis Krepps, the president of the condo owners' association. She had huge eyes, sad and alert, and she fixed them on him as if imploring mercy. Her voice, though, was resonant and in charge.

"I should like to set up a time in which you could speak to the residents, as a whole, about the city's protocol for fire inspections and evacuation procedures," she said. He eyed her quizzically. He rarely encountered formality in a conversation anymore.

"Yes, I know we heard from someone in your office when Herbie Bonebright gifted us with a grease fire the week he moved in," she said. "And I believe the person we talked to, at that time, raised some maintenance issues for the association to address."

Maki had two assistants who conducted inspections, and he tried to remember which one had mentioned any Pheasant Run problems to him.

"These maintenance issues have not been fully addressed," Mrs. Krepps said, "as there are several owners who think they are unnecessary expenses for the association to take on in these difficult times. That is, there was no intention to ignore the report and incur fines and so on, but simply to assess the scope of the repairs and so on, in order to proceed in a fiscally responsible fashion."

Maki had no idea what point she was trying to make. "And so...?" he prompted.

"And so, perhaps you and I should sit down in the next little while to discuss some other issues that might address the question of who is responsible, and who is not, for bringing the building fully up to code." She saw his puzzlement and looked around as if she thought the residents slowly pacing the sidewalk wore hidden microphones.

"It's possible," she said, lowering her voice, "that the building will change ownership. This is not written in stone, or is even close to the stone-writing stage, but it is a distinct possibility."

"Mrs. Krepps! Mavis!" came a voice from a knot of people just inside the open lobby door. A very pale man with electric white hair escaping from a stocking cap waved an arm for her attention.

He arrived at her side, breathing shallowly. Maki smelled turpentine, soap, recent sweat, and illness among a mélange of lesser smells. One of the fainter smells instantly conjured a memory of a terrible house fire he'd investigated out on the edge of town near the old fort, though the smell was plantlike and aromatic and had nothing to do with smoke or flames.

"Have they found Viola Six?" the man asked. Mrs. Krepps introduced him to Maki as Leo Uberti, a painter of landscapes, and said he lived on the same floor as the missing woman.

"I saw her this morning, not too long after seven," Uberti said. "She was getting into the elevator. She seemed fine, though she was wearing pajamas with some kind of jacket on top. Not so strange, really. I've seen her in that gear before, when she's going down to the lobby or

73

the storage area or someplace, and doesn't think anyone else is up and about yet. OK, a little eccentric, a little dramatic at times, but what? She just takes off without telling anyone? She just evaporates? I'm not buying it."

"I had the fire crew check her apartment again, just now, to see if she somehow got mixed up during the evacuation and went back there," Mrs. Krepps said in soothing tones. "And they checked the stairways, the parking garage, and so on. And she is not on the premises, Leo. I locked her apartment, and if she doesn't show up soon, we will bring in the police."

"And Herbie," Uberti said. "Our Mr. Bonebright. Where is he?"

"He didn't show up for his customary breakfast hour at the Den," Mrs. Krepps said. "I checked. And his car is not in the garage. So we don't know where he might be at the moment. Unfortunately, he's in for something of a shock when he comes home to find he's had a fire on his premises."

"Probably his fault," Uberti declared. "It wouldn't be the first time, would it? That popcorn grease event right after he moved in? Why wasn't he canned on the spot? He's a slob and a menace, and the owners' association is in a position to send him packing, and it doesn't."

Mrs. Krepps's mouth tightened, and she placed a hand on Uberti's forearm.

"Why don't you go talk to Cassie McMackin, Leo? She looks as if she could use a friend at the moment." She gestured toward a slim, very erect woman wearing a magenta shawl over a gold-colored robe. She'd wrapped the soft cloth around her tightly and gazed straight ahead. Her delicate face was a mask of sorrow. Her eyes were wide open, and tears ran down her cheeks. She made no effort to wipe them away. Looking at her, Maki felt a strange shock of shared grief, as if they were at a funeral for a mutual friend.

Uberti went over to her and rested a hand on her shoulder. She closed her eyes, then looked up at him and shook her head, incredulous.

"She's a friend of Viola's," Mrs. Krepps confided to Maki. "Maybe that's the trouble. She's worried."

This didn't look like straightforward worry to Maki, but he kept his thought to himself. Reviewing the photos he'd taken, he realized he didn't have Uberti or Cassie McMackin, so he summoned them over and briskly got it done, then mentioned that he'd be around quite a lot for the next few days and would want to talk with them both.

"I can tell you one thing someone should look into," Uberti said. "There has been a teenage kid on the premises who shouldn't have been here. Mrs. Rideout says he crashed in through the dumpster window when she was emptying her trash yesterday afternoon, then disappeared, then surfaced this morning outside the building during the evacuation. Ran like a shot when I called attention to him. Puffy kind of kid with a Star Wars T-shirt, carrying a sack of some kind. Could it be items that he robbed?"

Herbie Bonebright's apartment, scorched and soggy, was minimally furnished and none too clean. There was a single bedroom with a sagging, unmade bed and a plastic chair covered with dirty clothes and damp-looking towels. Some cords were tangled atop a card table but not connected to anything. Maki closed his eyes briefly and reminded himself to be on the lookout for additions and absences: anything inside that shouldn't be there and anything that should be there that wasn't.

As he always did, he identified the least affected area of the apartment—in this case the small bedroom and bath—and moved very slowly, in a counterclockwise fashion, around the spaces, taking a photo with every step. (The whispery sound of his phone made him realize again how much he missed his old Canon thirty-five millimeter with its decisive clack, its actual film. Digital photos were so easy to alter—in that way, they replicated memories—but they were the standard in fire inspections now, convenience and speed winning out, once again, over rigor.) The bathroom was filmed and stale. A toothbrush and a comb sat next to a ring of keys on the back of the toilet. Maki photographed the keys, then picked them up with gloved fingers and put them in a large Ziploc. From the bedroom closet's floor, discovered almost by accident behind a laundry hamper, he picked up an odd-looking object the size and shape of an egg. It was charcoal-colored and had a clip on the back. He put it in another bag.

The living room had a ripped faux-leather recliner, a TV table, dark-blue bedsheets for window curtains, and a large new flat-screen television, tuned to the sci-fi channel with the sound off. Tentacles the size of elephant trunks were slithering out the windows of a rusty school bus. There was a ratty old pillow on the recliner, and when Maki moved it, he found a shiny iPad partially wedged into the corner of the seat. He retrieved the largest Ziploc he'd brought and placed the iPad inside it.

The living room opened onto the galley kitchen, where the smells and scorching confirmed that he had reached the source.

Again Maki closed his eyes, this time to pay attention to his nose. The crowd of smells jostled for a few minutes, then grouped themselves into pods, some of them large and confident and familiar, others more mysterious, like the one that seemed to combine Coleman fuel and some kind of soft plastic.

The fire appeared to have started on the stove top and moved up the back wall to the ceiling and down to the floor. There was a charred pan on a back burner of the gas stove, but it had no residue in it of food or grease or anything else. The light bulb at the front of the fan had melted forward, suggesting a very hot, fast flame. He didn't touch the stove but took photos from a variety of angles and distances.

A charred area on the wall behind the stove looked blacker and deeper than it should have been. If a greasy hot pad had caught fire, or grease on the cupboard top had ignited, there would have been significant smoldering time. The mark on the wall also suggested a very hot fire. He picked at it with his knife to verify its depth.

Still, nothing he'd seen so far absolutely ruled out an accident of a slightly unconventional nature. He poked carefully through the ashes on the cupboard top, photographed them, and tweezered into a baggie a half inch of charred string and a sliver of wax.

The smell of Coleman fuel was strongest at the stove. He made another circle around the apartment, looking closely at the contents of the closets and cupboards, beneath the bed. No Coleman stove. No Coleman lantern or can of fuel. Perhaps the manager was a camper and kept those things in his car, or in the building's storage area. But why would he have brought the fuel to his apartment from somewhere else, and what would he have been using it for? Nothing about it made sense.

Maki sat in the recliner and thought about what he was smelling, seeing, feeling. The utter temporariness of the apartment's furnishings stayed front and center for some reason. The place felt like a room in a by-the-week motel. He held up the baggie with the large ring of keys in it. They had been removed from a belt loop clip, most likely, and Herbie Bonebright had left his apartment without them.

And yet what had the professor in the tracksuit told him about putting out the fire single-handedly? That he had grabbed the extinguisher and bashed in the locked door. Maki examined the door lock with some care. It was the kind that locked with a button from the inside and needed a key to unlock from the outside. And Herbie had left without his keys.

Back in the Volvo, Maki turned up the heater, rolled down the window, and smoked the day's second cigarette. Scattered debris blew down the street, and sleet ticked on the windshield. The temperature had dropped by at least fifteen degrees since early morning, and the sense of a benign November pause had given way to the first breaths of real winter.

Maki made his list: "1) Notify the police and highway patrol about the missing persons, Bonebright and

Six. See if their phones can be located and tracked. 2) Find the boy wearing the Star Wars T-shirt who was seen inside the building. 3) Get Bonebright's iPad to the geeks. 4) Get the lab work going. 5) Begin interviewing the Pheasant Run residents." He revved the Volvo a little and added a last item as an emotional nod to Rhonda and her ability to entertain the widest range of possibilities. "6) Rule nothing out."

Nightwalkers' Song

7

Cassie McMackin opened the curtains in her living room and sat in her velvet plum-colored armchair, which faced the window. The day's half-hearted storm had blown through, leaving the night sky, also plum colored, minutely punctured with icy stars. The season had turned, however, and now it would be winter.

She made herself a cup of hot chocolate with a shot of peppermint schnapps and returned to her cradling chair. It was night now. And she was alive.

The fire and evacuation had shocked her into terror first, and then into a sweeping sadness for those among her poor neighbors who, forbidden the elevator, had been herded whimpering down so many painful steps to stand outside in the morning's deepening chill. She needed some time to think about all this. She needed to find out what had happened to Viola.

From under a magazine on the side table, she retrieved her recorder, and she inserted a new cassette. Her voice low, she began to talk to Neil, as she had many times before.

"Strange developments in the aviary, Neil. This morning we had a fire. A shout, and heavy pounding on my door and on down the hall, and then firemen in their huge yellow uniforms were yelling at us to grab coats and shoes, and they marched us down the stairs that seemed endless, and out onto the sidewalk to mill like cattle in a pen. I kept watching for Viola, not finding her, and at some point I was told that she was missing, vanished. That her apartment had been empty when the men arrived, and no one—no one—had seen her after Leo Uberti spoke with her briefly, not long before the alarm blared and all became chaos. How does this happen? There is a lively, opinionated, feisty, hoping woman, and then there is an absence. When I thought about that, as we shivered and waited on the sidewalk, I became overwhelmed again by the idea that hope seems to exist only to march us toward utter, inevitable loss. And for what? What is served?"

She paused the machine to close her eyes, to pull her shawl close. He deserved to know. She depressed the recording button again.

"Before all this, I had a plan for today. I had a plan to go to sleep a final time. Right about now, I would be embracing oblivion, so to speak. Many reasons, love. Or maybe just a few or one. I'm sorting it out. And I'm reserving the option."

She felt involved suddenly in an argument, and she clicked the machine off. The laundry room would be empty this late, and she needed something to distract her long enough for her thoughts to sort themselves out. She wheeled her wire laundry basket from the closet and added a half dozen clean handkerchiefs of Neil's that she kept folded in drawer. A man with a clean white handkerchief, always. He carried one in his pajama pocket, his

pants pocket, his ski jacket pocket. His ski jacket zipped
to the chin as he stood on the top of their favorite mountain. One more missive for the evening:

"Remember how we stood atop the white mountain
on our skis, in our woolens, and the snow made caped
creatures of the pines and settled a grand hush on it all?
How the noises that remained were small and distant,
like rumors of themselves? The miniature clang of the
T-bars as they swung around the spool at the top? The
Strauss waltzes floating from the tinny speaker outside
the warming shack?

"We were so new to each other. We anticipated so much.

"Sometimes, on the mountain, the fog rolled in
and the swaddled trees fell back into it, fainted, and the
waltzes fainted, too, and all we heard was the chatter of
our long wooden skis, the scrape of the snow, an occasional small shout or whoop somewhere far away.

"Standing at the top—you, me—there was the knowledge of difficult terrain to navigate, a spectacular fall or
two or three to prepare for, challenge and travail and the
fast heart, and always a certain kind of necessary misery to
endure—the tight boots and soaked woolens, the glassed
eyelashes and wonky knee—but we careened down the
white mountain to arrive gasping on the level and ready to
do it all again. We couldn't wait."

She let the tape roll as she fetched the kitchen cloths
for the laundry. Someone down the hall turned up a talk
show that filled the outside corridor with aggrievement
before it was turned down.

"And remember that bright white day we rode the
small bus down the mountain because our car was dead

in the lot and we had to find someone in town to fix it? That beautiful, dark-haired woman in the bus, wrapped in a mink coat, wearing beaded sealskin boots and weeping? Huge sunglasses she had, and from beneath them tears dropping off her chin. Sometimes she blotted them with a tissue. Sometimes she didn't. She seemed transported from a nineteenth-century novel, in full costume and bearing a tragedy that we were supposed to decipher from her tears. She thrilled me. Where had she come from? Where was she going? Why was she so swaddled and alone? She wore thin black leather gloves pulled tight across the bulges of her rings.

"The driver let her off at the train station, and you asked him what her trouble was. Snow blindness, he said. All that light bouncing off all that snow, and she had no idea she couldn't be out in it with bare eyes. Some people, he said. And his voice was mean."

Thumbing through a *National Geographic* in the basement laundry room, Cassie listened to the dryer's tumble and tick and imagined Neil's handkerchiefs flying like white birds through the jungle heat. Always, he needed a clean pile of them. And she had happily obliged. It was a small thing to do, to launder and iron a dozen squares of cotton a week, and it mattered to him. So odd, in its way. Who could ever predict in the early years of a six-decade marriage how small gestures of care would count, especially toward the end?

She added them to her laundry simply to comfort herself with the ritual, to be reminded of the wit that had survived almost every mental depredation in Neil.

When she snapped at him, as she sometimes had done when it all seemed too much to weather, he liked to retrieve a handkerchief from his fleece vest and wave it as a flag of surrender. Sometimes it made them both smile. Sometimes it didn't.

They were nothing less than a fixation for him. Possibly it had to do with the fact that he'd had fierce nosebleeds as a child. That information had come from his mother, who said they occurred for a few years only but were exuberantly bloody when they happened and that stanching them could be dramatic and prolonged. That would scare a child—the idea that his blood was leaking from him and who knew when it would stop? Perhaps Neil later felt that his memories had become like that blood, escaping him, unstanchable. One day, watching the news of the latest massive oil spill, the earth hemorrhaging again, he had anxiously reached for a handkerchief and held it to his nose. His eyes over the top of the cloth were stretched with fear.

Cassie looked up, suddenly aware of someone in the room. A boy, a teenager, stood panting in the doorway. He sounded as if he had been running for days. His shoulders heaved. The hand that grasped the door frame was as delicate and articulate as a girl's. His rain-soaked backpack drooped heavily from his elbow, as if it were full of rocks. He wore a Star Wars T-shirt.

She folded her arms in a reflex of self-protection. He raised his hand like a traffic cop.

"Where did you come from?" she asked. It was rare to see any young people on the premises apart from the occasional visiting grandchild. He vaguely gestured upward. His breath was so labored he couldn't speak. It squeaked on the edges. A door slammed somewhere and he jumped. Cassie knew she should suspect the worst: that the boy had been rifling through a tenant's medicine cabinet or stealing a wallet left on a counter—that someone even now was on the phone to 911 or searching the hallways for his retreating back—but he looked so stripped and scared that she couldn't seem to feel him as any kind of threat.

"Sit down," she said. He flopped into a plastic chair as she shut the door to the laundry room, though they were unlikely to be disturbed this late in the day.

She studied him. His hair was dull and stood up from his head in rampant spikes and clumps. His skin was mottled. His eyes were large and brown and they moved quickly around the room. He was puffy and underdressed—thin T-shirt, ripped jeans, sad old sneakers. His foot tapped the floor. He smelled stale and oddly metallic.

"What's the trouble?" she asked quietly. "Why are you in here? What's after you?"

He avoided her eyes. Then he yawned, a huge yawn, as if it were the only way he could get enough breath.

"Sorry. I'm not bored. I can't help it." He looked up at her. "I'm on some meds that make me do that."

"You have health problems."

Perhaps that wild look meant he was on the verge of a seizure. She tried to remember what action was called for in such a case. A pen on the tongue, so the tongue couldn't be swallowed?

"Well, if a contaminated brain and being driven nuts by everyone in the world are health problems, well I guess

I have health problems." He stressed the last two words. His foot resumed its tapping.

"That's a peculiar term, isn't it?" Cassie said. "*Health problem*. It's sort of like saying, oh...*love trouble*. How can health be a kind of problem, or love be a kind of trouble? What's meant is problems *with* one's health or *with* a love situation. The shorthand isn't always so accurate, is it?"

The boy looked at her blankly. "Right," he said, wiping sweat off his face with the hem of his T-shirt. "Plus my girlfriend disappeared this evening. She's not answering texts or calls. I think she ran away somewhere."

"Would you like one of these?" Cassie asked, handing him a clean handkerchief.

"I'll destroy it," the boy said.

"So destroy it," Cassie said.

He scrubbed his face with the cloth. He looked ready to cry. "Her name is Raven," he said. "Like the bird."

Cassie didn't know what to say next, so she sat down on the chair next to the boy and pretended to get lost in her own thoughts. It was a method she'd discovered rather late in life for putting a stressed person at ease. You simply remove any obligation for that person to respond to you.

A few minutes passed. The dryer turned off. Cassie got up to retrieve the last of the clothes and began to fold them. The boy had tipped his head against the wall and closed his eyes.

"I just about got myself killed today," he said. "This guy at school hates me and he rounds up his friends and they come after me. They did it yesterday and I hit him and escaped. Then, today, when I went to school, I thought I was feeling, you know, up to them. I even went back to school this evening for band practice. But they cornered me and I broke away and they chased me. One other time there were six of them, and I ended up in the ER." He took a long breath. "But Josh Anderson doesn't have a clue about what I could do to him, if I really wanted to. If I just didn't care anymore, and really wanted to." His voice had taken on a peculiar lilt.

Cassie had a flashing moment in which her daughter's face, when she was embarking on a new assignment in a more dangerous region, wore the sound of the boy's new voice.

"Do your parents know that they are after you? Do they know you aren't safe at school?"

"'Safe at school'!" He shook his head as if he couldn't believe such gullibility existed. "And my parents. Well, my dad is shacked up with the half sister of the guy who wants to fucking kill me, and my mom spends most of her time trying not to go crazy from wanting to fucking kill my dad." He stood up briskly. "She goes to some kind of sweat yoga tonight." He consulted his phone, shook his head, and tapped out a brief text. "She doesn't know what to do with me.

"Sorry for the shitty language," he added as an afterthought.

"So why here?" Cassie asked. "Why this place?"

"Well, the guys who were after me aren't going to follow me into a building where people can see them jump me."

"Won't they wait outside?"

"Not if I stay here for a while."

"In the laundry room?"

"Well...somewhere," he said, gesturing vaguely. "It's pretty late for them to wait around, if they're out there. I think they'll leave pretty soon." He bent to retie a shoelace.

"You know," Cassie said, "There was a fire in the building early this morning, and one of the residents says she saw a kid in a Star Wars T-shirt enter the building yesterday afternoon—that he jumped through the garbage window when she was emptying her trash and ran down the hall. And then a man who lives on my floor says he saw that T-shirt on a kid who was outside the building right after the fire, when we were all evacuated. I'm going to guess that those people saw you."

The boy squinted at her. He shrugged.

"That fire inspector came over to the school," he said. "He already talked to me. The principal knew right away I was the one they wanted to talk to." He pointed to his T-shirt. "And he got me out of class to talk to that guy Maki."

"Well?" Cassie asked.

"He basically said I was going to have to account for my whereabouts during some certain hours. That I would need some proof of my whereabouts. He's going to talk to me again."

"And where were you?"

The boy considered this. "Not anyplace where anybody else saw me."

Cassie surprised herself with the thought that she should invite him to her apartment to eat something and gather himself. He seemed to need every kind of nourishment. She knew about needing nourishment. Then she surprised herself more.

"What if I said you were with me when that fire broke out?"

He looked at her as if she had said something embarrassing.

"Why would I be with you?" he asked so carefully that Cassie felt slapped.

"Because I went outside, early, before the fire, to see if the paperboy was in sight. And I saw you walking, and you looked very cold, or possibly injured, and I invited you to my apartment for a cup of hot chocolate."

"Oh," he said.

"And when the fire alarm went off, you ran off, down the stairs, and I didn't see you again."

She sounded crazy to herself, but she didn't care. She located the Post-it Note block that was left in the laundry room for messages among tenants ("Please remember to clean the lint catcher after every use!") and she wrote down her name and her phone number and gave them to him. He told her his name was Clayton.

"You can call this number anytime, and I'll answer it, Clayton," she said, as she placed her folded clothes in a wire basket with wheels, Neil's old handkerchiefs folded neatly on top. "Or if I don't, leave a message."

"What would I say?" he asked. His exhausted eyes made her look away.

"Anything you want to," she said as she pushed her folded clothes out of the room.

In her apartment, Cassie put away the laundry and poured herself a Gatorade. She needed the electrolytes. She needed something. The kid, Clayton, had appeared so suddenly and in such a state. It was as if the events of his day had hooked him out of home waters to leave him flopping and gasping on a riverbank. Or did he even have some equivalent of safe water, someplace that felt calm and familiar to him, someplace where he could swim and breathe? So many of the young fish seemed not to.

He had followed her from the laundry room to the elevator, waving in a stylized sort of way as the doors closed. Probably she should have made sure he was out of the building before it was locked for the night. Maybe he was quietly slipping into someone's bathroom right now, slipping past an old person napping in front of the TV and leaving with a handful of sleeping pills or painkillers. Possible. Not likely, though. She hadn't lived this long to end up with no instincts at all about another's intentions or criminal capabilities.

How utterly different, for instance, had been her visceral reaction to the boy as compared to her reaction to the lame-brained newcomer Herbie Bonebright. Why had she even listened to him when he passed her in the hall, a week ago, then turned to call her name?

He wore a pasted-on smile. His face was shiny with sweat. He put a hand on the wall and asked how everything was going for her, his tone so bored she knew it wasn't a question. And when she answered briefly, he just smiled and watched her.

"Mrs. McMackin," he said in a very low voice. "I've heard you make things up. I've heard that you and Mrs. Six tell lies, just to entertain yourselves. Is that right?" His eyes opened wider, and there was something in them that was frozen and virulent.

She felt the heat roar into her face.

"Who the hell do you think you are?" Cassie said very quietly. "You don't know anything about me. But what you should know is that some of the renters in this building have a problem with you. My friend John Quant who recently moved away, for instance."

"I'm sure he did," Herbie said, nodding gravely. He still blocked the door with his lumpy body. Down the hall, behind him, Cassie saw Viola Six standing outside her apartment door, eyes fixed on his threatening back.

Cassie raised her arm and called an adamant greeting to Viola. Herbie flinched. He turned on his heel, ignored Viola, who simply stared at him, and disappeared into the elevator.

"There is something wrong with that man," Viola called to Cassie. "There is something about him that reminds me of my old beau, Captain, who left me destitute." She thought for a moment. "Minus the charm."

Cassie put down her Gatorade, bent her head, and said a short prayer for the boy, Clayton. And then she prayed, as she did every day, for all the children, for her dead husband and her dead daughter, for John Quant, and for those she knew when she was young and had lost through time, distance, or death. She prayed for the groaning, hectically gorgeous, steaming world, which seemed, more and more often, to lurch and shudder on its planetary path, as if trying to correct its course—buildings tumbled then, oceans surged, hurricanes annihilated, wars and diseases erupted—before it resumed its ponderous spin, heavy under new layers of the innocent dead.

She prayed for surcease and hope and for the better instincts out there to triumph after she was gone. She prayed that she had lived well, by her lights as she had been able to know them. Then she prayed once more for the pale and sweaty boy who seemed to be hanging on by his fingernails.

Cassie prayed without the barest image of a deity. This was relatively recent. It was as if she had conducted, for decades, a lengthy call-and-response with an entity that, somewhere along the line, had installed a slowly evaporating hologram of itself and walked away. Or as if God had, for her, become a phantom limb, absent but extremely painful.

Part of the reason was that she had lost her faith in the Catholic Church, the institution she had embraced so long ago because of its very particular combination of texture, gravity, and practice. She had long felt that reckoning with suffering was the only credible function of religion, and that the Church took it on in a complex and artful way. How could one listen to Mozart's *Requiem*, for instance, and not hear in it the terror and rage of the dying young composer, his confusion and pity and yes, finally, a hint of his understanding of the nature of suffering and of God?

Her break, which she knew to be final, came swiftly on the heels of her realization that, theology and tradition and music quite apart, this was an institution that had protected the utterly corrupt and life-denying among its priests and nuns, that it had created suffering on a rather grand scale. And the victims were children—the innocent, the yearning, the idealistic, the vulnerable. She requested an explanation from the

95

entity she had addressed for so many decades, and she got nothing. "This is such bad timing," she complained to the blankness. "Now when I'm old, and could have used some blind faith."

The fire, the aftermath of the fire, Herbie Bonebright's disappearance, Viola's disappearance, and now the presence of this puffy tormented boy—it was such a welter. So many unfinished stories that seemed to want her to address them, but wouldn't say how.

It wasn't yet ten p.m. She decided to check Viola's apartment, on the long shot that she had simply left the building before the fire, for her own reasons, and had decided to return. She knocked, then ducked under the yellow strips the police had placed across the door and used the key Viola had given her to let herself in, calling as she went.

The apartment was spare and tidy, as it always was. Viola had placed crocheted doilies on the arms of the two chairs that faced the ancient rabbit-eared TV on a card table. Next to the television was a framed photograph of the young President Kennedy, grinning into the sun. The door to the small balcony was closed. A plastic vase on the coffee table held a profusion of paper tulips.

In the bedroom, Cassie studied the clothes on the bed and those in Viola's closet, arranged by function and color, feeling again the sadness that seemed so much a part of old age, sadness that had something to do with the fact, the *fact*, that the simplest of undertakings—getting dressed for a day—required a level of care and planning that approached the valiant. Nothing was casual anymore.

But why were some clothes laid out on the bed, as if she'd been preparing to dress but hadn't completed the job? Had the alarm interrupted her? And then what?

A Post-it Note on the bureau directed Viola to "Find lapis necklace!" Clearly it had been an unexpected gap, so panic-producing that Cassie felt a little surge of helpfulness and opened the top drawer, the one where everyone kept their necklaces, to see if the necklace had simply been overlooked.

There was a photograph in the drawer, turned facedown. On the backing cardboard, in Viola's handwriting, was a single word. *Italy.* She turned over the photo to find a radiant, clear-eyed woman wearing a satiated smile. She leaned against a white pillar that was darkly streaked with rust or erosion. Two pigeons at her feet pecked at the ground. It was a black-and-white photo, and the light was muted. A vendor with a tray of flowers seemed to be assessing the person snapping the photo.

The woman had Viola's thick hair, but in a tawny shade, long and wavy and swept back from her forehead. Her eyes were dark and widely spaced. She seemed loose-limbed and tall, the way she had casually but artfully tilted herself against the stone, so that a pretty leg parted her coat. The smile—that I-own-the-world smile—was, yes, Viola's. The same crooked eyetooth was there, and even an expression of pleased self-deprecation that Viola sometimes wore, as if she were mimicking someone she didn't feel herself to be, and, in fact, when all was said and done, didn't want to be.

The necklace, just visible at her throat, could have been lapis lazuli. One eyebrow was very slightly cocked, in worldly complicity with the viewer. She looked ready for anything.

When had this Italy visit occurred in Viola's life? Cassie had difficulty imagining it, and, as she struggled to, she experienced a wave of shame. She hadn't actually believed Viola's stories of her adventures, especially the more risqué ones. She had thought them to be wishful thinking because she herself evidently did not possess the imagination necessary to link them to the stolid, white-haired, bespectacled, opinionated, solitary woman who was her friend.

Would the photo have been taken before she came home to marry Ollie the mill worker? That seemed impossible. Who would set off for adventures abroad, fully alert to the world and its possibilities and her own considerable beauty, and come home to marry someone she'd known most of her life, someone who would, by her own admission, always have about him the feel of a small room without air?

Maybe she had discovered she was pregnant.

But would she have embarked on the adventures she told Cassie about after she had married and had a child to care for? Not likely. Not in that era, certainly. So had she waited, perhaps, until the child, the unlikable Rod, was out of the house, at which point Ollie suffered his untimely death in a mill accident, and she began to traverse the big wide world? She would perhaps have been only forty, with half of her life still ahead of her. Could this beauty in an Italian piazza be forty? Cassie squinted as she brought the image closer. Yes, she could.

—

She prepared for bed, exhausted, and placed her recorder on the nightstand. She had more to tell Neil's ghost. She wanted to offer some kind of summation of their years together, in a way that didn't discount the ordinary—the raising of their daughter, her own years as a librarian and a volunteer and a close friend to half a dozen now dead, and Neil's years as a high school history teacher and his flying of small planes and his passion for secret fly-fishing spots—but in a way that made it, instead, the summary of their moments of most-aliveness, separate and together. And the words wouldn't come. She turned on the recorder and went back to the day on the mountain.

"In the hotel bar that night, we had beers and burgers and stomped around in our after-ski boots. Some big guy in a plaid wool shirt and suspendered wool pants said something at the other end of the bar that made all the men laugh. His girlfriend or wife or date slapped him on the bicep and shook her head. Her face was flushed. Big new roars of laughter.

"The men, so many of them veterans of the war, two of them survivors of the POW camps, were adamant about the possibility of normalcy. The blur, the beer, the shouts, and yet they, you, had your own scorched eyes. You grieved to be hoping boys again, so you were unapologetic about becoming, when you felt like it, extra-boys.

"In the women's bathroom, a small window was cracked to the night. I pushed it open and sucked in the sharp air. The sky was black in the old way. The town was tiny and the streetlights made pale V shapes on the street. Fields of stars in that black sky fell together into an immense vault that reached further than I had ever seen

99

before. I felt I was looking up through an enormous bell. A train howled in the distance and a dog barked in the street. My muscles hurt.

"'Shall I?' I said aloud, testing it. 'Yes. I will have a child. She will be the freest part of me, my traveler, my joy. She will be the part of me that survives me, that moves into the future.'

"And, you know, at that moment I did see Marian as a child, and even as an adult. I saw her personality and her prospects, most of them, as strange as that may sound. I saw a lot of it, but not the end.

"Your voice made its way through the crowd sounds outside the door, jubilant, oblivious.

"The snow-blinded woman on the train in the night, speeding east, slept behind her dark glasses.

"She left me to it."

8

L eo Uberti in #402 arranged his easel and paint supplies near the curtainless window that framed the crown of a Chinese maple out on the boulevard, grateful again that he had landed a rental on the fourth floor, where his view was something better than tree trunks, parked cars, and teenagers shuffling off to school as if they had been tipped out of their beds onto a moving sidewalk, too sleepy to resist. In the early night, he could discern the tree's outlines and remember in detail how it looked in full sunlight. He removed the Emperor Concerto from its gray paper sleeve and placed the record on the hi-fi he had seen no reason to update. He liked his music with the delicious whisper of revolutions at the beginning, like a nervous performer breathing through his teeth.

He closed his eyes and ran his fingertips along the ribs of his right side. Still tender to the lightest touch. How stupid he had been to take on Herbie Bonebright over the issue of a leaking showerhead. Well, it hadn't really been about the showerhead at all, of course. It had been about Leo's right to ask whether Herbie knew anything at all about plumbing, and Herbie's refusal to answer. It had been about Leo's right to ask Herbie why

John Quant on the third floor had moved out so suddenly, after warning Leo to stay out of Herbie's way—the way Herbie had just laughed at that, bringing his wide face and his rank breath right up to Leo's face, to ignite the white rage that made Leo take a swipe at that face and get a hard chop to the ribs in exchange. White rage and such depletion afterward that he could scarcely move.

At least Herbie was off the premises now, and Pheasant Run's residents didn't have to add his presence to the stresses of the day. Didn't have to think about him at all, if they didn't want to.

The chaos around the fire in Herbie's apartment this morning had deeply unnerved Leo: the labored evacuation, the comings and goings of the engines and hoses and personnel, Mrs. Rideout's fall on the stairs and Jerry Olson's shortness of breath, the terrified eyes of his fellow tenants, a new and ominous tremor in his hands, his impending interview with the fire inspector, a raging headache, Viola Six's vanishing—all of it culminating in a state of near-panic that he hoped Beethoven might mitigate.

And that boy. Who was that boy, darting in and out of the building? What was his particular agenda?

The smudge-colored foliage this November intrigued him. He'd never seen anything like it—those clinging leaves, so far past their time to be gone. He felt they very nearly told him something important about displacement, about disparity, about a feeling that had provoked and mystified him most of his life. What was a physical entity when it became marooned from its customary location? An erratic. One of those boulders carried by white ice away from its original home. The leaves should have been mulch on the ground by now, but there they were, clinging, in the wrong place, at the wrong time. As perhaps he was, as well, and had been doing since he was a very young man.

Well, maybe those gray leaves could tell him something about the dislocations of his own life, about the incongruity of being a dark-skinned, dark-eyed Italian Jew in a white-bread college town in the American inland West. The shocking circumstances of his arrival. The slights out of nowhere, the muted disdain he'd endured all his years in the so-called land of the free. His emotional paralysis. The disjunction of being an elderly artist, a perceptive and discriminating person, in a country, an era, that wanted its elders, no matter what attributes they might possess, to be innocuous and erasable, especially if they were too poor or sick to line anyone's pockets.

He lowered his eyelids to produce a veiled gaze. Then he tried to move his mental stage lighting from the front, where he saw furred black branches against a deep evening sky, to the background, so that the scene might take on the additional depth that made it revelatory.

What he saw, when the shift occurred, was the low lights of a little city in the fog. They seemed to breathe in a shallow sort of way, their borders daintily expanding and contracting. Cristóbal. Cristóbal, Panama. Panama in the fog, every spot of light a tiny buoy, warning Leo and the other crew on the huge ship that their futures were going to be what they could never, in their wildest dreams, have imagined.

———

What a glitter-palace the *Conte Biancamano* had been when she carnivaled through the big waters with her several thousand passengers, her musicians, her dance floors, her champagne and swimming pools and movies. Leo had never tried to paint it, but if he did, he'd wash it all in a luminescent pink. Near dusk, the floor show singers warmed up in their cabins as the big engines thrummed, and the setting sun made the portholes rosy and excited looking, and it was easy to imagine the first-class passengers cast in that pink glow as they finished their dressing drinks and adjusted scarves, sequins, and collar studs for the evening ahead. Walking the upper deck after his shift in the kitchen, young Leo (just fifteen) liked to breathe in all the sounds: the floor show, the crooner in the first-class lounge, the spiking laughter, ruffles of clapping, the murmurs of the other deck-walkers he passed—all of it riding the deeper sound of ocean water churning and spraying as the festive little city cut its path from port to port.

And then to be interdicted in Cristóbal, Leo and the rest of the Italian crew ordered by the Allied forces to remain with the ship in that sweltering, gray place—sky gray, water gray, tempers gray and then worse. Meals became desultory affairs. Fights broke out. They felt they'd been detained on the flattened grass of a circus that had moved to the next town.

And after a year and a half of the motionless gray?

The presence of something colorless and coiled, ready to spring. Pranks, shouts, fights, booze, plots. Running feet at night in the long corridors. Talk of engine-smashing or ship-jumping. And himself, young Leo, escaping to the granular light of the ship's abandoned library to read anything he could find that had to do with gadgetry, gallantry, inventions, tricks, or Houdini.

Deeper in the ship: Wrenches banging on engine parts. Small fires springing to life. Tony, his hotheaded friend, bragging that he knew how to set one in which the ignition was delayed and he could be eight hands into a poker game when the alarm was raised.

And the color of Ellis Island after the emptying of the ship? Cement. And the barred train car that whistled across the vast and tawny American interior, taking Leo and some of the others to the internment camp somewhere in the mountains of the West? Yellow sunlight barred with black.

My striped chariot, Leo thought. *Bringing me to a former cavalry fort, just a few miles from this very room. From this room where I stand, more than seven decades off that train, to paint leaves that don't know what they are supposed to do.*

He kept his eyes squinted and dipped his brush in the cadmium white and began to make little lights on an anonymous vegetative color he'd mixed up a few days ago and laid down with a broad brush in impatient X's. Dab, dab, dab. His pinched motions made him feel small and angry. He didn't dare open his eyes fully to see how stupid and desperate the marks might look.

The fort's commander, Harold Tone, wasn't a terror. He didn't abuse anyone physically. Did he ever hit anyone? No. He was just quietly cruel. He had the ability to present one convincing face and manner to his equals, and another, entirely different, to the internees, especially the

Italians, who seemed to provoke in him a particular kind of vehemence. In that respect, he wasn't unlike Herbie Bonebright—so fawning with Pheasant Run's condo owners, such a bully with the renters. A personality split down the middle.

Tone, walking the grounds in the evenings, carrying a big Hasselblad and a tripod, taking his leisure in a way that was predatory, as if he were coercing his surroundings to deliver something to him. Leo, raking leaves, waiting for him and his obstreperous camera to move to a new place, and the way he remembers what happened next, to the very word.

"What do you want," Tone said.

"To get the last of the leaves," Leo said, pointing at the commander's feet.

Tone's face congealed. "You stupid wop," he said quietly. "Who the hell do you think you are?"

Leo felt dipped in acid. Everything burned. He ordered himself to stay silent, avoid the man's direct gaze.

Tone slowly folded up his gear and took a step toward Leo, the tripod shaft held like a weapon. Leo tightened his grip on the rake handle.

He came so close that Leo could smell his yeasty breath.

"Let me tell you something," Tone said. "You know, I could trade you off for a yellow dog."

He squinted into the distance.

"And then I could shoot the dog."

The fort and its grounds had a peaceable look with its handsome tall trees, the river flowing nearby, the mountains all round; and inside the fences were the sounds of string quartets, of hammers, of men speaking in Italian, and Japanese, and German.

Each nationality pretended the others didn't exist. So many of the Italians had been musicians aboard the ship that they staged performances most nights in the entertainment hall. *I pirati* with its slavering plunderers whipping machetes through the air. And what was the other musical in which the guy named Francisco donned a fluffy dress and played the ingenue? *Romanticismo.* What else? Leo had a brief vision of Francisco in his dress and huge booted feet ambling up the gravel path where several Japanese picked the pebbles they used to make pretty little pots. And the Germans? Leo couldn't remember what they did, the Germans, to pass the time, to move through the kind of time that made some of the men sick in the head. They flocked to the camp doctor with this strange headache, that case of the jitters, nightmares and sometimes weeping, all of it the more desperate, somehow, because the setting was so pleasant. Bella Vista, the Italians had instantly dubbed the fort.

During the church hour at Bella Vista, he liked to walk the grounds, slowing as he passed the tall house of Tone's second-in-command, Captain Whiston, because the captain's daughter, Mary, apparently a heathen like himself, was often on the porch at that hour, reading.

He called out to her once, asking if she could recommend whatever it was that seemed to absorb her so much. She called back that it was only a ladies' book and she was bored with it, and she might take a stroll around the grounds. Which she did. Which they did, keeping to a small path on the periphery where they weren't likely to be noticed. And that was the beginning, and the beginning of the end.

In his old age, the fort's cemetery was one of Leo's haunts. He liked its quietness, its smallness, the way the breezes tossed the branches of the big cottonwoods, the way the three sheep in the field next door made their timeless sheep sounds as they gobbled up the rampant knapweed. He thought then of Vasto on the Adriatic, and the sounds of bells and the sheep in the mornings as they were herded out to the hillsides.

Yesterday, pedaling his bicycle to the grocery store, he'd felt every nanosecond of his nearly ninety years. He knew they thought he shouldn't be riding his bicycle at all, the others in his building who watched him chain up his old Schwinn after an outing, his hands trembling with exhaustion. But what harm could he possibly do to anyone but himself? They were ones who thought nothing of jumping into their cars to engage their failing reflexes in fast traffic, to nick parking meters and occasionally terrorize bicyclists and pedestrians alike. He, on the other hand, did battle with nothing but the muscles in his legs, the disintegrating alveoli in his lungs. He was nothing but a potential victim, especially because he always made it a point to ride without a helmet because of his life insurance policy. If he was killed, some would find themselves showered in coin.

A few days ago in the grocery store, the background music—some kind of soft rock—had suddenly opened its curtain to admit the utterly old-fashioned sound of

"Greensleeves," and it had made him want to weep. It took the checkout girl with the metal bolt in her tongue a few throat clearings and small coughs to jolt him into handing over the money for his beans and orange juice.

He put them in his bicycle basket and pedaled slowly to the cemetery.

He and Mary were to meet behind the officers' quarters. She had said she'd give him her answer, adding teasingly that if he didn't show up, she'd know the worst. Mary. Mary of the long pale fingers. Mary of the sly laugh.

They were both eighteen, and would wait for the war to be over. They would marry, and stay in the mountain valley, and have four children, two boys and two girls. They would give all of them beautiful, antique names that could be shortened if the kids wanted something normal. Antigone. Ferdinand. They would love each other enough to erase the perfidies of the war, of all wars.

He walked toward their meeting place in the dusk under a wafer moon, and Leo knew joy, and thought it was his to keep.

There was a scrim of snow, light as talc. Warm lights glowed in the windows of the officers' houses, and smoke tendriled out of the chimneys. In the last house, a slouching shadow filled the back kitchen door, smoking a cigar.

Tone beckoned him over. He asked him what he was doing. Leo responded that he was taking a stroll before sleep, that it had been a long day and he was tired of his barracks mates and wanted just to walk and to think. He adamantly did not turn his gaze toward the small field behind the houses, the broad-crowned tree in its far corner where he knew she waited. He took a deep breath. Maybe an apology was coming from the commander.

"Take a load off your feet," Tone said, pointing to a splintery old bench next to the door.

"I will keep walking, I think," Leo said, trying to sound light, to sound genial.

"Take a load off your feet," said Tone. He patted the seat of the bench.

Leo took a few steps backward. He thought briefly about simply turning and walking away. But he could hear the soft, condensed fury in Tone's voice. Tone patted the bench again. Leo sat down. Tone gazed at a pale line of light on the horizon and took a long meditative pull on his cigar. And then they just waited. For a few minutes, for five, for perhaps fifteen. Leo made a tentative move to stand, and Tone placed the flat of his hand on Leo's head and pushed him back down.

More time. Much more time. Until it was full dark, and what had seemed a full hour or more, and suddenly Tone fixed Leo with an alert, even surprised look, and asked him what he was still doing on the bench. Didn't he have something better to do?

Leo couldn't speak past his anger. He said nothing. He pulled his sweater sleeves over his chilled hands and walked toward the barracks.

"Pleasant evening, old dog," Tone called.

When he circled back and made his way to the tree, she was not there. Could she really have decided he'd had second thoughts? He didn't think so, but he had no way to know, because in the morning word came to the barracks and flew around the entire compound that Captain Whiston's pretty daughter, the pale reader, had scarlet fever and was not expected to survive. In two days, she was gone.

For reasons still unclear to him, Leo was never able, after that, to imagine a life for himself that didn't have her at its center. He stayed in the little mountain city with the fort on its western edge. He educated himself, learned the insurance business, worked at a steady job, pursued his painting, made a few friends. He never married, never had children.

The fort grounds now housed a few offices and a museum. Its cemetery had very old graves, including that of Mary Whiston, dead at eighteen. Leo visited it weekly. He clipped the grass and weeds around it, and wiped away any dust or debris on the stone.

Leo had made a will that provided in part for ongoing upkeep of the grave and the little cemetery as a whole. He had a term life insurance policy that expired soon, and the other beneficiaries had been updated recently to include the maintenance fund of the condominium association of Pheasant Run. He wanted his old neighbors to have a safer building, and a less fearful one. He hadn't been a perfect person, a perfect neighbor. But he could do that much.

He would finish the painting he was working on, and then it would all start to happen.

9

Lander Maki lay half-awake in bed, Rhonda snoring softly at his side. As it sometimes did in his twilight states, a certain Minnesota night came back to him, as if wanting him to review it one last time before finally putting it to rest.

It is winter, a deep evening rimed with snow, the sky low and hard, like a lid. He is delivering flyers for the Lutheran church's upcoming pre-Christmas arts and crafts show, trying to do it on his bicycle, to get it over with, but the wheels keep wobbling and skidding on the ice and so he is forced to move more slowly than he would have on foot. It infuriates him, this thwarted fleetness. He feels he is wrestling with too many things at once: the bag of flyers slung across his shoulders; the treacherous dimming ice; the scarcity of streetlights on some blocks, so that he can't see any ice gleams on the ground; the stupid mission itself.

Why didn't the arts and crafts women just post the flyers in the neighborhoods, at grocery stores and on telephone poles, like everyone else did? It seems to him that all of them, his mother included, all of the quilters and crocheters, the baby-clothes makers and jewelry beaders and ski-cap knitters, that they all have such an oversize investment in fussy, colorful little comforts that they can't even tell people to come and buy them in a way that isn't fussy. They have to enlist their children to deliver the word to all those doors in person. Stuffed penguins! Embroidered hot pads!

But he is almost done. His flyer bag is almost empty. He can smell the damp canvas bottom of it. He is starving, as he has been starving, it seems, since the very day he became ten.

The light on the front of his bike isn't working. It flickered out a half hour ago. It is so cold he thinks maybe the batteries are frozen. Can batteries freeze? He can barely move his gloved fingers on the handlebars.

He has entered a neighborhood in which the houses are imposing brick, centered on huge lots behind boulevards planted thickly with maples. Four more blocks and he will be at the intersection where he can hang a right and speed the five minutes home. Golden lights glow behind curtained windows. The thick ground cover of accumulated snow forces all that solid, planted darkness into sharp relief. The maples lean their bare branches toward the street.

Now he is frightened. Because of his dead light, he can't see far ahead of him. There is no traffic moving on the streets. He feels that the big houses are saying, *Move on. You don't belong here. Our comforts are not your comforts. You live in a careful little bungalow with doilies on the chair arms, and your mother cleans and waxes the kitchen linoleum on her hands and knees, and you can't wear shoes in the house. And now you are late for warmed-over tuna casserole and a bowl of fruit cocktail. You are late, but she is more peeved than worried. She will want to know, first, if you delivered all the flyers. She will not ask if it was asking a bit too much of you, after a long school day, to embark on a chore that should have been hers.*

Without saying a word, she will manage to suggest to you that you failed to do something right. Not that you did something wrong, exactly, but that it was not quite right, either. It is what she does in order to suggest that you have placed yourself outside bounds that have never been described to you. You have no idea where they are located. Just that it's good to be inside them and bad to be outside, and you always seem to be just outside. Just beyond embrace.

At the intersection, he turns right, too fast, and his front wheel slides fast, to the left, and lays the bike and young Lander Maki flat on the icy road. The right handle grip somehow jams itself into his rib cage as he goes down, and when he stands up shakily he feels the sharp bite in a rib. He touches the bone and nothing seems out of place, but it grabs him with each breath. The big houses seem to walk backward, to retreat from this spectacle. A car approaches, slows, and the driver asks if he is all right. Yes, he says. No problem. Need to get my breath.

After the car turns out of sight, he leans to pick up his bike and nearly cries out. He can't imagine lifting his leg over the bar to get back on, the way he'd have to torque his upper body just that much. He bends over slowly and rights it, and walks it to a large bush on the boulevard where he can drop it so that it is almost out of sight, to be retrieved tomorrow. Then he starts walking toward his house.

In his mind, he runs. He flies down the street, wind in his ears, the big trees whispering encouragement, the now-visible winter moon increasing the speed of its path across the blackness to pull him on. In real, body time, he walks very slowly, trying not to move his rib cage any more than necessary. Inside, he leaps and dodges and cries out to those on the other end that he is on his way. The blocks inch past and put him in a neighborhood that he recognizes, and finally there is the filling station and the shadowed corner market, and, two long blocks farther, his street. His breath chugs. His fingers are numb. The yard light is on.

As he walks up the steps to the shallow porch, his mother's shadow appears behind the curtained glass. He takes a very small breath, trying not to move his ribs. She opens the door.

"What?" she says. "Why are you just standing there? Why are you so late? Can it take that long to deliver a few flyers?" She runs exasperated fingers through her permed hair.

He stands there. Shrugs a little. Waits for her to perceive his injury, his immense ordeal. He thinks of making up an exciting story: a speeding driver, attack dogs, a hobo who stole his bike. He wants to give her something huge. Something that will make her say, *How horrible! How worried I was about you! How completely amazing that you made it home!*

She looks distractedly over her shoulder and calls to his sister to check the stove and feed the old dog. Her housedress smells old. She reaches toward him impatiently, to pull him inside, and he backs away and puts up his hand like a traffic cop.

"Don't touch me," he says. "I'm hurt."

She narrows her eyes as if to laser through his obstinance to something he is hiding.

"I'm hurt," he repeats.

"You're not hurt," she says. "You just say things like that."

10

In the evening, after all the tumult around the fire, Professor Emeritus Rydell Clovis in #410 paced his apartment, then sat himself down, hoping for some noirish old police procedural on the classic movies channel, only to discover that a surfing musical was all he could expect. He popped his shirt cuffs and stared at the backs of his hands. Two more red splotches. Senile purpura, his toddler-faced doctor had smirked, and nothing to worry about, and, yes, well, it was an ugly-sounding name, and, yes, it could be said to be insulting, but, bottom line, the name was a lot worse than the reality, so go home and don't worry about it. The patronizing little moron.

For most of the two years since he'd retired from the English department, Clovis had been adamantly upbeat. He began each day with ten minutes of stretching and flexing to the electric hum of Tibetan monks. Then he racewalked through the halls and stairways of Pheasant Run for a half hour, making sure, via his enhanced activity tracker, that his pulse topped 65 percent of the maximum for his age. For breakfast, he brewed a mug of sencha tea and ate multigrain cereal topped with goji berries while he listened to NPR and read the ever-thinner newspaper, after which he scrubbed himself in the shower with a loofah, sometimes followed by a vigorous evocation of a hot tub experience he'd had with a pair of stoned minxes from his Chaucer seminar in the spring of 1976. And then a long final rinse and he was ready for whatever came his way.

At some point, however, the pallor of his circumstances had become unignorable. Here he was, in something not unlike a second prime, occupying a cramped apartment in a ridiculously named residence for senior citizens, and why? Because, due to a series of unfortunate investments and too many early withdrawals from his retirement fund, he couldn't afford anything better than an apartment for himself and another, in the same building, to rent out so that he could adequately supplement his modest fixed income going forward. And what a renter—the hysterical, nearly indigent Mrs. Six, who seemed now to have taken a powder. Whatever a powder might mean in the universe of Viola Six.

Still. All this—the doughty old ones, the sketchy new building manager, the pathetically earnest and hapless condominium owners' board—would be behind him very soon, if the stars lined up right. And why shouldn't they?

Clovis had been more than surprised when he was notified, a month ago, that he was one of three finalists for director of the university's proposed new Center for Ethics and the Digital Humanities. He was a literature man, but yes, he had made himself technically proficient before his not-entirely-voluntary retirement, to the point of serving on several university-wide committees aimed at bringing the institution into the twenty-first century and the digital universe on a minimal budget with lean and mean staffing. As it turned out, "lean and mean" included a 60 percent cut in English faculty, including a few modest buyouts—Clovis among them—and threats from the provost to eliminate all junior faculty if the remaining warhorses didn't gracefully retire earlier than they might have planned.

And then, it seemed, a donor had come along, and planning for the center got underway, and Clovis applied for the director's job on a whim. It seemed he hadn't been forgotten as thoroughly as he'd thought, because, to his frank surprise, he had now survived all the winnowing except the last round of it, and the job could very well be his. His prospects, and his financial future, had lit up like the opening footlights at a musical revue. And he was not even that old, physiologically, and there was time for a new life. So why was he so terrified that it might all be some cosmic joke?

He began to pace again, but when he felt his pulse rate skip ahead of his steps, he forced himself, again, to sit, and he turned on the surfing musical. As he watched the ridiculous spectacle, 95 percent bikinis to 5 percent waves, with bouts of execrable singing thrown in for laughs, he relaxed into the nonsense and began to drift.

When and if he got the job, he'd have enough money to go to high-end beach resorts and come back with a compelling tan, and, not impossibly, would cross paths with a classy, lithe woman with stilettos and a big mane of glossy auburn hair, a fellow divorced person perhaps, but no, more likely a widow. A youngish wealthy widow with pooling eyes who might want to redeem her years with a fat-cat, philandering husband by taking up with the director of an entity with a lofty name. And per- haps—again not impossible, surely—he'd hire a lovely discreet intern who was conflicted enough to be especially receptive to his mentoring for a period of time, to their mutual benefit, he thought he hoped.

It wasn't out of the realm. The other two finalists for the job were academic hipsters with blurry sexual orien- tations who'd been brought in from a couple of no-count campuses in the Midwest, and were so cant-ridden and vacuous in their presentations to the all-campus forum that the conclusion was, he hoped, inevitable. Because, face it, the director's main job would be to lend tone and a certain gravitas to encounters with high-minded, deep-pocketed potential donors. And if some silver-hairs with money to burn were going to support a center that explored topics like the ones he had proposed on a for-instance basis to the search committee—"The Poetics of Triggered Hedge Investing" and "Coding the Imagination"—then they were going to want to allay their nervousness by putting it in the palm of a calm, techno-savvy and seasoned guy who seemed not at all shaken in his cultural and academic foundations, attentive though he was to the cutting-edge currents at hand.

Clovis had to admit to himself that he would be hard put to explain to someone outside academia—a beer stocker at a 7-Eleven, say—what exactly the center would do, day by day. But he had found, in his university career, that titles tended to create content and function. So not to worry. He genuinely felt himself to be a human- ist as a result of his literary studies and his long belief in the capacity of the human to realize himself (or her-self!) via reason and historical perspective, rather than divine or psychic lightning bolts. And then, well, nice tension there between ethics studies and the digital zeitgeist with its cold, rapid-fire efficiency, its rampant rebraining of the human universe. Shove the two ideas together and you had a big old capacious tent with room enough inside for any number of circus animals to mill around.

The surfing musical ended in a riot of song, dance, skin, and waves against a lurid Pacific sunset, rousing Clovis and leaving him short of air. He threw back his living room curtains and opened the window a few inches. He knelt on the rug and rested his chin on the sill to breathe in the new and wintry night. Just barely, he could make out the creeping form of the black cat that frequented the neighborhood rooftops, descending now, like slow ink, to the ground. *What next for that cat?* he thought. Was this the beginning of its day's excitements, or the end?

He tried to meditate, to clarify, to do something in his head that would isolate and address the sources of his unease. OK, a small one was that he had lost his activity and mindfulness tracker sometime today. The device had simply come untethered from his waistband at some point. Before the fire? After the fire? When he made a quick afternoon trip to the little grocery for chai and shaving cream?

And here came another nagging worry. Two members of the search committee, both of them profes-sors in the School of Business, had made a point at the post-interview reception of verifying where he lived. Where he lived! This wasn't kosher and they knew it. Because he was unable to think of any plausible reason for the question, Clovis had decided that his interrogators wanted some evidence from him that he was tuned into the economic conditions of the community, including housing availability, perhaps because they envisioned that the center ultimately would draw faculty, students, and visiting scholars whose decisions to relocate might be affected by their housing options.

And so he had launched into an overly elaborate description of Pheasant Run, his very temporary dwelling place, and its occupants and the sorts of people who lived there. He had described the half-owner/half-renter situation, and the deferred maintenance, and the pressures on the owners to make up for declining condo values by raising the rents of their tenants, nearly all of them on modest fixed incomes. And he also offered the information that rumors of a mass buyout were circulating, though he, Clovis, was skeptical that the owners would go for it. Where would they move? Where would the renters go?

"Well, they—you—might be wise to think about it," one of his interrogators advised. "Speaking from a strictly business standpoint, I'm saying you owners should be thinking in those terms. Someone comes along and offers a decent enough price for undermaintained property, you might want to think about it."

"It takes leadership, though," the other chimed in. "Any kind of group, a homeowners' association, a university center, is going to be best off when they have a real leader piloting the ship."

Reviewing that brief conversation, Clovis could hear the gear sprockets engaging. He'd been issued an ultimatum of sorts. Certain persons connected with the university—perhaps the university itself—wanted to acquire Pheasant Run, and the directorship hinged on Clovis's willingness to help that process along. Whether the two faculty members wanted it for private real estate speculation or the university hoped to acquire a nondescript off-campus building at a bargain price, with minimum fuss and publicity—for its cybersecurity program? For animal experiments? For lucrative resale?—seemed almost beside the point. What mattered was that they were verifying that Clovis could help to make it happen. Was that what his candidacy had been all about from the beginning?

If so, he was happy to fudge his ethics a tad and try to accommodate them. At the very least, he could urge the condo association to seriously consider a buyout. Before he had second thoughts, he sat down at his computer and composed an email to Mavis Krepps and sent it with a maestro's flourish.

And now he had only to make sure the search committee knew he'd done so. A casual mention would do the trick.

But there was another problem, and he'd known what it was from the beginning of his candidacy. It concerned the Bad Old Days and the possibility they would come to light while he was still under consideration for the director's job. Would it really matter that he had, more than half a century ago, engaged in some petty thievery and a car-burning with a few other bad actors, not long before he met the inestimable public defender Bonnie Jo Archer, who kept him out of jail, got the charges expunged from his record, supported him through college, married him, and eventually pretended she'd never known him as anything other than a scholar of medieval literature? Bonnie had been out of the picture for years, and he couldn't think of any reason she'd try to do him out of the director's job—the divorce settlement had been grossly skewed in her favor—but who knew?

And now it also seemed possible that the moronic Herbie Bonebright, who very likely had his own criminal record, might have somehow uncovered some information about Clovis's mishaps back in the mists of time and be prepared to come forward with them for money.

Just two days ago, Herbie had unsuccessfully addressed a dripping kitchen faucet in Clovis's condo by doing a lot of swearing and wrench-banging, which prompted some sharp words from Clovis, maybe sharper than was strictly necessary. Herbie then said a peculiar thing.

"You should try to remember that you and I are in this together," he said. "And I know a couple of things about you that don't exactly add up to a great personal reputation, I guess I'd say. So you might want to think about the best way to get along with me. That's all."

"In what together, may I ask?" Clovis had said as icily as he could.

Herbie shrugged elaborately and ambled to the door, flip-flops slapping. He zipped up his puffy vest, then glanced down at the newspaper on the hall table. It was folded open to the second page, which had a photo of Clovis and the other finalists for the director's job. He studied it.

"Hey," he said. "There you are. You probably wish the whole thing was over, eh? Get the whole thing over and done. Get the job."

Every detail of that conversation came back as Clovis tried to recover from the exertions of putting out the fire in Herbie's apartment, the chaotic evacuation and milling around, the fire inspector's request for an interview. Herbie knew something, and he was prepared to use it against Clovis. But what, exactly? And how? And what was this "together" business? He and Herbie Bonebright had about as much in common as a jaguar and a two-toed sloth.

His exercise routine for the day was in shambles, but Clovis felt as if he had been running since dawn. To calm down, he did some hamstring stretches and drank some valerian tea. He reviewed every step he'd taken since he went out his door at dawn. Every step. He bent over because he suddenly felt light-headed. Old and light-headed and afflicted with some kind of unnamable craving.

He drank a tall glass of water, then retrieved a stale packet of Top Ramen from the back of his cupboard, yielding to a perverse craving for pure salt. As he dipped his finger in the spice packet and touched it in a contemplative way to his tongue, a cold rain pocked with sleet began to tap against his windows. Public radio was playing some kind of whining Celtic dirge. He stared down at the sidewalk, where two hunched walkers moved among the pale streaks of near-ice as if they swung among silver ropes in a slow dream.

Somewhere a violin played. Live or recorded, he couldn't tell because the sound was too faint. It was probably from an iPad. But it had, at its heart, a yearning quality that pierced him. Which of his old neighbors was listening to the violin to calm down after the day's shocks and disruptions? He couldn't begin to guess. The violin stopped and dread bloomed.

Knees splayed, he closed his eyes and rested his hands on his knees. *I am here*, he thought, *and my lives are over there*. He couldn't have said where *there* was, but it seemed to exist beyond a glass wall and it held his past life, his future life, and—the realization made his whole body clench—his current life. He leaned back in his leather chair and shook his head slowly from side to side. He dug his clenched fists into his eyes like a furious, exhausted child.

11

Viola Six stood alone under the stars at an unpeopled rest stop on the Continental Divide. She was shivering hard, partly from the cold and partly from the strain of the call she'd just made to say she'd been abandoned in her pajamas and ski jacket, high on a mountain pass, and needed help very soon.

The rest stop lot was framed with leaning halogen lights that seemed to be humming messages to each other. Or maybe not. She couldn't let her imagination run away with her, or she might become convinced that she inhabited a murmuring anteroom of the afterlife and would stand, too soon, before the monstrously whimsical judge she had managed not to believe in for most of her life.

A car, very long and low in the old way, crested the rise of the highway and followed the arrow of its headlights into the haloed lot. All that Viola could see of the driver was a nest of black hair that barely topped the steering wheel. This wasn't an officer of the law.

The car stopped and the driver got out, leaving the engine rumbling. She was a teenager, maybe fifteen, with blue-black hair, kohl-rimmed eyes, and tattooed sentences snaking across her forearms and hands. She circled the car slowly, kicked a tire, and squatted to look closely at another. Only then did she walk over to Viola and look her up and down in a way that suggested she was not unfamiliar with the bizarre. Her eyes were swollen and red. Everything about her seemed aggrieved. Now and then she glanced over her shoulder at the empty road, the sentinel pines.

Viola needed to think. Almost as soon as she had completed her call, she had realized that she could very well be in some kind of psychiatric holding pen by dawn. Who would believe her story? That it was true didn't mean it wasn't preposterous.

She made her frozen feet step carefully back from the girl as she thought about how to present herself and her situation. Her phone buzzed. It was the dispatcher she'd just spoken with, seeking more information, telling her to shelter herself in the restroom, verifying details of her physical surroundings, all with an oily patience that was worse than outright accusation.

The girl walked back to the car as if she didn't want to intrude. She opened the passenger door and stood by it.

Viola nodded. She pointed the phone at the salty stars. The miniaturized voice beeped and cheeped before Viola pressed the red icon and dropped it in a nearby dumpster.

As she got into the car, she explained that she had been the victim of an unsuccessful abduction and would now like to proceed to California. The girl sniffed and nodded. She said California was fine with her. They'd go back to Butte and take I-15 south, then cut west someplace in Utah. Viola settled her cold feet under a warm blast of air. They drove, without speaking, into the quiet black night. Near the outskirts of Butte, a garbage truck with undimmed lights pulled up behind them too fast, then lurched into the other lane, passed them, and roared down the highway, taillights scribbling.

"Nice," said the girl. "Dim your dumb lights, you drunk punk."

"I couldn't agree more," Viola said.

At a complicated and lit-up truck stop, the girl gassed up and returned to the car with moccasins, face wipes, a toothbrush, a gray T-shirt with an elk on it, and gray sweatpants printed with tiny pink dinosaurs. She handed it all to Viola. Out from behind the wheel, she looked older and more confident, and she pulled rolled money from her cowboy boot to pay for things.

She drove fast, pulling over every several hours to take the briefest of naps. Otherwise, they stopped only for fuel, gas station food, and restrooms. Viola changed into her new clothes and was pleased to find that they all fit. No one, anywhere, gave them much notice. She fell into a deep sense of relaxation and inevitability, sleeping in spurts and waking rested. The miles flew away, and there was no need to decide anything for a while. The girl clearly had her own wild troubles, but no apparent interest in sharing them, which was a relief. The hot dogs they consumed with stale corn chips evoked in Viola a not-unpleasant memory of a county fair with a spinning ride that pressed her child-body against a wall like a huge hand and stuck her there while the floor fell away.

The West became tweedy with snow, then seriously white in the higher reaches. She felt amazed to be on the move. And she was moving toward something she fervently wanted: a new life in a warm place by the ocean. A place where the temperature varied only ten to fifteen degrees through the seasons, and gregarious flowers spilled over rock walls, and the Franciscan mission bell on its high knoll chimed the hours, as it had done for a couple of centuries.

If Rebecca Tweet from Seniors could find a life, a niche, in Santa Barbara, so could Viola. She would count on Rebecca to help her get situated, but she wouldn't presume on her ongoing hospitality or companionship, because it wasn't company she was looking for; it was the experience of feeling intact and safe in a place she had chosen for herself. A place far away from Pheasant Run and its lurid troubles. She would miss dear Cassie McMackin, and maybe courtly Leo Uberti. Her typewriter she might miss. But that was about it.

Somewhere in northern Nevada, she and the girl began to converse in fits and starts. The girl identified herself as Raven and said she had decided, as they drove, that she would go to Los Angeles, as a first resort anyway. She said she would like to see anyone try to find her there. Viola said Santa Barbara was where she wanted to go.

They discovered that they had been living in the same small city and, in that moment, eyed each other at length, mutually relieved to experience not a glimmer of recognition.

Raven said she was escaping the place because she was afraid some big trouble was brewing that could involve her. She threw a wary glance at Viola.

"This kid I know, I just found out he's got a gun, and he's got enemies at school and thinks they insulted me. I need to get away because he might try to turn into a super-hero if I'm around. And then, last straw, some home shit I don't need. My stepdad. Toby the terrible." Her face closed. Viola noticed that she was driving with her eyes shut. For five, ten seconds she didn't open them to blink. She had done this several times before, producing in Viola some curiosity, but not alarm. It seemed a technique for conserving energy, if nothing else, and there weren't that many other vehicles to worry about, as they had now abandoned the interstates, where they might be easier to find.

Pheasant Run, Viola's home for the past decade, faded with each mile they covered. By the time they were climbing toward Tonopah, it seemed like a place she had only heard about. And the freedom of that distance made her want to talk about it.

She turned to Raven. "Do you find that putting a lot of miles between yourself and trouble can somehow make the trouble seem as if it belongs to someone else?"

"Nope," said Raven. "Absolutely not. Trouble catches up with you. Don't kid yourself about that. My personal goal is just to give it a run for its money."

"That sounds…would you say…a little bleak?"

Raven shrugged. "You think it doesn't?" she said. "Find you? You think you're going to get to wherever you're going and find that your troubles have stayed back in Clowntown, Montana, USA?" For the first time in the trip, she was ruffled. Viola wasn't sure if that was a good thing or a bad thing. It did seem that the climate of the car, its air, was circulating in a livelier way.

"I was abducted from my building yesterday morning," she told the girl. "I knew I was in danger, and it turned out I was."

Raven gave her a long look and pressed her lips together.

"He drove all over for a while, saying all kinds of crazy things, and I thought I was going to be killed," Viola said. "Hours and hours on various roads and back roads, like he was looking for the perfect place to do the deed, and then eventually we were back on the interstate and he let me out at the rest stop to use the restroom, and when I came out he was gone. Second thoughts, or maybe something scared him? Somebody maybe drove into the lot and gave him a curious look before driving away, and he thought he better hit the road."

Raven closed her eyes for a few seconds. "For sure," she said.

"I knew about some things that some very powerful people didn't want me to know, and they ordered my abductor to get rid of me, is my theory."

Raven lit a cigarette. "Let's not talk for a while," she suggested. "I don't think it helps anything. Maybe in a year, we'll both look around and go, *Well, hey. Things turned out OK*. But maybe not. Point is, we're moving, and it's all we can do, and all we should do, and I think we oughta just sit back and do the ride." She closed her eyes and draped her thin hand with its gnomic scribbles over the top of the steering wheel, where it made minute, automatic adjustments to the shapes of the road.

"At one point I heard whimpering just like a little hurt dog," Viola said quietly. "And I realized it was me."

In Santa Barbara, she'd need only a room, really. She could find a room. She would take the bus to the beach every time she felt like walking on the sand. She'd gather lemons from a small tree in the yard of the handsome house where she rented the room. She would have her morning coffee on a small terrace outside the French doors of her room, a separate terrace from the ones the homeowners used. Theirs was on the other side of the house and had a firepit and a water feature.

Her mind, in the room by the lemon tree, or outside on her terrace, would untangle itself so that the fears and worries and suspicions that had lodged themselves inside the knots would be free to float into the blank blue sky. She would wake no more in a sweat of dread about being evicted as part of a plot devised by cold-eyed capitalists to make a pile of money off a piece of real estate that needed only to be rid of its elderly occupants in order to quintuple in value.

She would be free of her role as the town crier, the Klaxon, the alarmist; free of the fear that she would be killed because of the danger she presented to the plans of the capitalists. She had tried to stop them. She had almost paid with her life. And now she was happy, more than happy, to be many miles from a place that had begun to feel hellish to her.

They turned toward the coast at Bakersfield and drove into Santa Barbara at mid-afternoon. The water glittered. The gulls cried. The little city hummed to the tune of another perfect day.

Inside a public restroom near Stearns Wharf, Viola washed her hands and face and examined herself in the mirror. She felt oddly pleased that the dinosaurs on her new pants matched her ski jacket. She didn't need the jacket, but she decided to tie the arms around her waist because she didn't know about the evenings yet.

She thanked Raven, who was going on to Los Angeles right away. She wished her well. Raven reached into her boot and retrieved her roll of bills. She peeled off $300 in fifties and put them in Viola's hand and rolled Viola's fingers around the money with her own.

"You can thank terrible Toby," she said. "The guy who thinks the perfect ATM password is his dog's name."

"Not necessary, but thank you so much," Viola protested. "I have my emergency credit card. I also have a son who owes me some money, and maybe there will be a miracle and he'll get it to me somehow. Stranger things have happened." She retrieved an envelope from her pocket. It was addressed to Cassie McMackin in #412 at Pheasant Run.

She examined the seal as if she might open it, then quickly handed it to Raven.

"There is more I could add to this, but I will write a follow-up. Mail this when you get to the City of Angels," she said. "I'm counting on you to do that."

Raven nodded. She slid behind the wheel of the long car and lifted her scribbled hand to Viola.

"You will be pretty much OK, then," she said.

Viola nodded and the car moved away.

"I won't remember you, if you won't remember me," Raven called out the open window as she rumbled onto the road that would take her south to the metropolis.

———

Viola returned to the restroom to verify that she looked presentable and smelled relatively clean. Then she walked slowly along the waterfront. The November air was soft and lucid and filled with sparkles and a light breeze. A group of elders performed trancelike movements on the beach. Tall palms flanked the walking path like auditioning showgirls, and the terra-cotta roofs of the little city rose gently from the water toward low hills. All was containment and ease. At the harbor, boats in their slips looked freshly painted in the bright sunshine, and there were the fake pleadings of the gulls and sometimes small bells or the faint chatter of talk radio. A dog stood at the prow of one of the boats and barked at her in an inviting and friendly way.

She bought fried clams and coffee at a place with sidewalk tables, ate slowly, and ordered more. She was famished. She would have to fortify herself to find Rebecca, an enterprise that suddenly felt overwhelming. In her postcards, Rebecca had never included a return address, but she had once remarked that she was in the phone book, should Viola ever decide to abandon the endless northern winters and dabble her toes in some salt water.

She asked the waitress for a phone book, which the girl had some difficulty locating, and which turned out to be three years old, so there would be no Rebecca in it. She asked if she could use the restaurant's phone, and called information, and lucked out. There was a number for an R. Tweet. Viola wrote it down and decided to wait a few hours to call.

Along the harbor street she caught the first metro bus that came along and rode it for several miles, maybe more, until she realized she was in another part of the city, thickly planted and hushed with wealth, and when two middle-aged women ahead of her got off, she did, too. They were a half block from the entrance to a parking lot, and there was a sign at the turnoff that said "Lotusland."

For the flash of a moment, Viola felt she was in a child's dream. But the two women were pragmatic, stolid-looking sorts, and they walked with purpose toward a small group of other middle-aged and older people who were gathered around a tall, broad-shouldered woman with a name tag and a mane of electrified-looking hair to her shoulders. She wore a safari hat and was checking a list. There was a low building behind her, restrooms and a gift shop. Viola reminded herself that she looked very nearly respectable and summoned the will to approach the tall woman, who informed her that tours of Lotusland were by reservation only but, since it was the very end of the season and three people hadn't showed, she was welcome to join them by paying the fee inside.

Lotusland felt like the inside of a fierce and agitated mind, all looming fronds and deep shadows, statues of twisted dwarves, giant cacti, aggressive palms. Even the peaceful interludes—the Japanese garden, the allée with its roof of winding lemon-heavy branches—had something about them of the mind instructing itself to stay within the bounds of control. Viola was sorry she had come and quickly weary to her bones. The guide told them the heiress who designed the place had imported the world's most exotic flora, but she couldn't seem to retrieve the botanical names of anything. She looked as if she had had a bad night.

When they were at long last near the end of the tour and within sight of the visitors' center, Viola slipped away from the group to rest for a few minutes on a broad rock near the blue garden. And then she must have dozed, because when she opened her eyes and rose to catch the group, it was gone.

She felt watched by eyes far back in the leafy surround. What kinds of animals might live in this sort of place? Did they go in and out of Lotusland, sunning in the late-day dappled light, napping on a gargoyle, taking their leisure in the place after the tour groups had left for the day? How did they get in? How did they get out? She sat on the rock again, to capture a little more strength so that she could proceed with her day.

She stood up quickly, suddenly afraid that the group would forget all about her and the grounds would be locked with her inside. The world tilted sideways. She flailed her arms to right herself. And all the blue plants came rushing toward her.

She surfaced to the sound of a woman explaining where they were. The day had proceeded without her. Late-afternoon light now filtered through the tall plants. The voice she heard was lovely and low, and it stayed ahead of a multitude of whispering footsteps and lesser beings asking questions. The voice seemed not to want to speak in real sentences or convey any ordinary sort of information. When someone in the inaudible distance asked another question, the guide said a number of words, but they all seemed to frame and support the best ones in the center. "Bromeliad," she said. And then "Shade palm." Every word that made its way to Viola—*topiary, succulent, aloe, pavilion, blue*—gave her a little shock of recognition and grief. How had she failed, all these years, to appreciate the tensile grace of her own language?

Her body felt crooked and inert. It was arranged on a loamy substance and curtained by the high plants. Her head was next to a large rock and was paralyzed with pain. She felt planted, as she couldn't seem to move. Only the lids of her eyes. Only the tiny rasp of her breath, as rapid and shallow as that of the small lizard that stared at her from under a drooping fern. Her voice was out of the question. It had done all of its speaking. *Pavilion.* She could only think it. *Topiary.*

Long, benign light warmed her shoulder. The people whispered into the distance, their guide's voice like a gentle gong that they carried on a litter, around some far corner, into the ongoing world. Wouldn't they miss her? Wouldn't they give her a thought?

The patron saint of gravediggers. The phrase came to her from one of Rebecca's postcards.

"Saint Barbara was a very beautiful young woman who lived in the second century AD. When she was beheaded by her father for becoming a Christian, he was instantly struck dead by lightning. She is the patron saint of gravediggers and architects, and protects against lightning, sudden death, and impenitence."

When Rebecca moved to California and wrote her postcards, it was deep winter back in Montana. Everything felt like expired food in a refrigerator.

"A Chinese man who lived here a century ago was famous all over the country for predicting the weather. He called his forecasts 'celestial morsels.'"

The soft, towel-swaddled form of Rebecca lay on a chaise, nibbling daintily at a large shrimp that had been scooped up that very morning from the sea.

"But what the Chinese man had to forecast is a mystery to me. The weather here does not require thinking about or preparing for or guarding against or running inside from or hoping for. It is constant meteorological kindness."

In the winter in Montana, Rebecca had worn a stiff woolen jacket and fake fur hat, donations she'd confiscated from the Seniors thrift store, and stern leather laced boots to which she had attached climbers' crampons to keep her from falling on the eternal ice.

"The stations of the cross at the mission are so darkly painted, and so small and high on the wall, that it is impossible to see what kind of suffering is being shown. Only the very lightest parts are visible at all, such as a raised arm or a band of silver at the horizon beneath a black sky."

Viola wandered with Rebecca under a black sky. A smoky forest surrounded them and blocked their passage to the ocean, a silver line in the far distance. The cracking and hissing of a fire grew louder. Ash intensified the silver tones in the plants that towered above her and above the lizard, who hadn't moved. *More than anything*, she thought. *More than anything, I want the tiny living creature to stay. Aloe. 'Allo. Abide.* A trickle of liquid left her ear, slow and jammy. The lizard blinked. It had turned from a leafy green to the palest blue. It held her in its tiny stare.

THE PRESENCE

OF AN ABSENCE

12

Maki had completed his initial interviews at Pheasant Run. He had also intended to have another chat with the teenager who'd been lurking around the building, but Cassie McMackin had provided an alibi for the boy and a brief explanation of his troubled circumstances, so he'd put that one on the back burner.

There was something about Cassie that felt so familiar to him that he had found himself engaging in a conversation that went in many other directions than the fire and its complexities. They talked about Little Boy and his latest, and wondered, almost at the same time, how long the frightening nonsense would last. She asked Maki questions about his work and his life, and when he told her a bit about Rhonda and her animals, she laughed in the way you do about the propensities of a longtime and beloved friend.

Sitting in his parked Volvo, he tried to reside for a while in the part of his mind that skittered and whispered just beneath his full consciousness. His cell rang. Rhonda had news. Their limbless lizard, Roscoe, seemed to be dying. Maki trained his sights on a little boy across the street who was executing perfect figure eights on his skateboard, looking entirely unburdened by the day-to-day.

They'd rescued Roscoe the day before from PetSmart. The creature, which looked like a snake, had Morse-tapped its snaky little snout on the glass of its cage as Rhonda and Maki were walking past it toward the dog food. Rhonda felt an immediate affiliation and began to quiz a nearby clerk, who told them the reptile was a so-called glass lizard with unique self-protection abilities that she didn't specify. Ten minutes later, the clerk, Shilo, had filled them in on the reasons a snake could be technically a lizard—movable eyelids, external ear openings, and almost invisible appendages near "the rear vent"—and Roscoe was in the back of the car in a cardboard box.

"At first, I thought Roscoe was just shivering in place because Sid had fake-pounced at him like he does—that way he raises his paws in the air and brings them down hard, just close enough to make him seem serious?" Rhonda said.

"Well, you might seize up, too, if a hairy beast two hundred times your size did something like that."

"We're not talking about me," Rhonda said in her arguing voice, though what there was to argue about Maki wasn't sure. "In fact, he seemed to recover and was blinking and moving his head around. And then! I went to make some tea, and when I came back to his little pen, maybe a third of him had broken off and was in a separate part of the cage."

Maki digested this for a few moments. "Various pieces, or a single piece?" he asked.

"Various," Rhonda said. "Shilo said not a thing about this possibility."

"And I don't want to be indelicate, but do any of the pieces happen to contain the critical rear vent?"

"Oh ha ha," Rhonda snapped. "I haven't done a microscopic exam. And I haven't told you the worst part." ·

Tell me there is something worse than getting your ass broken off, Maki thought better of saying.

"The parts are moving," Rhonda said, glum. "And the rest of Roscoe is alive, but just looks, I don't know. Unable to proceed with his life. And Sid's pouncing at the parts. Which are definitely twitching."

Maki tried to give all this his single-minded concentration. He understood the feeling of being unable to proceed with a life. The boy on the skateboard wiped out spectacularly but regained his feet in one fluid move.

"Do you want me to come home?" he asked.

"Of course not," Rhonda said. "I just want you to know what you're facing when you do."

There goes my mulling time, Maki thought as he placed the phone in his pocket. There went his chance to repair to the backyard to his thinking shed with the space heater, where he would try to put together the pieces of the Pheasant Run fire as he could identify them at present. There went the phosphorescent particles of near-knowledge that had started to gain some steam and climb to the surface of his mind. *Gain some steam.* He felt a sharp pang of nostalgia for the idea of an era powered largely by boiling water.

Although idly cruising the internet was against his rules for himself when he was on the job, he typed in "glass lizard."

The word from Wikipedia was that glass lizards, also referred to as glass snakes, are so named because they "have the ability to deter predation by dropping off part of the tail which can break into several pieces, like glass. The tail remains mobile, distracting the predator, while the lizard becomes motionless, allowing eventual escape. This serious loss of body mass requires a considerable effort to replace, and the new tail is usually smaller in size than the original."

Maki pretended he was in his thinking shed and shut his eyes. At first he saw the panting Siddhartha jubilantly crouched over the moving tail parts. And then he saw a huge rally of some kind. The figure at the center wriggled around the stage, out there in the spotlight, shaking outstretched hands, giving the thumbs-up, engaging in high fives. And off to the side, some human figures in the shadows watched the antics, turned away, whispered among themselves in a way that chilled.

He gave his head a shake and reminded himself to cut down on the melatonin.

When he got home, Rhonda waved a weary arm in the direction of the lizard's cage without lifting her eyes from her computer screen. She told Maki she was with a client. The toes of her slippers were duck heads, and they pecked nervously as she typed. Her hair was limp and her face was drawn.

The lizard was indeed in a segmented state, the head and torso cowering frozen in the corner, the remaining parts gyrating on the other side of the cage.

"Jeez," Maki said. Siddhartha, banished to the mudroom, whined piteously.

"That cat I was conversing with the morning of the fire?" Rhonda said, head cocked, fingers flying across the computer keys. "The one on the rooftop?"

"Righto," Maki said. He really needed to go to his shed.

"She told me just now that a guy came out of Pheasant Run during the evacuation and ran off toward the high school. She said he stepped behind a tall bush and pulled a gun from his backpack and pointed it straight at her." Her fingers quit moving. "She said she felt her heart stop." Rhonda's face took on a distant, remembering aspect.

"Sweetheart," Maki said. "Why don't you take Sid for a drive? He really needs not to feel like a dog for a while. He needs to sit in the front seat and look around at the big world, and forget about pouncing at lizard parts. Don't you think?"

She searched his face, then let Sid into the room. While she got her jacket and purse, the dog leaped at the lizard cage until she pulled him out the front door by his collar, claws clattering across the floor.

"Did you eat lunch?" Maki asked as he accompanied them down the walk. She said she had, but had a headache that wouldn't seem to go away.

"I'll make something so delicious for dinner that you'll thank me in a dozen interesting ways," he said. She rolled her eyes and opened the passenger door for Sid, who took up his position, haunches to shoulders like a holy man, head tipped out the open window.

Maki watched the two of them heading into the afternoon, their valiant profiles plowing the steely day. He worried excessively on the infrequent occasions when Rhonda seemed seriously below par, then tried to talk himself out of it because he knew he was worrying as much about himself—about losing the fuel she gave him—as he was about her. It was time for him to shake off the pall and do his work.

Some kind of knowledge was waiting for him to deserve it—*it* being some real insight into what might have transpired at Pheasant Run. He knew he needed to cultivate a state in which his inner eye could move alertly among the random facts and images that presented themselves. Only then would the edges of those facts and images become portals, rather than a frame that constituted the limit of what he knew.

In his interview with Cassie McMackin, he had put it this way: "We're looking at something that was destroyed, and we have to be able to put it back together again, either in the mind or physically, to determine the origin and cause." Cassie told him, without further explanation, that she felt she was doing much the same thing in her own life.

To prepare himself for the process, he needed some food energy. Not a lot, but it had to be the right kind. There were similarities, he'd found, between really fine cooking and investigating a suspicious fire. In each, you wanted to follow an adopted method but keep your mind elastic enough that unexpected avenues of investigation could present themselves.

From the top cupboard shelf, he retrieved the pretty ceramic bowl with the vermillion glaze. He minced some scallions and leeks and quickly stir-fried the leeks in sesame oil until they were curling and crisp. He left the scallions raw because their cool grassiness so perfectly offset the hot crackle of their cousins. He was about to dice a red bell pepper when he saw that shredding it finely would open much more surface and allow it to cook just the right amount of time in the broth to come. He boiled some water, poured it into the bowl, and stirred in the shredded pepper and a dollop of miso paste. He sprinkled the top with the scallions and leeks, then ground black pepper (for acuity) over it all. Smoky, meadowy, pungent, thoughtful, ancient. He drank from the bowl and licked up the dregs.

In his shed, Maki lit a Kool and sharpened two pencils to needle points. He found a fresh legal pad and placed one pencil on either side of it. The space heater hummed away, eager to assist.

He squinted and thought about the old people in their four-story building. An early-morning fire breaks out in the manager's second-floor apartment. The manager is absent, presumably eating his customary breakfast at the sports bar. The smoke alarm in the hall goes off. Professor Emeritus Rydell Clovis, strenuously speed-walking as per his daily routine, finds himself in the area, grabs an extinguisher, gains entry, snuffs the blaze. The firefighters come sirening in and mop up. The bar reports that Herbie never arrived for his breakfast. His car is not in the Pheasant Run garage. Attempts to locate his phone are unsuccessful.

Maki had sent photographs and what little physical evidence he had to the insurance company people, to be reviewed and forwarded to the lab. He'd consulted with the detectives who were trying to locate the missing Herbie and the missing Viola, and handed off Herbie's iPad to the geeks. So there was a lot to be discovered.

The biggest development, of course, was that an elderly woman using Viola Six's phone had made a call to 911 late the day of the fire. She said she'd been abducted, and then she seemed to vanish into the ether. Her phone had been zigzagging across the state for the two days since then and still hadn't been located. By the time the highway patrol got to its most recent location, it would be gone. So how was Viola Six traveling, if the caller had indeed been Viola Six? Of her own volition? It didn't seem likely.

And what about the fire itself? His gut feeling was arson. The lab evidence, so far, was more suggestive than conclusive: a test suggesting the presence of something that could have been soft plastic, Coleman fuel traces in an apartment that didn't have a Coleman stove, too hot a blaze for a simple grease fire, and there were still a few last refinements of the tests to be run. The lab was analyzing what it could of the burned material—Professor Clovis had done a regrettably thorough job of coating it all with extinguishing foam— but there was scarcely a cinder.

For Maki, though, the strongest evidence for arson was the absence of any evidence that suggested an accidental cause. It was what he liked to think of as a black hole arson: a large absence that itself was a powerful presence. Where was the grease residue? The fragments of trash that a junk-filled apartment would have in the kitchen?

By everyone's account, Herbie was an out-and-out slob. He couldn't adjust a thermostat without making a mess. Every part of his apartment, with the exception of the kitchen, was littered with old newspapers, balled-up tissues, plates of half-eaten food, dirty socks, tattered towels, fast-food sacks and containers. French fries were embedded in the carpet near the TV-watching chair. Why, then, would the kitchen be so clean?

Where were the traces of greasy hot pads, Chicken McNuggets, paper napkins—all the stuff that would have littered the countertops of someone like Herbie? If they had been there, someone had removed them. And if someone had removed them, it meant that the person had taken pains to make sure the fire didn't get too large too fast, wanted it contained enough that it wouldn't spread to the rest of the apartment or any other part of the building. A rather sophisticated undertaking. The person in question knew the habits of fire and trusted his own skills.

Would Herbie Bonebright have a motive to set it, even if he happened to have those skills? A second fire in his place could only hurt his prospects of retaining his job. Why would he want that to happen? And if he had set it, would he have left his new iPad on the premises? Not likely. And if he'd set it to terrorize the building's residents, why take pains to make it so strictly contained?

Had one of the building's residents set the fire to take revenge on Herbie for something he'd said or done to them? It was difficult to imagine a bent, white-haired person scanning the long hall like a hawk before entering Bonebright's unit to concoct a very sophisticated, self-limiting, delayed-ignition revenge fire that would seem to have been caused by Herbie's carelessness and get him fired. But who knew? Maki had seen a lot of things in his career.

In any case, something unspoken and weighty was going on in that building. During his interviews, Maki had been struck by the residents' independence, intelligence, and lucidity. They were extraordinarily on top of it for their ages, especially given their obvious physical fragility in some cases and the fact that the majority of them lived alone.

And yet, when asked about Herbie Bonebright's general habits and his capabilities as a building manager, a number of the tenants (all of them renters) had answered in an extremely guarded manner. They looked scared, as if something had knocked and they were afraid to open the door.

And what about Professor Clovis, the hero of the moment? Both the professor and his story bothered Maki. There was the matter of the lock. In all likelihood, Herbie Bonebright had left his apartment unlocked when he went to breakfast, as was his habit, according to several tenants. If he'd locked it, he would have needed a key to unlock it upon his return, and he'd left his ring of keys in his bathroom.

So why did Clovis say the door had been locked? Maki consulted his notes. Yes, unequivocally, the apartment, according to Clovis, had been locked, and he had had to bash the door open with the extinguisher. He'd shown Maki how he had struck it like a murderer.

There was a general fishiness about the man. Nothing he said or did seemed entirely sincere. He had also taken pains to let Maki know he was about to take the reins of a new center of some sort that was being hatched over at the university—that he was a man of some considerable standing, should Maki have somehow missed that fact.

Maki tried to envision Clovis's smile again, the way it was an offering, not a response, and was therefore entirely strategic. He wanted something or he was deflecting something. Mirth was not even in the equation.

He had a strong feeling that, despite his education and credentials and tweedy manner, Clovis had been an abused child or had even done some prison time. It was that smile, partly, but also a quality of alertness that was utterly divorced from curiosity, that was purely self-protective. Or maybe many years at a university could make you that way. He'd heard stories.

The professor reminded Maki of what Sid was like when they first brought him home, and poor, declawed Rosemary the Manx, before the fatal raccoon. They'd had several rescue animals who had arrived with convict alertness, who had paused just a nanosecond in every exchange to assess the degree of threat. Most had eventually seemed to understand that their surroundings, their people, had pleasures and comfort to offer. But it could take quite a while, and in a few cases, it had never happened.

Maki closed his eyes and let it all twirl and amble in his head. He turned off the space heater and did a few stretches. His knees popped. It was time to make dinner.

He wanted something that would comfort Rhonda and make her forget her wretched first marriage, the man at the mall with his gun, the lizard falling to pieces, all the world's troubled and chatty animals. Something vegetarian and earthy, then, with a dessert that smelled like a storybook grandmother's kitchen.

Linguini with vodka sauce. Toasted sourdough baguette brushed with emulsified garlic in walnut oil. His special chopped salad with the fennel, red onion, and macadamia nuts. Pear clafouti, warm from the oven, topped with soft folds of whipped cream spiked with vanilla and a whisper of cognac. A shot of the freezer-chilled Absolut first, with chopped pickled herring and fresh dill on rye toasts. A glass or two of that rowdy Malbec with the linguini.

"A symphony of tastes and textures," he said to the cat on the windowsill. He found himself unable to check on the condition of the lizard. The cage was very quiet.

As he slowly stirred the vodka sauce and listened to The Decemberists, he examined the patched crack in the ceiling above the stove. Time for some paint touch-ups around the place. He put the lid halfway on the sauce and turned it to a very low burble. He looked again at the ceiling. Something about it was pricking at him. What was it? And then he pictured the cupboard over the stove in Herbie Bonebright's apartment. He had focused intensely on the burn pattern when he was there, but now he remembered something else. There was a small hook attached to the bottom of that cupboard, directly over the stove. A little, charred hook.

As he tried to think about why someone would put a hook in that place, a hook that was far too small to hold a pot or pan or even a cooking utensil, Rhonda blew in with the dog. They both looked as if they had engaged in some exciting minor larceny. A few leaves were caught in Rhonda's curly hair. Sid ran into the kitchen, wriggling with excitement. He had an orange balloon tied to his collar.

"Something in here smells not unlike heaven," Rhonda called from the vicinity of the coat closet.

"Hello, creatures," Maki said, pouring the icy vodka into shot glasses he'd placed on a small tray next to the herring toasts. He set the tray on the coffee table near the pellet stove, which emitted a toasty aura, stole a look at the lizard, which was still two-thirds frozen and one-third segmented and mobile, and threw a towel over the cage, leaving a little room for air. The dog seemed to have forgotten about it. He was studying the balloon as if waiting for it to leap at his throat.

"Some kids at the park were dressed up like medieval knights and having a sword fight," Rhonda said. "They had a bunch of balloons tied to the picnic table for some reason, and one of them fetched this one and presented it to me with a big knight-in-shining-armor bow." She sipped the vodka and smiled. "He had a good bow."

Sid pawed the balloon into a corner of the room, then tried to stare it down. Maki thought about kitchen ceilings and studied Sid.

"You know," he said. "It's possible to set a delayed fire with a balloon."

"Don't put felonious ideas in Sid's head," Rhonda said. "There isn't room." Sid turned to gaze at them with rapt, mouth-breathing tenderness.

"Some pissed-off person fills a balloon with fuel, knots the top with a string, and breaks into his enemy's place. He tacks the balloon to the ceiling or some other surface with a small hook and places a lit candle on the cupboard or stove directly below, with some combustibles—newspapers, telephone book, and so on—nearby. Then he sets the balloon swinging widely, exits the place, and has been in a bar down the street for more than a quarter of an hour when the fire is reported. He has calibrated it just right. It took at least fifteen minutes for the balloon to come to rest directly over the flame. A few moments more and...whoosh."

Outlandish as it was, he had a scenario that would account for the faint smell of soft plastic, undetected by anyone else at the scene, and for a few shards of wax among the remains.

Maki's phone did its text gurgle. Detective Hanrahan wanted a call.

Stacy Hanrahan was six feet tall and 260 pounds, a former bull-riding champion from some scraped and howling part of Wyoming. In his early forties, he still moved remarkably fast for his size. He had a reputation as a ladies' man, and when he wasn't hard on a case, he was a Saturday night regular at the Cabin out on the edge of town, where a band called the Laid-Off Cowhands played all the old schottisches in addition to a rock repertoire that stopped at about 1959. Maki and Rhonda had seen him out there a time or two, pounding Dr Peppers and escorting a sequence of lovelies around the dance floor in the side-by-side shuffle that requires such extraordinary finesse and lightness of foot, and which paradoxically seems to attract oversize men with big guts emblazoned with big buckles, who tend to execute the movements perfectly.

Detective Stacy Hanrahan seemed to know, from the first cases he and Maki had worked on together, that Maki's real interest was always in the why rather than the how of a potential arson. The how was evidence, analysis, comparisons, records, a certain kind of intuition. But the why was human yearnings, resentments, scheming, desperation, even, not infrequently, a kind of evil.

So, over time and as they came to like and trust each other, Hanrahan brought Maki in on the police end of certain investigations, confident that he wouldn't overstep his authority and sympathetic to his wish to know where the trail was leading.

Hanrahan also had a zest for his work that affected Maki in somewhat the way that Rhonda did. Basically, he felt happier in their presence. More alert. And they both made him laugh, especially, in Hanrahan's case, because he channeled the speech patterns of almost everyone he dealt with in a professional capacity. Sometimes it was almost uncanny, the way he became the ventriloquist's dummy.

"We know more about Mrs. Six's phone than we did," Hanrahan told Maki. "So OK, it was on Homestake Pass the evening of her disappearance. Call it six or six thirty or so when a woman made a call from that phone during that time, to 911. As you will remember, she said she was inside the women's restroom at that rest stop. The dispatcher called her back for more info and got cut off, so the patrol headed up there pronto. They said the rest stop was totally empty, really dark by then, of course, and witch-tit cold. They looked around for quite a while and saw a few footprints and tire marks, not many, but nothing else. They combed the place. Nothin'."

"And then the phone is moving erratically."

"Well, it was at the rest area or in the vicinity after the woman's call, then it started moving west on 90 and then down all these county roads, all over the damn place, as you know. Get a bead on it, and off it went again. That's why it's been taking all this dad-blast time."

"And now?"

"Well, the Billings patrol apprehended an extremely drunk person of interest, the driver of a garbage removal truck. He's picking up garbage on Homestake Pass the evening of the day Viola Six disappears. His girlfriend texts him that she's taken off for parts unknown with his best friend from childhood that he was blood brothers with. Next stop for our boy is that shitty little road bar near Rocker, where he leaves with a couple fifths of Black Velvet and proceeds to drown his sorrows while driving a mammoth garbage truck all over the damn state for a couple of days, with Mrs. Viola Six's phone buried back there in all the crap. Not a pretty job, but they found it."

They both mulled silently for a few moments, then agreed to reconnoiter the next day and map out some potentials.

Before he went to bed, Maki checked his emails, knowing he shouldn't. He almost always found something that churned him up and kept him awake.

There was a very short one from Daphne, saying their mother was not doing so well, that she was leaving garbage all over their parents' living area, not noticing or caring about the mess, and putting weird things in the refrigerator, like her face cream, and that she kept repeating, with much laughter, a story in which her own mother had called her "too dang big for her boots."

Maki couldn't fashion this person from the image he retained of their mother's fastidiousness and propriety, her utter lack of joy. Age had produced an impersonation, it seemed to him. He had nothing to say, so he didn't respond.

Another email was from Professor Clovis to Mrs. Krepps, who had forwarded it with no comment.

Dear Mrs. Krepps,

Just a note to extend my support to someone who is doing a difficult job in difficult times, and to say (in all modesty) that I have become something of a "layperson/expert" on real estate finances and trends in this long wake of the 2008 slump and subsequent "corrective" legislation that impacts us all. Although the condo market has gained viability in certain areas, Pheasant Run suffers, as we all know, from certain issues regarding maintenance, occupancy rates, and so on. It's my belief that the long-term personal and financial interests of the owners might, at this point, be best served by being very open to the possibility of negotiating the sale of the building to a qualified buyer. You have suggested that such a buyer might exist, and we in the association hope to learn more about that very soon. Let me just say at this point that I believe the association should seriously entertain any credible offers that are forthcoming.

We are sitting on an uneasy condo market and facing expensive structural repairs to the building. Perhaps this is the time to negotiate a sale that is advantageous to all.

Let me know what you think, Mavis (if I may).
Very sincerely yours,
Rydell

Maki noticed that the email had been sent to her the day of the fire, late in the evening. *Busy, busy*, he thought.

There was a brief message from one of the geeks who had retrieved all the recent searches and all the messages sent or received or scrubbed on Herbie's iPad.

"One email Mr. Bonebright thought he'd scrubbed appears to be a threat. It is addressed to Felix Wingate, who is general manager of Longleap Enterprises. Bonebright threatens to reveal damaging information about Longleap unless he is paid a sufficient sum to stay quiet. Details at the morning meeting! P.S. The guy spells worst than my little neece whose 4."

"Well, well," Maki said to Rhonda, who was reading the newspaper in bed.

"They've found four new species of legless lizards in California," she announced. "A couple of famous reptile professors did. They thought there was only one species—I'm guessing Roscoe's—but they searched and searched and found some others. Guess where?"

Maki raised his eyebrows.

"At the end of a runway at LAX, in a vacant lot in downtown Bakersfield, on the edge of the Mojave Desert, and among some oil derricks in the lower San Joaquin Valley."

"You're not alone!" she called to Roscoe before returning to the newspaper. "'The biologists are trying to determine whether the lizards need protected status,'" she read.

"We all need protected status," Maki said.

13

Just after daylight, Maki and Hanrahan met in the basement of city hall to chat with the geeks. The technical staff, as they preferred to be called, were three exceedingly pale, round-shouldered young men who shared so many gestures and physical traits they could have been triplets. Even their voices, wry and singsongy, sounded alike.

The two rooms in which they labored were low-ceilinged and filled with computer equipment, cardboard boxes, reference manuals, cords, wires, and junk. The overhead neon buzzed faintly, and an enormous espresso machine on a corner table hissed and sputtered.

The one named Harley handed two printouts to Maki and Hanrahan and moved boxes and papers off a couple of chairs for them to sit on. The one named Charlie brought them espressos and stale powdered sugar doughnuts.

One printout was Herbie Bonebright's iPad email to Felix Wingate at Longleap. "You did not pay me when you said, and yet I have been doing my job as agreed. I suggest that you quit your threts and pay me imedialy with a bonus for my efforts or I will have to take some action."

The other printout was a record of recent searches on the iPad, the majority of them having to do with long-ago charges involving property destruction and criminal mischief in someplace called Bryan, Ohio.

One of the geeks brought forth a plastic bag containing the egg-shaped entity Maki had discovered on the floor of Herbie Bonebright's clothes closet.

"I know what that thing is," Hanrahan said. "I do my research."

"An amulet carried by a member of a lost space tribe?" Maki said.

"This," Hanrahan announced, "is a mindfulness and activity tracker. A hundred and twenty-four bucks at Amazon."

"And that buys me…what, exactly?"

"Mindfulness and productivity. You clip it to your waistband or whatever and head into your day, and every time your breathing gets tense, it emits a gentle little bleat." He bleated quietly. "It also tracks your steps, counts your calories, and monitors your heart rate and other sorts of respiration patterns besides the tension ones. Connect it to your phone and you can get some meditation sessions thrown in. Charges on a charging plate, which wasn't in the closet or anywhere else in Herbie's place. I checked that out."

"I don't know," Maki said. "My vision of Herbie Bonebright doesn't fit with the mindfulness part. Or with paying a bunch of money to track whatever mindfulness is. Or with keeping track of physical activity at all, for that matter. You know what I'm saying?"

Hanrahan bleated.

"But it does fit a little better with Professor Clovis, the fitness buff and fire extinguisher wielder. Yes?"

Another small bleat.

On their way to Pheasant Run, Hanrahan told Maki he'd contacted Longleap in hopes of getting Herbie Bonebright's work history, address history, emergency contacts, and recommendations prior to his employment at Longleap. The office administrator, an extremely thin and thin-voiced woman of an uncertain age, had reluctantly retrieved the file.

It was skimpy at best. Several previous jobs were mentioned: security guard, delivery driver for a beer company, manager of a bowling alley in another state, employee of a carpet cleaning company. He was forty-one years old. Born in Finch, Ontario, Canada. No felonies registered. No chauffeur's license. In case of emergency, contact a woman in Ontario named Edith Bonebright. Hanrahan had located her last residence and discovered she'd been dead for a decade.

He asked the office administrator whether Herbie had any previous property management experience, and whether Longleap had verified the "no felonies" information.

At that point, the woman had become quite huffy, he said, and had launched into a weird little speech—he imitated a high-pitched voice—in which she affirmed that she was not in charge of hiring, that she merely made sure the records were in good order, and that she left it up to her higher-ups, most particularly Mr. Felix Wingate, to handle personnel matters directly, which was his preference, those matters including all hiring, and that the idea that she would know, for instance, whether or not a criminal record had been investigated thoroughly was preposterous, as that was not her job, and was not a job she would want, whether it was offered to her or not, he could be sure of that.

None of it made much sense, and, in fact, Hanrahan had concluded that Longleap seemed to have more than its share of so-called eccentrics, to put it most kindly, and he wondered how they managed to stay in business, and why anyone would enlist their services. So he'd begun to poke around.

"For now, I'll just say that Felix Wingate and his associates seem to have done business under a few other corporate names in a few other states."

"Property management?" Maki asked.

"Well, yes, seemingly," Hanrahan said. "But the properties are always in prime locations and are always occupied by older people on fixed incomes. And, what do you know, those people start selling or moving out, and suddenly there is an empty building in a good location getting bought by a developer and turned into extremely high-end real estate. Luxury condominiums. Boutique memory care. Who knows what else?

"And you think Herbie was the hit man at Pheasant Run, so to speak. The enforcer. The terrorist."

"That might explain a mindfulness tracker in his closet," Hanrahan drawled. "Stressful work."

At Pheasant Run, they took the elevator up to the fourth floor. It thumped and shuddered before the doors opened. As they waited for Clovis to answer the door, Hanrahan adjusted his cuffs and whistled through his teeth. As usual, he wore a pressed white shirt, leather vest, and blue jeans with a crease ironed into them. Instead of the boots that would have completed the look, he preferred dazzling white running shoes because he felt they gave him that extra edge, should he ever have to run. It didn't happen often in his line of work, but it happened.

Clovis's greeting was curt. He looked disheveled in an unidentifiable way, nothing about him obviously out of place, but the whole package a little blurry at the seams. His face darkened when Maki introduced Hanrahan as a police detective, and he lifted his hands in fake surrender.

Hanrahan strolled across the living room and took a look out the window, his belt buckle glinting as he turned to survey the room. There was a photograph of a large ram on a precipice, its curled horns blaring. A wine-colored leather chair. An etching of Oxford in some previous century. Fewer books than you might expect for an English professor. A few odd ones. Secrets of various sorts of winners, biographies of athletes.

Clovis indicated the couch as if he were flicking an insect away. He emitted an ostentatious sigh.

"First off, remind me again what you were doing immediately before the fire alarm went off," Maki said, extracting a notebook from his shirt pocket.

"My daily routine, my exercise routine. It's a half hour and includes a program of racewalking, stairs up, racewalking backwards, stairs down—basically consistent cardio."

"Just keep on keeping on, eh?" Maki said. "Do you start the minute you leave your place?"

"No," Clovis snapped. "First I take a nap in the hall. Of course I start when I leave my place."

"And just keep on keeping on," Maki repeated like a machine. "Do you keep track of what it's all adding up to with some kind of gizmo? I don't know much about the latest gadgets, the really elaborate ones, but there are these Fitbits and chronometers and such, right, that can track everything to the minute."

"Right," Clovis said.

"In fact, don't they have things now that can test your mentality and also tell you when you should drink some water, maybe both at the same time? And then someone told me there is a computer app that can make your refrigerator also be a stereo and a photo album. Did you know that?"

"Why would a person want to do that?" Clovis asked.

"You tell me," Maki said. "But you use some kind of device to monitor your morning exertions, pure and simple, is that right?"

"That's right," Clovis said.

"And I suppose it keeps you moving pretty steadily, and at a darn fast pace," Maki said.

"That's the point."

"What's confusing me a little is that Mrs. Riddle down on the second floor said she saw you walking pretty slowly down the hall in the vicinity of Mr. Bonebright's apartment, shortly after seven on the morning of the fire. She thought she heard something at her door and looked through the peephole and saw you walking by, slow as mud."

Clovis took this in.

"Well, I am seventy." He held up his hand like a traffic cop. "Don't say it: I don't look it. But that's a fact, and very occasionally during my workout I have been known to take a breather."

Hanrahan walked over to the window. "Look at that cat on the very top of that steep roof over there," he said. "Good traction. Must have sticky stuff on its foot pads."

He appraised his large white shoes as if they were suddenly wanting.

He looked up quickly and drilled a look into Clovis.

"We've found evidence that Herbie might have had something on his employer, Longleap Enterprises, and wanted money to keep quiet about it. Do you have any idea what that might be?"

Clovis shook his head, as if he couldn't believe the stupidity he was forced to acknowledge. "I know you gentlemen might not believe it, but I have better things to do than to listen to speculative rubbish. I really do. In fact, I have a meeting at the university in less than an hour."

"Oh yes," Hanrahan said. "You're a finalist for a job over there. Some center for something or other, am I right?"

"For Ethics and the Digital Humanities," Clovis said slowly, as if he were spelling it out to a child.

"See?" Hanrahan announced to Maki. "I *do* do my homework." He sat down in the big leather chair. "Maybe you could enlighten us as to the mission of the place, or group, or whatever it is. Just for background and whatever."

"Let's just say in basic layman's terms that I—the new director, I should say—will supervise a series of initiatives aimed at exploring the potential interface of ethics studies and the digital zeitgeist, especially as it relates to what we used to call contemporary literature."

"Katie bar the door," Hanrahan said.

"Actually," Clovis said, taking the smaller visitor's chair, "we're talking about no less than a rebraining of the human universe, a process that is happening at such speed that the old intellectual fiefdoms, segregated from

each other by walls they've enthusiastically built themselves, simply aren't up to the task of offering anyone help
in living their lives in a mindful sort of way."

"So when I want to make an appointment for a mindful rebraining, can I come to you?" Hanrahan said, slowly
unwrapping a toothpick from its paper sleeve. He stuck it
in his mouth and wiggled it up and down.

"I'm guessing it's too late," Clovis said airily, consulting
his phone.

Maki extracted a printout from his vest pocket.

"You sent an email to the president of the condo association, Mrs. Mavis Krepps, suggesting that the group
consider selling the building to an interested buyer,
should one step forth." He handed the printout to Clovis,
who read it slowly. The tips of his ears turned a faint pink.
He coughed.

"We've asked Mrs. Krepps to forward to us any communications she gets regarding the building or its tenants,"
Maki said.

"Well, this place has its problems, in case you haven't
noticed," Clovis said. "I think we'd all be smart to sell to
some person or group with the money to make this building what it could be."

"That's the thought that warranted an email to the
association president late on the day of the fire? Couldn't
it wait?"

Clovis shrugged.

"Our technical staff also discovered that Herbie was
researching your early days and found that you were
something short of an angel as a youth," Maki added. "A
firebombed car was involved, if I remember right."

Clovis stood, then turned on his heel and walked to his little kitchen. He returned with a glass of water and set it down carefully on a side table.

"They found a search record?" Clovis asked.

"They did," Hanrahan said. "It took some doing, but the geeks finally unearthed it."

Hanrahan let the quiet come into the room and stay. Maki knew better than to say anything. No one was better than Stacy Hanrahan at sitting with the kind of silence that becomes so weighty it feels permanent.

"I did have a juvenile record of sorts," Clovis finally said. "Though for God's sake, that stuff happened when I was a very lost lad, what, some fifty-five years ago. A half century! And to my knowledge, my lawyer got it expunged from my record, and it was gone, done, buried."

"Not deep enough," Hanrahan said.

"Given Mr. Bonebright's extortionist tendencies, I'm wondering if he ever brought up the fact of your misspent youth with you," Maki said. "And if he did—just saying—I think I'd want to know just how far he'd gone with his own research. In fact, I'd almost be tempted to get a look at Herbie's iPad, just to see what all he'd been up to. That is, if I could get into his account by, I don't know, knowing his password or using some kind of all-purpose one? Do they have those? The geeks seem to be able to do it, eh, Hanrahan?"

"Geeks are geeks," Hanrahan pronounced. "The university has a pack of them, too."

Maki took the egg-shaped tracker from his pocket and put it on a coffee table in front of Clovis, who squinted as if it wouldn't come into focus. He yawned with his eyes open.

"OK," he said. "You can stop. I did go into Herbie's apartment, about ten or fifteen minutes after he left for breakfast the morning of the fire. His door was, not surprisingly, unlocked. I looked for the iPad just to check his search record. I found nothing." He looked hard at Hanrahan.

"Well, our geeks might be a step up from you in the cyber realm," Hanrahan said with an elaborate shrug.

"I heard someone coming, hid in the closet," Clovis said in a newly soft voice. "Waited. Fidgeted with my tracker because I was very tense and was afraid some beeping was about to go off, and it must have loosed from my waistband and dropped somewhere in that hellhole unbeknownst to me. Someone was in the kitchen doing something, and then they were gone, and I was out of there like a shot."

"Taking just a second or two to lock the door from the inside."

"If I saw someone in the hall, I wanted to be able to say I'd tried his door—wanted to talk to him about something, whatever, even though I was pretty sure he'd left for the Den—and it was locked. That way, I couldn't be placed inside the apartment at any time."

"Who did you think was going to try to place you inside the apartment?"

Clovis yawned widely. He stood up.

"Well, look," he said. "Whoever came in after me was up to something in the kitchen, and it wasn't baking cookies. I could hear whoever it was testing the burners, and there was a smell of some type of fuel, then some tapping and raspy swearing, and he was out of there. I wanted out of there, too, before the place blew up."

"But it didn't," Maki said. "There was something of a wait before the fire occurred."

"And I was ready for it, alert to the possibility shall we say, and I put the damn thing out," Clovis said, aggrieved. "And this is the thanks I get."

Hanrahan had been studying the photo of the ram on the precipice, focusing closely on the way its hooves were placed at the very edge.

"That whispered swearing, or however you described it," he said. "You ever heard that voice before? You remember the words?"

"Well, people sound different when they're whispering, so, no, I really couldn't say I recognized the voice or what it was saying."

They all considered this for a few moments.

"And you didn't bother to take a good look at the kitchen on your way out?"

"No."

"Well, OK," Hanrahan said. "Food for thought. Food for thought."

"Oh, please," Clovis said. "Just get out."

14

Without the plodding presence of Herbie Bonebright, Pheasant Run took on a suspended aspect. Whatever he was—fraudulent or just moody, inept or sinister, a doughy no-count or, as Viola Six would have it, an ex-con with an agenda—his duck-footed presence as he walked the halls in his beach clothes had grounded many of the Pheasant Run residents in the day at hand. It was difficult to drift into ethereal sadness or regret, or to stew in long-ago memories, or to dwell on the sinister nature of new aches and pains, or to tease out the tendrils of the circumstances that had left you utterly alone in a cackling and money-mad world when there was a figure like Herbie moving in all his dim corporeality across your line of sight. He was like a slow reptile in an old terrarium, unsavory but strangely absorbing.

Now that he was gone, vanished it seemed, some of the residents found themselves listening for his thumping walk or the roar of his leaf blower or the talk radio that emanated from his apartment door when he left it open a few inches to tend to something somewhere else in the building. Others found themselves rereading his ridiculously contorted missives—"Please! After garbage, binn lid is closed and window above lock tite!!"—simply to remind themselves again that their own diminishments and sagging fortunes didn't include outright illiteracy.

For a week now, Herbie's apartment door had opened only to admit or relinquish various investigators. There was a piece of yellow plastic ribbon across it ordering others to stay clear. A sign told anyone who needed assistance with repairs or lost keys to contact Longleap and to be aware that the cost for delivery of a replacement key would be twenty-five dollars. The investigators had walked out with plastic containers for a few days, and then they stopped arriving much at all.

This morning's mail contained a letter to all the residents from Mrs. Krepps, who had been fielding queries about the investigations into the whereabouts of Viola and Herbie, particularly whether any information had surfaced that suggested foul play.

Dear Pheasant Run Residents,

Regarding the whereabouts of our resident manager Mr. Herbie Bonebright and our long-time neighbor Mrs. Viola Six, may I suggest, as president of the Pheasant Run Condominium Association, that we take stock of our good fortunes in life and leave the authorities to their work? They have assured me that little has surfaced that sheds light on either disappearance, and that, when and if it does, we shall be informed promptly.

———

Meanwhile, we must remind ourselves as a group to keep our collective wits about us and proceed with our lives in a calm and regular manner.

To that end, I have appointed an interim building manager from among the building's tenants, Mrs. Lydia Wishcamper. She is the person you should see about any concerns relating to the maintenance and upkeep of your units. She has employed an on-call handyman to address small maintenance concerns, and will relay larger ones to our property management firm, Longleap Enterprises. Mrs. Wishcamper was more than generous to take on these duties for what amounts to a token salary, and it would behoove everyone to thank her in whatever way seems appropriate.

I also have new information about the potential purchase of the building. Be reassured that nothing is imminent, and that any purchase will, of course, depend upon a unanimous vote of the building's condo owners. I invite all owners to make appointments to meet with me separately regarding additional terms and details of the potential buyout.

Finally, I would remind all occupants of the building that any holiday decorations you wish to put on your doors or in the common lobby area must be flameproof according to the condo association regulations and, I believe, city ordinances. Also,

any guests that you may be entertaining must be
reminded that this is a smoke-free building and
that any cigarette smoking they may wish to engage in must be done twenty feet or more from
the building. And finally, the recent "thumping"
of the elevator was investigated by the elevator
company repair people, who extricated a foreign
object from the shaft that was apparently causing
the noise and represented no immediate danger
to elevator users. I believe it was a stocking.

Kind regards,
Mavis Krepps

In her mail, Cassie also had a single thick letter with no
return address, but with a handwritten order to "Open
Immediately Upon Receipt." Cassie recognized Viola's
writing. It had been mailed three days earlier in Los Angeles. The letter was dated November 12, two days before
the fire. There it was: evidence that her friend was at least
well enough, safe enough, to post a letter. She found herself trembling slightly as she opened it.

Dear Cassie,

I hope this doesn't sound to you like the ravings
of someone who is "off her rocker." I continue to
stay on my rocker, and, in fact, feel very calm and
levelheaded at the moment, despite my awareness
that something eerie and dangerous is going on
at Pheasant Run. I hope to be able to have a cup

of coffee with you soon and spell it out from A to Z, but I might have to leave the premises quite suddenly. In that case, I won't post this until I am so far away, and in such a populous locale, that I won't be easily found.

There are unscrupulous people out there who want to empty Pheasant Run of its owners and renters and buy it for a song. Then they will resell it for a handsome profit to purchasers who have deep pockets and special needs. That's the short and long of it. We are entirely expendable to these ruthless people in the wings who hope to profit from our gullibility and our fears. I alerted our property manager, Longleap, that I knew they were likely involved somehow, then realized, too late, that I may have put myself in considerable danger.

There are many dots that connect.

Meanwhile, dear Cassie, when you get this, I will be far far away from Pheasant Run. My son Rod won't know where I am, but my friend Rebecca Tweet has moved to Santa Barbara, California, and she will have heard from me and can confirm that I am safe. If you hear that I have moved (or been moved) because I can't live independently anymore, know that the facts are otherwise.

Your friend,
Viola

Cassie read the letter again. Though it seemed proof that Viola was alive, or had been several days ago, the contents seemed overheated in a way that made her worry. Was it possible Viola had fashioned this disappearance simply to insert drama into her life, the way she had perhaps concocted personal adventures that seemed unlikely at best? Had she really had a sojourn in Athens with a handsome businessman who was a secret gunrunner? A journey on a tramp steamer in the company of a bohemian crowd that included not one but three soon-to-be-famous poets, all sleeping with each other? Maybe the stories had become her antidote to a tedious marriage to a carpenter named Ollie and a subsequent alliance with a fool who let a con man erase her savings, not to mention the existence of her hapless and infuriating only child, skipping from surefire deal to surefire deal, everything a disaster, and then he was there again at his mother's door, whining about his fortunes and convincing her to hand over money she couldn't spare.

But there was also that ravishing photo of Viola in Italy. So who really knew?

And where was Viola now? Where could she possibly be?

Cassie called Inspector Maki to tell him she had heard from the missing woman. He was working closely now with the police and would know where to direct it. She left a message on his voice mail that he was welcome to pick up the letter at his convenience. And then she read it again, and folded it tenderly into the envelope, which she placed under a paperweight next to the photos of her husband and daughter.

Rereading the newspaper, she came across a tidbit she'd marked with a big check, and recorded the information on her little machine.

"Note from the larger world: it seems that large chunks of ice from melting glaciers are being airlifted to Antarctica for safekeeping because the glaciers are predicted to entirely disappear in the decades to come. Since bubbles in these ancient glaciers are frozen records of our past atmosphere, scientists have constructed an Antarctic ice bunker to keep them safe for future research.

"Time is kept safe. Time is transported. Time is melting."

Several mornings a week, Cassie walked from Pheasant Run to a coffee shop on the other side of the downtown river bridge. It was the most she could manage without feeling slightly weak-kneed, and she didn't attempt it when the sidewalks were wet or icy. This autumn, so dry and warm after the shocking October deep freeze, had delivered an unbroken sequence of walkable days. She liked to leave fairly early, and to proceed in such a way that all her senses were as fully engaged as she could make them. This required a certain slowness and a willingness to stop at times to let her sensations find a place to alight, deep within her. Her brain, yes, but also her fingertips, her nose, her retinas, the delicate hairs and bones of her inner ears.

When she got to the coffee shop, she found an inconspicuous corner table if she could, and she ordered Earl Grey and an oval cookie sprinkled with sugar crystals and orange zest. Then she took a small notebook from her purse, and her silver Eversharp, and pretended to write things down. This was a way to deflect the pity of strangers who might be tempted to see her as a frail isolate with nothing in her day that she really had to do. She could be making a grocery list, or a Christmas card list. She could be jotting down remembered lines from a lecture she had attended at the university the night before. She could be compiling a list of possible donors for a pressing cause in which she was involved. Or making an intricate little drawing because she was a brilliant, largely unrecognized artist who drew, who conjured, in a manner habitual and necessary, like breathing. And then, when her cookie and tea were over, she liked to replace the notebook and pencil in her purse with a tinge of regret, as if the contingencies of the unfolding day spared her only these brief islands of repose.

The morning that Viola's letter arrived, she walked downtown on a day that had quickly taken on an anemic cast and an unengaged gray. But the flatness seemed to push the river and the vegetation on its banks into sharper relief. Standing at the railing of the bridge, two stories above river level, she could make out bright-red berries on the bushes, clouds of them here and there, and, in between, some white ones that seemed almost translucent. From a half block away came the toasty smells of the bagel place.

Despite the pallid weather, she was feeling uncustomarily alive. Twenty years earlier, the feeling would have produced a spring in her steps. She thought about the boy in the laundry room, Clayton, and realized that her buoyancy had much to do with their conversation. How long had it been since she had conversed with someone who seemed to want, to need her company? And Viola's letter, too, wasn't making her sad now. It meant, she trusted, that her friend had been alive to mail it. She decided to believe in Viola Six's resilience.

The fact that Cassie had created a workable alibi for the boy was not bothering her as she had feared it might. He had his troubles, certainly, but she would stake her last dime on her belief that he was no arsonist—if, in fact, the fire did turn out to have been criminally ignited, as Lander Maki now seemed close to confirming. And the boy seemed so desperate in general, so fragile and hunted, that she had feared for his stability should he become, officially, a suspect.

Inspector Maki seemed to believe her. She saw no need to revisit the issue. And maybe, years down the road, Clayton Spooner would remember the lengths to which she had gone for him, and think of her, not for the first time, as the person who had halted a downward spiral that could have killed him. As the person who had reversed the course of his life.

The river was extraordinarily clear, clear and low, and she was reminded, as she watched it, of how pleasurable it is to see moving translucence atop a bed of rocks, the way the translucence keeps altering the colors of those rocks, just slightly, so that they become moving things themselves.

The ringing bell of the Catholic church over beyond the courthouse reached Cassie and the river and the river's bridge. That old sound. That measured, measuring, lovely old sound arrived, then fell gently to the river to be taken west. She hoped no one would get rid of the bell, or alter it in a terrible fashion, as with the electronic version she'd once heard in a strip mall, where it emerged from behind a big clock sounding as if it were a real bell that had been hit on the head and was staggering around, stunned. It had made her feel bleak, to the point that she decided against the shopping mission and went home.

A bicyclist whooshed past her on the street. She could feel his air. She passed a woman with a leashed dog, a big dog with a yellow bandanna around its neck, who looked up at Cassie without interest.

The bridge began to slope downward and extend beyond the river, over a grassy area and concrete lot that were the site of the Saturday morning markets, bright and clotted and jolly, but were empty now. The lot gave way to stairs that ascended to street level. Two willows and a large pine had been planted in a concrete balcony that bordered the stairs.

Cassie stopped to make sure she hadn't forgotten her wallet again. She seemed to be doing that too much lately. It was there, in its allotted corner of her purse. She retrieved her bills and counted them, to remind herself, then replaced the wallet and looked down at her feet to make sure she hadn't dropped any bills, though she was certain she hadn't.

Her feet were near the edge of the sidewalk. A small paper rectangle, damp-looking, seemed pasted to the walk near her right toe. It said "English Oriental," only that, which made Cassie wonder what it could possibly have been attached to. A piece of crockery? A can of tea? She bent closer to read it again. She could see the dirt beneath the willows and the plump pine, and below their branches she saw something else, quite close, on the ground, just six or eight feet below her feet.

It was a young man in a sleeping bag that was zipped to his chin. He was on his back. He wore glasses, and the hair on his forehead looked trimmed and clean, and his eyes were open and he was watching her. He blinked. His face wore no expression that she could discern. Not menace. Not fear.

She was so startled she didn't know what to do. She felt embarrassed, somehow, that she had intruded upon the cave he had discovered so near the traffic sounds, the footsteps, the dogs and bicycles of the bridge, the shadowed cave that perched above any danger coming at him from below.

He blinked and rubbed a finger across the lenses of his glasses. Then he looked up at her, still mild, still absent any expression.

"Aren't you cold at night?" Cassie blurted out.

He turned his head away and extricated an arm from the bag. He raised it as if to push her back.

Cassie stood up straight and fixed her gaze on the moving river.

"Are you hungry?" she said to the river, as a young mother wheeling a baby cart maneuvered around her.

The young woman stopped.

"Hungry?" she said, interested and incredulous.

"Go on," said Cassie. "I wasn't talking to you. I talk to other people when I feel like it, even if they don't answer. Don't worry about it. Go on."

The woman patted her carefully on the arm and rolled away slowly. "You take care," she called, picking up speed. "You have a good day."

The man in the sleeping bag had begun to mutter. She bent to hear him, hoping he might tell her how she could help him. Sometimes a person just needed a listener. The man clawed his glasses off his face and threw them toward her. He was hissing slightly now, as he talked, and the words that came from him were vile, rapacious, wit's end. He wanted her destroyed. He wanted her out of his glasses. He began to bark, or hiccup, and she fled.

In the coffee shop, Cassie found herself crying. Just a little. Just enough that the girl who brought her tea gave her a pat on the arm and asked if she couldn't bring Cassie anything else. They were out of the lovely orange-zest cookies, and this felt like a quick blow. The tears started again. The waitress took some time to reassure her that the cookies would be back in the morning, and they'd be better than ever.

15

The door slammed and Carla Spooner's old Saab revved loudly, and then she was gone. Clayton took a long breath and hauled himself out of bed.

On the breakfast counter were a protein shake and his pills. He took a long drink and watched Foster run back and forth along the front yard fence, as silent and mechanical as a toy. Because the neighbors had complained about his morning frenzies, Carla had bought him a collar that emitted a burst of strong lemon scent every time he barked, and it was working. Clayton imagined the helpless stutter of the dog's little heart as it ran, terrified of the lemon blast, paws leaping forward on their own to pull the little beast behind them. He put his pills, as he had for the past few days, down the garbage disposal.

When he had showered and dressed, he retrieved the gun from beneath a pile of sweaters in the furthest reaches of his closet. He took it out and wrapped it in a sweater to place at the bottom of his backpack. He had come to love the grave weight of it against the small of his back.

The morning of the fire at Pheasant Run, he had returned to school with the gun. At lunchtime, smoking with Raven in the alley, he invited her to reach inside the pack and see what was at the bottom of it. Her reaction was amazing. For the first time since he had met her, she seemed fully alive to his presence. Her face dropped its mask of ennui and remove, and her black-rimmed eyes opened wide. She searched his face, then closed the backpack and placed it very slowly at Clayton's feet. He waited for her to say something. She took a couple of long drags on her cigarette and threw it abruptly onto the gravel.

"So," she said, her voice as airy and distant as ever. "So what's the story with that?"

The story was simple, Clayton told her. He'd found it. He intended to keep it.

"Why? Because of Chaser and his morons?"

"Call him Josh," Clayton said. "It's his name. I don't like the way he orders you around."

"So you come back with a gun," she said.

"Well, he might treat both of us different, with this. Anyway, I just wanted to show it to you. I think it looks awesome. Like from some other century. One of the cool centuries."

"Well, listen to me," she said. "Don't bring it to school. I've seen it. I'm impressed. Now take it home, and throw it away, and forget about it."

Clayton shrugged. He didn't know what he had expected, but this surprised him. He felt a little sick.

"Listen again," Raven said. "I'm going to get out of town in a few hours. I'm having some stupid and scary shit going on at home, and I have to get out of here for a while."

"Where?"

"I don't know. The Twin Cities. California, maybe. Someplace with a lot of people who don't give a shit about me one way or another. Just for a while."

Clayton wanted her to ask him to come along. They could strike out on an adventure together. They could get to know each other in the real world, beyond shared cigarettes and complaints about school, get to know each other in the minute sorts of ways Clayton had imagined for them, when the time was right. But he knew, almost as soon as the wish came to him, that there would be no asking. Her face was set. She was agitated in an exclusionary sort of way.

To recall her to him, he told her that the principal had called him into the office, about an hour after he got to school, and said the fire inspector was looking for a student in a Star Wars T-shirt. That he wanted to talk to him about why some people saw him outside the tall building down the block just after a kitchen fire in one of the apartments early that morning. He said he probably would tell the guy the honest truth: that he'd hidden inside the building to save his life and knew absolutely nothing about any criminal incidents. Raven simply shrugged.

"Why don't you get in touch when you get wherever you're going?" he said, hating the faint pleading in his voice. "Or not. Whatever." He wanted to give her a raincoat. He wanted to give her a bag of gold and her own jet.

"I will," she said. "I'm all organized about this. It's been coming for a while." They heard the bell inside the school building. She waved in that direction and started off in the other.

"Lose it!" she called over her shoulder.

A week later, and the gun still accompanied him to school. He had no bullets for it, but they'd be here soon. He had spent some time online determining what kind he would need and where he could get them, then scrubbed his search history and used a public computer at the library to order them, using a credit card he'd lifted from Carla's wallet. She always came home long after the mail arrived, so he'd intercept the bullets, and when the bill arrived, he would deny any knowledge, hoping she would conclude that someone at work had stolen and replaced the card. It had happened before.

With bullets, the effect of the hidden weapon would intensify, he knew. Because this was what had already happened in just a few days: Josh and his friends—clueless about the contents of his backpack—had begun to treat him in a slightly altered manner. The change wasn't dramatic—they still snickered and murmured when he passed; they still called and texted insults, and feigned accidental stumbles that pushed him off balance in the halls—but there was something distinctly different about their attentions now, a stylized, almost bored, aspect that made the pack of them seem brittle and light, when they had formerly seemed all meat and muscle and intention. Clayton suspected the change had to do with some new sheen of steadiness and power, some new armor, on him. Maybe it was the thrown-away pills. Maybe it was the presence of the gun in his backpack. Maybe his old shrink would have called it incipient bipolar grandiosity. Whatever it was, he liked it. It was getting him through the days feeling almost fine.

In the time since he had stopped playing video games with Steiner and Mack, Clayton had turned to his small, out-of-date, single-player stash. In one game, he exhausted himself by shooting many of the enemy in the far reaches of the Afghan desert, then pushed on to play a tier in which he had to figure out which of his buddies had betrayed him to the captain they all knew was an intelligence agent for the mujahideen. He clicked on the virtual envelope that had been slid under the floor mat of his Humvee and learned that torture of the betrayer might be involved and was he game for it? He was allowed a question. "Do the stakes warrant it?" he typed. "What do you think?" came the reply, which appeared against a collage background that contained exploding fireworks, photos of ordinary family-type people in sepia tones, and a huge American flag that billowed in languid time to the national anthem.

His next decision was to choose the soldier he would interrogate first. (There was a Hispanic, a Black man, and a carrot-topped Caucasian.) He chose the carrottop and got down to some fairly complicated business.

At the end of the game, the screen was blaring his victory, two former friends were dead, one was seriously and permanently maimed, and it was time for his avatar to drive his Humvee into the sunset, contemplating the next best use for his gifts. In the melee, the captain had been spirited away by a pair of infiltrators, then outed as a double agent, and he was presumably getting stoned to death at the moment. (He could click on that and make sure, but at this point in the game, he always felt it was time to turn his thoughts to the future.)

He drove slowly. He was alone, as all strong men are inevitably alone. The screen changed from a khaki-colored sky with some dust storm squiggles on the horizon into a clean, inscrutable blue. His vehicle threw a long shadow across the stern desert, and the sky morphed into lilac with a peach-colored blush at the horizon line. A drop-down gave him his choice of music to mull by. Everything was now aglow, including his perfect strong hand on the wheel, its soldierly square tips lined up just right. He felt his heart slow into a calm, intelligent rhythm. The world around him was its own entity, and it was impervious and gorgeous. Clayton felt as if he could drive forever, a man who had accomplished justice, who had risked his life and who drove forth boldly into the violet and the gold and the pink of alien terrain.

He thought about what he had summoned in himself to eliminate men who had been comrades, at least on the surface. He had the stuff, clearly. It would have been nothing to do the same to an enemy.

To relax from the rigors of killing, Clayton increasingly turned to *Call of Duty: Modern Warfare 2*, which had its share of firefights and swarming ambushes, but which also had its lulls, in which your avatar could simply explore buildings that had been inhabited but were empty now, except for the occasional body in a pool of old blood. One decrepit house, thought to be the periodic hideout of a terrorist, had books on a bedroom bookshelf: *The Jungle*

Book, a biography of Karl Marx, and *Atlas Shrugged*. Physical objects seemed designed to contain clues. There were suitcases and boxes and crates. You only had to shoot at them to see their contents fly out.

On the third story of that silvery old house, blushed by backlight, was a conservatory full of plants that seemed to be fueled by acid-green blood. They glowed; they grew and tendriled before your eyes, they drooped above velvet, jewel-toned furniture and baroquely framed portraits that hung on the old-gold walls. They seemed to be having a demented sort of fun.

There was a drop-down that could change the time of day. Clayton changed the scene from noon to dusk. The long shard of light that had arrowed into the room from the top of a mullioned window dropped lower and changed in color from wheat to old brass. The furniture threw shadows, and the plants took on various gradations of blue. A huge fern that canopied an entire corner of the room lost its predatory look and became a sheltering silver fan. Orchid blooms on metal-colored foliage became heirlooms instead of decor. Horizon gray. That was Carla's favorite color for staging rooms—the name an apt description because it was a gray that expanded instead of enclosed, soothed but didn't lull. The plants in the conservatory now were various shades of horizon gray.

The portraits, in heavy bronze frames, were three: one of a pair of children with a white, long-nosed dog on a bright sward of grass; one of a young woman with reddish hair falling in a profusion of wild ringlets down the thin white material of her blouse; the last of an

elderly woman with large, beautiful green-gray eyes
and a wreath of gauzy white hair. She had the kindest,
most knowing face Clayton had ever seen. She seemed
to look directly at him, and to like and admire what
she saw. Next to her portrait, pale-yellow curtains billowed in the breeze from a tall window, open to admit
a landscape of burnished hills and endless lavender sky.
Clayton wanted to sit on that windowsill and rest his
exhausted head against old bricks. The breeze sounded
like feathers.

Someone must have offered the school administration
a plausible explanation for Raven's absence, because, in
the week she'd been gone, no one had remarked on it. At
lunch, Clayton walked alone to the pizza place for a slice.
He hoped he'd catch sight of Raven's only female friend,
Courtney, so they could speculate together about where
she might be. He knew she would call him soon, maybe
with a report about California, the parts of it that seemed
cool or uncool, or whatever, and there might be a hint of
something in her voice that suggested she missed him, or
that she had these ideas, maybe, about someplace down
there where they could hang out together and plot their
next moves.

He caught sight of Courtney standing by herself
against a tree in the pocket park across from the school
building. She was a tall, spectrally thin girl with stringy
hair that she had somehow dyed in dots for a leopard
look. Her snaky arms were wrapped around her torso.
He crossed the street, trying to look nonchalant, and
deposited the greasy paper from his pizza in the bin

nearest her. She didn't move. Her eyes were closed and her face was clenched, drawn into itself, in a way that looked like fierce, blind concentration, or as if she had just heard terrible news.

He drew closer. He cleared his throat, summoned everything he had. "Wazzup?" he asked, as her eyes slowly opened. Suddenly, as if he had pressed a switch, tears fell down her face. She didn't wipe them away. She didn't close her eyes. She started to say something, and all that came out was a chirp of pain, as if she'd been poked in the ribs.

They heard the inside bell ring faintly behind the big doors. The park was empty.

"Raven called me," Courtney said in a near-whisper. "She isn't coming back, ever. I can't believe it. She wouldn't do this to me." She took a long, shuddering breath.

"Do what?" Clayton asked. He felt that he had walked into a movie that he'd never be able to describe, even to himself.

"Do what she's doing," Courtney said. "You don't know us. You don't know anything about us. You have a few smokes with her and you think maybe you have some kind of, I don't know, bond or something. Right?"

"I don't know. No. What am I supposed to say?"

"That you're sorry," she hissed. "That you're sorry I'm going through this."

"Through what?" Clayton asked. She shook her head at the impossibility of his very presence.

"She called from a pay phone so she couldn't be tracked," Courtney said. "You know the whole situation with the stepfather, right?" Clayton shrugged. He realized he and Raven had never made conversation a priority.

"She said she got down to California and had this vision of doing something really awful to him. Or getting someone else to. She hates his guts." The tears started again. She swiped at them as if they were insects.

"I would have," she wailed. "I would have done anything for her. But now she says she's going to put everything behind her." She fastened her wide wet eyes on Clayton. "Because she's met someone. This guy Ralph who is letting her stay in his house rent-free."

Clayton couldn't digest any of it. He felt as if he were listening to a story about someone he'd never met.

"He has a gardener and a cleaning woman who comes every day for four hours," Courtney said. "She called her mom and stepdad, and they told her she's making her bed and she can lie in it with the rest of the barnyard animals, or something. Whatever."

"How did she get there?" Clayton asked. The question seemed almost too big to voice.

"Stole a car," Courtney said. "It was parked and running outside Freddy's Market while the driver ran in for wine or something, and she just got behind the wheel and said adios and eat my shit. She dumped it somewhere near some beach after she met the guy with the gardener and shit."

There was a long silence. He touched her lightly on her shoulder.

"You should go home and get some rest," he said, like a doctor. "I'm going to Spanish."

She gathered up her book bag and ran distracted fingers through her wild hair.

"*Muchas gracias,*" she said bleakly. "Tell Señora Kirschenbalm *yo tengo catarro.*"

198

"Yo," said Clayton. It was the last word he could manage.

In his desk during fifth-period Spanish, he texted Carla and told her that, it being Friday, he wanted to chill at Steiner's house and probably spend the night, and it was OK with Steiner's mom. He hadn't actually spoken to Steiner in a couple of weeks, but Carla didn't know that, and she had been so frazzled this morning that he knew she would want, badly, some time alone with a dumb novel in an aromatherapeutic bath, and wouldn't be likely to check up on the arrangement. She had begun to cry softly in the bath sometimes—he heard her when he tiptoed past the door to his room to wall himself off from it all—and he couldn't bear the sound. There was something in it that seemed ongoing and biological, like breathing.

To his surprise, Clayton saw that he had a text from his dad. He was just "checking in." Another pinged its arrival, again from his dad, clearly about to propose some kind of bonding activity to ease his guilt. For a few seconds, Clayton couldn't decide whether to read it all, his throat so tight he couldn't take a real breath. It was the same way he'd felt in English when the teacher quoted some poet from three centuries ago writing about his dead son: "Farewell, thou child of my right hand, and joy; / My sin was too much hope of thee, lov'd boy."

He swiped the text away and tried to summon again the wild autonomy of his Humvee in the desert, the peace of the conservatory windowsill. He tried to see the sentences on Raven's hands, to remember some of the words. He tried to conjure her face, but it hurt too much to look.

—

After his last class, he decided to return to Pheasant Run. He could see no one in the lobby area, so he walked straight in through the unlocked front door. From there, it was just a few steps to the door that led down a flight of stairs to the basement and the storage cubicles.

No one had fixed the lock. His small space welcomed him back. He felt that he'd arrived from another era, another galaxy. All the smells and textures were redolent of a reality he seemed to have encountered only in his furthest dreams. There was the leather saddle tipped on its horn in a corner. Beneath it was a blanket made from sheepskin. The old patchwork quilt with its dusty, old-flower smell welcomed him back. He spread it on the floor and lay down on it, his head on the sheepskin blanket, the saddle propped behind it like a shallow enclosing shell. Its smell was ancient leather and what the boy presumed was horse. He had never seen a horse up close. The horse part was grassy and woody, like warm tree bark, with a little sweet salt on the edge. The ghost of a horse or horses dead now for many decades. And still the smell remained.

The saddle was heavy. Almost everything he discovered in the storage cubicle by the light of his phone was heavy. The soft herby quilt was filled with heavy cotton or wool. The Christmas lights in a large paper sack were as big as robins' eggs. The binoculars on a dusty shelf seemed to be made of iron. The phonograph records in a warped cardboard box were red and heavy and thick. The gun, now his, had left the other objects behind, but remained the heaviest object of all.

Raven would love this place. He would show it to her when she decided she was through with California and hated Ralph and his house and wanted to come home, for a while at least. At school, Josh and his friends would treat her with respect because the person at her side, Clayton Spooner, had a new look about him that said, *One* fucking *word, and you will pay dearly.*

His thoughts circled back to the old lady he'd encountered last week in the laundry room. She seemed to contain a deep calm, a kind of watchful stillness that he yearned to have for himself. She also seemed to be someone who had been through battles, the way he had been through battles. She felt like a fellow warrior. And it seemed her story about his alibi had been swallowed hook, line, and sinker by Maki, the fire investigator, because after that first brief interview, he hadn't heard a word from him.

Slowly he scrolled down his short contact list to Cassie McMackin's number. He wanted to see her. He wanted her to explain what needed explaining. He wanted to sit on her windowsill and listen to her talk.

Her voice when she answered was pale and kind. She hesitated only a moment or two.

"Well, yes," she said. "Let's have a chat. When you get to the building, take the elevator to the fourth floor and come to 412."

He waited and, in his mind, walked toward the building from several blocks away.

In the lobby, he hit the elevator button. Nothing happened. He hit it again, fast, faster.

16

He was pale, puffy, sloppily dressed, the way he had been when she met him in the laundry room on the day of the fire. He stood in the doorway, looking sleepy and ashamed and ill at ease. There was a long abrasion on his forehead.

Cassie had slept scarcely at all the night before—she'd had fire dreams and homeless dreams. She had a dream in which the Pheasant Run residents were being driven onto the street by fumigators who used things that looked like Fourth of July sparklers to do the trick, very dainty things that shot out thin streams of smoke—it seemed to be only smoke, but maybe it was mixed with some kind of drug or poison. They walked down the hallways in stocking feet, these fumigators (yes, there was something in the smoke that killed vermin or disease) and wafted, so daintily, the sparklers back and forth in front of the door locks, sending the very thin smoke through the mechanism to bloom on the other side. And they called out something innocuous. "Up and at 'em." As her mother had.

So she felt, as she greeted Clayton, a little dismantled still, a little ephemeral, from the rancid dream and the night of so little sleep.

"I'm glad you're here. Come, sit down."

He shuffled in and wrangled his overloaded backpack off his shoulders. It was in a camouflage print. Maybe he liked it because it seemed military, made him feel like a soldier. Though the rest of him—the grimy T-shirt, the low-slung cargo pants, the dirty sneakers—worked against the effect. He reeked of cigarette smoke. Or probably, Cassie corrected her impression, he smelled exactly as she and all her friends had smelled in high school, not to mention their parents, everyone on the bus, even some teachers who lit up before they embarked on the day's instruction. It was a smell that had been integral to the environment, and then it wasn't. It was gone. Cassie couldn't remember if she had even noticed it when it was there.

His head fell back against the couch and he closed his eyes. Cassie waited a few moments. She studied the skinned forehead.

"Are they still giving you a bad time?" she asked.

"One of them knocked me against a wall a few days ago," he said, touching his forehead lightly. "Now they are sort of backing off." He consulted his backpack. "At least they were today.

"There is really one main guy," he added. "And his sister is shacked up with my dad. I don't think I told you that." He glanced at her, then away.

"Is that what he's furious about? Your dad and his sister?"

"Oh no," Clayton said. "He likes it that his sister can wrap older guys around her little finger or whatever. Plus she gives him information about me, some of it a bunch of lies, that he uses against me."

He closed his eyes again. "Their mom had a different first husband. The sister is seven years older than Josh. Like, twenty-two, I think."

"An older woman," Cassie said. "What does your dad say about all this?"

A flush crept over the boy's face. He took a long breath that had a shudder at the edges, then squeezed his eyes tightly shut.

"Oh…fuck!" he said. "Nothing! Too much! Everything that comes out of his mouth sounds so lame and stupid, I want to hit him. He's like a snot-nosed little kid. I feel like his parent. And I wish he would just…get out of town. He keeps wanting to do something together so that he doesn't have to feel me hate him so much. Or, I don't know, so he can say he tried."

He lifted his stripped face. "Tried *what*?" he wailed. Then he was hunched over, face in his hands, shoulders shaking.

Cassie walked over to him and rested her palm on the top of his head. Then she stood by the window and looked out at the neighborhood roofs. It was a steely afternoon, the light already fading. Someone in an upper story of one of the houses turned on a lamp. Someone on her floor was cooking hamburger.

She wouldn't ask about the mother. What was there about her situation that Cassie couldn't guess? She had read somewhere about a group, a cult, something that demanded the strictest monogamy of its married members, with the exception of a six-week period every year when everyone was free—was encouraged—to fornicate to their fill, with as many partners as they wanted or could handle. Rules of hygiene and safety to be observed, of course. Or maybe it was some kind of sociosexual group experiment. She couldn't remember the details. What she did remember was that quite a few in the group went for it in the beginning, avidly and imaginatively, but that, in the end, six weeks was too long. They started drifting back earlier to their husbands and wives and children, often within a few days of their so-called freedom. They didn't deny that the hiatus was a good idea, but, because they had another shot at it in a year, they didn't feel obligated to follow through fully at the moment. Over time, the experiment basically ran itself out.

Was this another thing she thought she had concluded, somewhat gradually, over her long life? That the prospect of experimentation becomes not so alluring once it's condoned, codified, endorsed? Or that perhaps it's not sex at all, but transgression that forges the kinds of bonds that can obliterate the past?

Clayton got up and paced the room, shaking his hands as if they were covered with cobwebs or feathers. He slumped. He shook his greasy head. His shoelaces were untied, and he flipped each step almost imperceptibly to keep them off to the side.

He bent to examine the photos of Neil and Marian on the end table. Neil wore his Scotch-plaid driving hat, the brim tilted above his beautiful shaggy white eyebrows, his laugh-crinkled eyes. His smile was alert, knowing, wry, happy. There were two of Marian. In one she was a topknotted child planting a big kiss on the wooden ear

of a merry-go-round pony. In the other she was standing in front of a khaki-colored tent, a foot on the fender
of a Jeep, reporter's notebook on her knee, writing. She
had wild graying hair pulled into a haphazard ponytail.
Presumably she was interviewing someone, but that person wasn't in the photo. Or maybe she was amplifying
and clarifying notes she had taken fast, on the fly. Her
head was bent. She wore very dark sunglasses. Beyond
the tent, the little that was visible was glaring and empty
and white-hot.

At first, soon after she got the news, Cassie almost
banished that photo to a box or the trash, leaving only
the charming everything-is-funny image of the child
Marian. But every time she removed the war zone
photo, she put it back, the reason having something to
do with an obvious symmetry between that utterly engaged person and her fully present father that Cassie
could not bear to disrupt.

"Where is he?" Clayton asked, startling Cassie.

"Where is he?"

"Your husband. Is that him? Where is he?"

"Stop saying that," Cassie said. "He's dead."

"Oh," he said.

"But if I hadn't answered when you called, you would
have heard his voice on the machine," she said. "I've kept
it there. For quite a few years, actually. I like to think
that it sends a signal to callers with any bad intentions,
or even just something to sell. Back off. There is a man
in the house."

"Yeah. I guess."

"Your girlfriend with the bird name," Cassie began. "Does she feel that way? Does she feel safer in a man's company, or is that completely old-fashioned?"

"Raven," the boy said dully. "No. I don't think so. Not at all, actually. I think her stepdad, like, thinks she's hot. And she doesn't feel safe at all with him as the man of the house."

"The man of the house," Cassie echoed, her voice a little drifty. Ordinary turns of phrase were, more and more, sounding strained, even tortured, to her.

"She hasn't even texted me," Clayton said, his voice very quiet. "She said she would, if she didn't throw out her phone. I think she must have thrown out her phone. So no one could find her."

Maybe that's what Viola did, Cassie thought.

"Her friend Courtney told me Raven called her from a phone booth and told her she's staying with some guy in California. Courtney is actually sort of mentally ill. She says anything. Plus she's jealous of me and Raven, so she's just going to do anything to get to me."

"Are people looking for Raven, like perhaps her mother and the stepdad?" Cassie broached. "I mean, has an accident or something like that been ruled out? Are the authorities involved?"

"Like declaring her a missing person? I don't think so. Courtney says Raven called them and they said like, whatever. She has run away other times. It's like that boy that could have been in some kind of danger, like from a fox or a lion, but no one believed him because he had done it so many times before."

"Wolf," Cassie said, suddenly drained. "The boy who cried wolf."

"Whatever, yeah, that sounds right," Clayton said. "Some animal." He hoisted the backpack onto his soft shoulders.

"That looks heavy and awkward," Cassie said. "Like you're carrying tools around."

"I sort of am," he said, suddenly eager, as if he wanted her to press the issue.

"You're heading home?" Cassie asked, trying to mask her relief. All she wanted at the moment was her chair, her feet elevated, a cup of peppermint tea, herself to herself. She also wanted to feel as if she had provided something to this strange kid, but he seemed to drift beyond the range of possible contact.

"So that Maki guy believed you about being with me when that fire happened, must be," Clayton said. "He hasn't been back in touch with me."

"Good," Cassie said. "I'm going to trust that you had nothing to do with it."

"Oh yeah, no worries," he said. "I had plenty of reasons to be inside this building that didn't have anything to do with setting random fires. Like one reason was I'd get destroyed if Josh and those others caught me. Maybe almost killed. That would make them happier, almost killed. Because I'd feel it more."

At the door, he lifted his hand.

"See you around," he said.

"Take care," she said. "See you around."

He turned away.

"Come back sometime," she said, surprising herself. "Get some sleep. Don't do anything you haven't thought through."

The door shut and he was gone.

"OK?" she called.

Silence. Breathe. Breathe again.

She leafed through the small pile of newspaper clippings on her coffee table. So many strangenesses. Small strangenesses. This one felt worth recording, for what reason she didn't know. She pressed the button and leaned close.

"From the Earthweek column in today's paper:

"'One audible legacy of Ukraine's 1986 Chernobyl disaster is that the woods surrounding the derelict nuclear reactor are filled with songs of lonely male birds.

"'Very high levels of radioactive contamination have killed far more of the female birds, mainly due to the stressful combination of coping with the radiation while reproducing.

"'Writing in the journal *PLOS One*, biologist Timothy Mousseau of the University of South Carolina says that after counting the number of females to males around Chernobyl, researchers conclude that lonely bachelors are spending more time calling out for mates that just aren't there. The study also found more yearlings than mature birds, meaning the survival rate is relatively low in the contaminated zone.'"

17

During the evening shift change, Viola Six woke from a delicious nap to hear two nurses in the hall talking about arrangements to take her to something called "transitional living." It had a terrifying sound to it. Transition to what? Whom would she be living with? What kinds of new skills would she be expected to master?

Viola's head was swathed and throbbing, but she didn't have a fractured skull. In fact, the blow from her fall on rocky ground among the towering blue plants had done relatively little structural damage. The doctors speculated that she had gone down so fast and completely because of her age, possible exhaustion, and severe dehydration.

Viola hadn't been saying much to anyone. She assumed her driver's license was still where she'd put it before she got on the bus to Lotusland, under the inner sole of her right moccasin with Rebecca's phone number and the cash from Raven. Hospital staff popped into her room from time to time to ask who she was, where she lived, who were her next of kin, whether she knew anyone in Santa Barbara. She told them she couldn't remember much of anything.

She didn't want a single detail to change for a while. She wanted to stay in her white room and be tended to;

she wanted people to ask how she was feeling, whether her thoughts were becoming more clear. She wanted to rest in a safe place, to be anonymous, to be asked what sounded good for lunch. She pretended, at times, to be unresponsive or confused, so this swaddling twilight would continue.

Now, though, the reference to transitional living had spooked her, and she decided to come fully around. She told the night nurse, Devon, her full name, where she was from, and what her son's phone number was. She asked for her moccasins and retrieved the driver's license and Rebecca Tweet's phone number.

"My plans," she told the nurse as crisply as she could, "are to stay here in Santa Barbara with an old friend. I have no intention of returning to Montana. Certain conditions in Montana are quite dangerous to me." She could see his antennae go up.

"It's not paranoia," she reassured him. "It's a living situation in which I was likely to be injured. Rotten maintenance. Stairs. Ice..." She turned her hand in a vague circle that included many dangers too tedious to mention. "I have an old friend here in Santa Barbara, and I'd like to call her, if I may."

"Be my guest," Devon said.

The phone rang and it rang. Seven, eight...and then a woman's small voice.

"I told you to stop bothering me," it said, in a near-whisper. "I have no nephews needing bail money in Nigeria."

"Rebecca?"

"No Rebeccas at this number."

"Rebecca, it's Viola Six. Your friend from Seniors. You sent me all those postcards. I'm here."

There was a long silence.

"I need your help," Viola said. "I've been injured and I need someplace to go for a little while or they'll put me in transitional living."

"Take me off your list," came the shrunken voice. "You people are always bothering me. Don't call again. Take me right off your list." The phone clicked dead.

Devon stepped into the room with an armful of clean sheets.

"Was your friend glad to hear from you?" he urged.

Viola nodded. "But she's very hard of hearing," she said. "It makes conversation difficult."

She thought for a while. She called her son. He answered warily.

"Where are you?" she asked.

"Jackpot. Still here in Jackpot. Working things out."

"Why haven't you or anyone else come looking for me?" She realized, as she said it, how utterly abandoned she felt. "It's been days now since I've been in my apartment, and no one has come looking for me. Including you."

"Someone from your building called, but I didn't have anything to tell them. How could I know where to look? Where are you? Are you back home?"

"No! I'm in a hospital in Santa Barbara, California."

"Why?"

"Because I have a concussion and contusions!"

"Were you able to come up with your rent money? Or stall the landlord? I really needed it, and my business deal went south, and I've pawned a few things so I hope I can get the cash to you pretty soon."

Viola answered with a long silence.

"Why would you be in Santa Barbara?" Rod asked.

She sighed as audibly as she could. "Because I was kidnapped. Abducted. That's why."

"In Santa Barbara?"

She didn't have the energy to keep answering stupid questions.

"You have to come and get me," she said. "You have to be helpful to me. Just once, you have to try to make my life a little better."

This time, the silence was so long that she thought he had disconnected.

"It sounds like a complicated story," Rod said. 'How did all this start?"

"Just get here, please," she said. "I will review it for you in detail."

Another long silence.

"I'll need you to cover the gas," he said.

Viola gave herself twenty-four hours to think about nothing connected to her next steps. She knew she had to recharge herself, and she knew they weren't going to discharge her for the next couple of days. So she could invest all her energy, temporarily, in the sweet routines of being attended to. What to order them to bring her on a lunch tray. Yes, good, time now for a pill and a nap. A brief, solemn assessment before she checked which face on the wall chart represented her level of pain. (She hated the one with the severely down-turned mouth, the drawn brows, the sweat drops flying off into the air, minuscule capsules of sheer pain.) The chatterings of the nurses and aides, the solemn Madonna face of the phlebotomist as she bent over the needle. The change of the bed. The solicitous arm on hers as she walked the hall. The waking up in the night to the sounds of purposeful steps, murmuring voices at the desk down the hall, knowing that she had only to press a button and someone would come to talk to her about any concern she might have.

It would be different, she knew, if she were lying there disoriented, in serious pain, or with a dreadful, or even iffy, prognosis. If she were just holding on, alone, in a hospital in a strange city, perched at the top of a nonnegotiable, unequivocal descent—yes, then she would feel something like terror. But this was not that. She was going to recover, she'd been assured by the young professionals with tired eyes and untroubled brows who stopped by in the mornings. Her cognitive powers were now functioning pretty well, given her age. She was ready for transitional living, probably by the weekend.

After her twenty-four-hour reprieve from thinking, she asked for a pen and paper, and she wrote a note to Cassie McMackin. She had not been able to get out of her mind the possibility that Cassie, upon receipt of her first letter, which outlined the problems at Pheasant Run, might have taken it upon herself to register a complaint with Longleap, or to request that the owners' association investigate more closely the buyout offer and who might be behind it. If she had, then she, too, might be a target of violence. Herbie had his marching orders, and she was sure they weren't restricted to her.

She would, yes, write a note to Cassie, and she'd add the information about how she got taken away from her home. Cassie would pass on this information to the authorities. She would know what to do.

She would miss Santa Barbara, though she had been granted only a few hours to walk around and take it in. She would miss the celebratory wintertime birds, the benign light, and the flashing ocean. The pretty buildings and handsome houses she would miss. But none of it would miss her, she realized. Everything would stand back, arms folded, and watch her go.

Rod would arrive and Viola would be on her way back to Pheasant Run. He would want the details, the chronology, so she began to think about what she would tell him and how he would react.

For someone who didn't have the vaguest idea about how to order his own life, Rod was stunningly unhesitant about questioning the conduct of hers. Even as a child, he was constantly asking Viola why she had done this and not that, why she wore what she wore and drove how she drove and bought the food she bought.

As an adult, he only got worse. There had been her trip to Italy when he was stumbling through his first and only year of junior college, and did she get so much as a question from him about the experience? Not that she would have felt comfortable sharing the most memorable details, especially in the realm of romance, but you would think he could have summoned a sort of brute curiosity about people and places that were unfamiliar to him.

And her few years with Captain and the disaster that he'd turned out to be? Rod had professed permanent

speechlessness at the scope and consequences of her mis-
judgment—this all while he was trying to extricate himself from his joke of a marriage to the Slovakian teenager
who had convinced him that she was a wealthy young
woman of virtue who needed only a green card to facili-
tate Rod's access to the complicated monetary assets she
wanted them to share as a couple.

She knew that none of that would stop him from be-
rating her for landing, contused, in a California hospital
1,300 miles from her home. So she tried to mentally line
up the circumstances in a way that seemed simple enough
for him to comprehend and traumatic enough to encourage a little empathy.

She had, that early morning a week ago, made preparations
to flee her apartment in order to avoid harm that might
befall her as a result of what she knew about skullduggery
at Pheasant Run. (The details of it she would skip, because Rod wouldn't care anyway.) And then came the hard
knock at her door, and the sound of a key in the lock, and
the voice of Herbie Bonebright in her living room.

She felt she should call out, but her voice wasn't
working properly, and she could manage only a squeak.
Footsteps now, and Herbie stood at the doorway to her
bedroom. Her first thought was that evil intent comes,
so often, in stupid-looking packages. No wonder so many
children were afraid of clowns.

Herbie's Steelers cap was pulled low over his eyes, so
she couldn't really see an expression. He stood with his
legs spread like a football coach and wore the large plastic
clogs that constituted his winter footwear.

He told her to get a coat, his voice pitched higher than usual. He said they were going for a drive.

She asked him why.

Just do it, he said, and don't bother about shoes. She wouldn't be taking any long walks that day.

He walked her to the elevator and they took it to the basement, where a door opened onto the alley. She recognized the parked car, his turquoise Honda Civic.

She asked him why he wasn't having breakfast at the Den, as he did every day at this time.

He didn't answer to her, he said, and now they would go for a little drive.

Viola's whole body became very quiet. He pushed her into the front passenger seat, where she struggled briefly with the seat belt before she realized the irony of self-protection. Nothing could protect her now. She felt quite sure she wouldn't see the end of the day, or maybe the next hour. Would Rod have the slightest comprehension of the terror in that?

Herbie drove slowly toward the interstate entrance, then gunned it when they were leaving town. The landscape flew by. Trees, glint of river, trees, tawny mountainside, billboard, fence, river. The sky was wide, silvery, impervious. As they traveled, it turned low and tired.

November and its short light, Viola thought. *My life and its short light*. Tears welled in her old eyes. What had it all amounted to? She felt the urgency of trying to answer that question in whatever time she had left—minutes, hours. And she felt, too, a slowly growing sense of something oddly like victory. Whatever else she had done or not done, whatever mistakes and misjudgments she had made along the way, whatever her death might feel like when it happened, she would know that she wasn't dying a victim. Near the likely end of her long life, she had stood her ground against some kind of evil afoot. She would like Rod to understand that.

She had been a force, a threat, her suspicions clearly expressed and clearly on the mark. And for that, she was going to pay the ultimate price.

Finally she had summoned the courage to try for some answers from Herbie. The moment returned to her, engraved.

"Why are you doing this?" she asked. "Not me. I don't mean taking me out on the road like this to terrorize me. I know that's what they expect you to do. But why are you doing the bidding of that sleazy company you work for? They must pay you a lot."

"Longleap Enterprises pays shit," Herbie said, his voice flat. "They need to clean up their act."

Viola looked at him sharply.

"What they need to do is make it worth my while to do my job, instead of threatening to terminate my employment."

"Have you told them that?" Viola asked carefully, as if they were confidantes.

"Shut up, Mrs. Six," Herbie said. "Shut. The. Fuck. Up."

He fished a plastic liter of Diet Pepsi from beneath the seat, clasped it between his legs, and twisted the top off with some difficulty. "Fucker!" he said to it. He took an oblong pill from his vest pocket and swallowed it with the Pepsi. He had a white-knuckle grasp of the wheel and had started huffing.

"Maybe we should just turn back and start the day over again," Viola suggested. "You're expected back at the building about now. People will wonder where you are. Or do you have to find someplace to knock me out and dump me in the river first?" She hoped she sounded calming and self-mocking.

"There's an idea," Herbie said, pulling into a rest stop near a river. He got out, locked her in the car, and paced the parking lot, checking his phone. She guessed he was checking in with Longleap, maybe reminding it that he was upping his terror campaign against the tenants of Pheasant Run, and she was the proof. She felt weariness, like a huge hand, pushing her into the seat back. She discovered that she was crying. She stared at her slippered feet and felt a wash of pity for them.

Herbie returned to the car hissing through his teeth. She asked to use the restroom. The only other people in the lot were a couple of stoned-looking teenagers at a picnic table, so he let her. After she peed, she removed her phone from her jacket pocket and stared at it. Was there one button to summon help, or did she just press 911?

"Out!" yelled Herbie, pounding on the restroom door.

She slipped the phone into the waistband of her underpants, opened the door, and walked with him back to the car. Herbie hissed again.

"Is there a reason you're making that sound?" she asked, trying to sound polite. He gaped at her, as if she were some wild creature who'd bounded in from the woods, panting and unpredictable.

"I'm making that sound because Longleap just fired me. There's been a fire in my apartment at Pheasant Run, and it's going to get me canned by the condo association anyway, they said. Well, it's going to get them canned, too, but maybe they didn't think of that yet."

Viola clenched her eyes and covered her face with her hands.

"Shut up!" Herbie said. "No one's hurt. No big deal. But I can tell you this, Mrs. Six. Both of us have gone missing, haven't we? They cleared the building, and we turned up missing, and now they are looking for us."

He stared at the phone in his hand. And he walked to the bank of the river and threw it in.

"Get out," he called. Then he thrust his hands in the pockets of Viola's ski jacket, a move that shocked her almost as much as if he had hit her.

"Phone check," he said, coming out empty-handed. "Good girl."

She returned to her seat and curled into its corner. For many miles they traveled an untrafficked state highway. The tawny foothill country was glazed with snow that began to take on shadows as the day moved into the light violet of late afternoon. They said nothing. Herbie appeared to be working out a very complicated puzzle in his head. His lips moved.

Eventually they circled back to the interstate, passed through Butte, its mine gallows etched black on the hills above town. Traveling east, the Civic labored up the long mountain pass, lurching as it geared down. It was dusk.

"We've been driving around all day," Viola said. "Aren't you starving?"

"Shut up," Herbie said.

Viola told him she was desperate again for a rest stop.

At the top of the pass, they pulled into one. A green sign said they were at 6,355 feet above sea level, and on the Continental Divide. A single semi idled on the far side of the otherwise empty lot.

"Get in there and make it quick," he said. "I don't want any accidents in my car. And remember, if anyone's in there and you say anything, they'll think you're batshit. I mean, look at you."

She ran her eyes down her ski jacket, her pajamas, to her slippered feet. In the restroom, she went to the farthest stall and locked herself inside. She retrieved the phone and stared at it. She poked at it and the screen lit up, so she swiped it as Rod had shown her. The keypad that came up had an "emergency call" square, so she pressed it. Her heart began to chatter. She pressed it again. "Go somewhere," she whispered. A voice came on.

She listened. She told it what it wanted to know, and then she pressed the red phone icon that stopped the call. She found the button that turned off the phone entirely, then returned it to her waistband, washed her hands, and opened the door.

Herbie's car was gone. The semi, too. Taillights were dropping down the steep slope to the east, fast. Something had made him leave in a hurry.

She was alone atop the Continental Divide under a sky that was partly scarved with clouds and partly clear, the blackness littered with stars. A chilly wind harried trash scraps across the lot. Herbie was gone. People were looking for her. She had to decide on her next steps.

The rest of the trip with the girl Raven, and her fall in the strange blue garden, she would summarize very briefly. Rod would just have to believe her about it all. She wondered if he would. She wondered, if he believed her, whether he'd care much at all about what she'd experienced.

For the first time in many years, her answer to that question felt like grief.

VERGES

18

Rhonda's confidence notwithstanding, Maki seriously doubted that the blue butterfly around his neck was doing much to mitigate his general unease, especially his guilt about his parents. But he did find that he was able to call his sister more frequently than he had in the past, in order to inquire about her circumstances and theirs. Before he called, he fortified himself with a smoke and a cup of steaming chai, sometimes enhanced with a shot of rum, though he had to watch the booze in his exchanges with Daphne because he sometimes found his voice turning hectoring or his eyes, amazingly, filming briefly with tears.

The information Daphne provided about her own life was comprised mostly of reported alterations, usually minimal, in her daily patterns. (Maki thought this might be a defining characteristic of a certain kind of aging: an iron-tight embrace of the usual, a suspicion of any break in the routine.) She was still driving the school bus, but she had a new route that required a dangerous U-turn at one point in the process of delivering her charges, and she was making no headway with management in getting this changed, though it was an unnecessary and stupid move on its face. And her cat Critter was no longer disgorging furballs with alarming frequency, having mysteriously resumed his previous hairball-less pattern, but he was now drinking more water than he used to, and she wondered if he might have some cat version of diabetes. And if so, then what? Daily monitoring? Shots?

Daphne had talked once about coming to Montana for Christmas—Rhonda had insisted on the invitation—but it developed that her habit of briefly visiting their parents every other day at five fifteen was so fixed that she feared any change would produce anxious behavior on everyone's part, and then the assisted-living company might jump on their parents' changed behavior as a reason to insist on a higher, costlier level of "amenities," such as a person to make sure they were both taking their five or seven daily medications.

There was no margin for an increase in their living costs, Daphne had pronounced. In fact, they had about two years' worth of assisted living at their current level of amenities, even with the sale of the house, and then they were looking at Medicaid and a nursing home, if there was space in any of the facilities nearby and if they would qualify for Medicaid under what she referred to as "the changing world order."

Certainly her own condo was far too small. So the parents might have to go further afield, to Montana maybe, or to Costa Rica, where she thought their younger brother the Christian wellness person was still living, though no one had heard a word from him in several years. Presumably someone had contact information, and they would have been notified if he were dead.

When Daphne was a young girl, she was so wiry and loud, skinny and wild. Their mother, especially, feared for her safety and her reputation well into her teenage years, with justifiable cause. At nineteen or twenty, however, something happened. She seemed to stop in place. There was a stab at community college courses in accounting, and another at being a recreation assistant at a girls' summer camp. And then she got a chauffeur's license and began to drive the bus, and embraced a solitary life that eventually left her heavy and humorless and utterly without spontaneity of any kind. What had happened? Their mother told Maki at one point that Daphne seemed to have had a serious "romantic reversal," but Daphne herself never alluded to anything of the sort, and their father declared that she was merely a female version of the bachelor uncle everyone seemed to have in their family—solitary and stoic—and that to investigate her life and her choices any further would be a fool's errand.

Maki swallowed the last of his unspiked chai, stubbed out his Kool, and contacted Daphne for the monthly update. The butterfly felt oddly warm against his chest, but maybe that was the chai.

She told him their mother was in the hospital. Several weeks earlier, she had been moved at the direction of Forest Glen's manager into the memory-care portion of their facility after a couple of episodes of nighttime wandering, including one that had resulted in a fall and a severely sprained knee. The director hadn't bothered to tell Daphne that the bill for this memory-care stint was going to be triple what the regular quarters cost. And Daphne hadn't bothered to tell Maki any of it because the arrangement seemed temporary and she wanted something solid to report. The so-called memory-care area, she added, was really no different from the regular assisted-living apartments—maybe a few more grab bars in the bathroom and along the hall—and the staff was sparse and included no real medical types that she could discern.

So Daphne had, a few days ago, brought their mother back to the couple's apartment in an adjacent building, and it was then that the bedsores were discovered. They were deep and on the verge of necrosis. And they meant that their mother, when Daphne wasn't there on a stop-by, had basically been left in a bed. Not once had she said anything to her daughter, though she must have been in extreme pain.

"Can you imagine," Daphne said, and it wasn't a question.

Maki felt sick. He quizzed her about who was ultimately responsible for this transfer decision, and why hadn't anyone been informed about the extra cost, and what was the nature of the company, ElderIntegrity, that owned Forest Glen, and how could it cause such neglect to occur? Had it ever been sued for negligence at Forest Glen or at any of the hundreds of other assisted-living facilities it owned? Daphne didn't know. She said the hospital expected their mother to heal up in a week or so, with luck, and she'd go back to the apartment she shared with her husband, and everyone would hope that their Medicare gap would cover the medical bill and that there would be no mental issues surging up again. Daphne sounded very tired.

"Care!" she scoffed.

When Maki hung up, he went to the computer and started poking around. He felt a white anger. He wanted to take ElderIntegrity to the cleaners. He *would* take them to the cleaners if it seemed they were engaged in systematic neglect of this kind.

Increasingly, he discovered, assisted-living companies were converting a portion of their facilities into higher-cost memory-care units. More income out of the same bed. They offered housing and "daily care," but rarely medical attention, to the occupants.

He also discovered online that ElderIntegrity, one of the giants in assisted-living facilities across the country, had been the defendant in several lawsuits charging that profits had taken precedence over care, resulting in death or injury to several elderly tenants. One jury had awarded a victim's family $19 million in punitive damages, a decision ElderIntegrity had immediately appealed.

Enough was enough. Maki tuned up Ravi Shankar on YouTube and played spider solitaire and tried as hard as he could to think about nothing at all.

An hour later, he drove to the Cabin to review the status of the Pheasant Run investigation with Hanrahan. It was late afternoon, and the day shift was wiping down tables and changing out the cash registers for the next crew. Weak, late-day sun filtered through the small, high windows on the building's west side, giving the interior a cloistered, intimate atmosphere. A few day drinkers murmured to each other up at the bar, but the place was otherwise empty, which was why Maki and Hanrahan liked to meet there on business from time to time.

Hanrahan texted Maki that he'd be a half hour late. Maki ordered a light beer and inhaled. The place smelled like tap beer, slightly dirty bar rags, peanuts, and bleach, with undertones of hair spray and hamburger wrappers.

The unruly jumble of smells reminded him that he had learned something important about Leo Uberti the minute he stepped into his apartment.

To all immediate appearances the apartment was cluttered and chaotic. An easel was set up near the window atop a paint-spattered cloth that covered half the small living room. On a rickety card table were a pile of old newspapers and an open can of turpentine. His paints, mineral spirits, and varnishes were stored on the shelves of an old wooden bookcase. The entire opposite wall was floor-to-ceiling bookcases filled with books. A single large chair next to a good reading lamp filled one corner, facing a hi-fi flanked by boxes of LPs.

As they spoke, Maki did what he always did in an interview: he split himself into an avid listener and a subtle but thorough noticer. And what he noticed was that everything Uberti might want to use—as a painter or a reader or a hi-fi user—was impeccably ordered. The books were arranged by subject matter, and, within those categories, alphabetically by author. Although he couldn't examine the LPs as closely, he suspected the raised markers in the boxes indicated a similar cataloguing technique. The boxes of paint supplies were arranged in their own categories—brush cleaners, paints, rags and gloves, framing materials—all of them labeled in small clear letters.

The range of book categories was broad and eclectic, and included World War II, World War II in Italy, three biographies of Houdini, magician's manuals, infamous criminals, battlefield strategies, a history of life insurance, European internment camps, American internment camps, Arthur Conan Doyle in three volumes, Maerz and Paul's *A Dictionary of Color*, illustrated biographies of the painter Bonnard and the photographer Leiter, and a collection of grave rubbings from small-town cemeteries in the West.

Uberti had answered the door in casual clothes and stocking feet. He struck Maki as exceptionally fit for his age, which he gave as eighty-nine. He confirmed that, yes, he owned a bicycle and rode it regularly around town and to the cemetery near the old fort, where he liked to sketch the old gravestones, sometimes as studies for paintings. He stored his finished paintings in his basement storage unit, he said, or he gave them away to anyone who would have them. He couldn't seem to summon what he called "an instinct for commerce" and painted mainly for himself because it helped him "see better" in his old age. Maki didn't ask what he meant, because he felt he knew.

Uberti had large, brown, slightly hooded eyes and a deep, resonant voice with just the barest trace of an accent. His manner was courtly, reserved, and, in some way Maki couldn't quite identify, calming. He understood instinctively why other Pheasant Run residents spoke so highly of him, of his reserve and kindness, his formality and quiet warmth.

Uberti offered coffee and brought a tray to the little table just off the galley kitchen where he and Maki could sit. On it he had arranged the cups and saucers as well as a small pitcher of cream, sugar, and two small spoons. He picked up Maki's spoon, examined it under the light, and returned it to the drawer for another. He washed his hands and dried them carefully before he poured the coffee, which was excellent.

Their talk yielded no helpful information. Uberti had seen Viola before the fire. He had no fond feelings for Herbie and wasn't sad that he'd gone missing. Beyond that, nothing.

When Maki rose to go, he asked to use the bathroom. This was something he'd done at the end of every interview.

He noticed nothing remarkable in the room, or in the medicine cabinet. A pair of tennis shoes had been placed on the edge of the tub, soles up, as if they'd been washed. Maki sniffed them and smelled the residue of grass, dirt, and some kind of pungent weed. Sage, perhaps.

He was thinking about that clean, weedy smell and trying to decide whether his beer glass had actually been washed when Hanrahan arrived and apologized. He ordered a Dr Pepper with a Dr Pepper back and slid his chair away from the table to give his big legs room to stretch.

Maki found himself reviewing the situation with his parents and what he'd dug up about ElderIntegrity without half trying.

"Scumbags," Hanrahan said. "Yellow-bellied snakes. And they're everywhere, it seems, especially now that the boomers are marching in massive battalions straight into their so-called golden years. You want to make a pile of dough? Let me count the ways." He spread thick fingers and jabbed at them, one by one. "Memory care! Boutique memory care! Luxury condos! Luxury condos in genteel and intellectually stimulating environments! Gated golf communities!" He clenched his fist, then fanned his fingers to count again. "Personal trainers! Rehab facilities! Plastic surgery! Joint replacements! Gourmet food-delivery services!"

He took a long swig of his drink.

"What I'm sure you've noticed, Maki, is that this consumer market is a very special one. Shall we call them the one percent? The five or ten percent? The elderly members themselves, or those who are responsible for them, are loaded. So there is big money to divest them of, and the so-called entrepreneurs are going to make sure they do. And if they have to pull the rug out from the rest of the old people to do it, that's, by golly, what they will do."

Hanrahan held up his Dr Pepper to the dim light. "Dangerous stuff," he said. "Makes me into a screamin' preacher."

They sat with their own thoughts for a while.

"So, Longleap," Maki said. "They're in the business of ousting old people from their homes, perhaps to make way for other old people who will pay some developer a fortune to live in a retooled version of said home?"

"That's one scenario," Hanrahan said. "Basically the Longleaps of the world are in the business of delivering real estate empty and unencumbered. But you or I will have all kinds of trouble proving that agenda. Because, hey! People move out of buildings all the time for every kind of reason. People sell their places for every kind of reason. So what you're looking at is a conspiracy, if that is in fact what's going on, and conspiracies are notoriously difficult to prove because they are crimes of the mind, not the deed. Maybe Herbie Bonebright made the folks at Pheasant Run feel afraid enough, in some cases, to move out. But what did he do that constitutes a chargeable crime? And maybe our Professor Clovis, who very much wants a job at the university, sees that it's to his advantage in some way to encourage the sale of the building to the university or someone connected to it. But maybe he really believes it's a good idea."

"And what benefit would the university see in an emptied-out Pheasant Run?"

"Research dollars," Hanrahan said flatly. "There are certain so-called educational enterprises that require a certain kind of cover, so to speak. Someplace near the campus, preferably, but masked to the general public. Animal experiments. Cybersecurity labs. And if the institution can deliver it, the research money follows. So hell, maybe the center for ethics and whatever would be housed on the bottom floor as a front, and the dirty work would take place upstairs." He shrugged elaborately. "Or maybe they just want to obtain it cheap and sell it high. To support the higher education enterprise.

"Actually," he added, "Mrs. Krepps says that, though she's aware of a possible buyout offer, the so-called new information she mentioned to the residents is that she still doesn't have concrete information about who that buyer might be. Longleap simply presents itself as a generous-minded broker of any deal that would be to the advantage of all parties. Not exactly property management in the strictest sense of the word, but oh well. They assure her that any potential purchaser would be honest and credible and all that hoo-ha, but none of the owners really knows squat, at this point."

Hanrahan got up to use the restroom, making his way doggedly across the dance floor, white shoes aglow even in the far dim recesses of the big room.

When he returned, he was listening to his phone. He looked disgusted. He wanted a where. He wanted a when. He wanted the names of the lead investigator and the highway patrol at the scene. He wanted to know exactly where to look on a topographical map. He wanted a callback when someone knew anything more. He grunted, swore, disconnected.

"Well for fuck's sake," he said. "Herbie Bonebright's been stone dead for the past week."

Maki experienced a ruffle of shock. He quickly realized that he hadn't believed that Bonebright—what he knew of him—was important enough to be dead. The thought made no sense whatsoever, but he couldn't shake it. He also felt a trickle of something like dread. That, too, made no sense.

Hanrahan told him he'd been talking to a sheriff named Bang Scofield over in the eastern end of the state in Rosebud County. A couple of fishermen on the Yellowstone River had hooked themselves a turquoise Civic, and when it was hauled out of the water, a bloated male body took up most of the front seat. The license was run, and Herbie's name and address came up. Because

Hanrahan and Scofield had done some investigatory work together a few years earlier, Hanrahan got the call.

Tire marks showed that the car left the interstate just short of flyspeck Forsyth. There were brake marks on the concrete for a short stretch, then wavery tire lines off the shoulder in the dirt and grass, but the vehicle had apparently been traveling at such a high speed that Bonebright sailed right off the riverbank and landed well away from shore. Anyone passing by on the interstate would have been unable to see the car, which had floated a way downstream, then nosed down in deeper waters.

"Time of death is a guesstimate at the moment," Hanrahan told Maki. "But it probably was six, seven days ago. Not so long after the fire in his apartment."

"Huh," Maki said.

"My sentiments, to a T," Hanrahan said.

That evening, Maki got a call from Hanrahan, who said Herbie's body and the car were on their way back to town.

He had another piece of news: Viola Six had been located in Santa Barbara, hospitalized for a fall and some temporary memory problems but otherwise OK.

"She says Herbie Bonebright forced her into his car and drove her all over hell and gone before stopping on Homestake Pass to let her use the facilities. When she came out, he was gone. This was the day of the fire, but she says neither of them had any awareness of any fire when they started their journey, and Herbie only found out about it from a text he got from Longleap sometime that afternoon when they were wandering around the highways and byways. Or so he said."

"Lots to talk about with Mrs. Six," Maki said. "But first: Did she just spread her wings and fly from a Montana mountain pass to lovely Santa-Barbara-by-the-sea?"

"In her pj's, yet. Well, she says a young gal in a big old-fashioned Buick or something pulled into the rest stop and they sort of decided to be road warriors together and get themselves to California where they could think about something other than their troubles for a while. That's the short version."

"And do we know who the young gal is?"

"Yes. Her name is Beth-Ann Felska but she goes by Raven, and she ran away from home a week ago. That's a longer story, too, but, bottom line, after some interviews with the cops and lawyers about what exactly happened when she got to LA, she will be coming back here, too."

"And that goofball Bonebright will get autopsied here, and the car examined for any problems," Maki said.

Hanrahan nodded. "Former goofball," he said. "Mrs. Six said he talked to Longleap when they were on the road, and then he seemed to be fleeing the dogs of war. Or maybe it was the hounds of hell. Something extremely unfun."

19

Carla still got the morning newspaper, though she never had time to read it until she got home from work, and by then the news might as well have been last week's. She liked that about it. She told Clayton she liked to thumb through large sheets of paper and find everything in its place, like a table set for a holiday: her horoscope, the funnies, the car ads, the national news, the local news. It calmed her down to be in the presence of information that didn't come to her sounding telegraphed, breathless, and pursued.

The front page of this morning's paper had a story about the Pit over in Butte, seven hundred acres filled with fifty billion gallons of acid and heavy-metal runoff from defunct copper mines, growing by the year and now, these past few days, a death lake for hundreds of migrating snow geese that had landed there in the face of an impending winter storm. Landed there to die, to get their throats burned out, though most of the story was given over to the sound of company officials sputtering about all the efforts they'd made to keep this from happening once again. (Several hundred geese had died years earlier in a similar scenario.) Loud noises were employed, they said. Gunshots were fired and drones buzzed the cough syrup-colored water because, during the past two decades, the banks of the lake had become so eroded that it was impossible to lower crews in rowboats onto the toxic stew to haze the birds away.

"Is this real?" Clayton whispered. "Fifty billion gallons?"

He sat down heavily and read the entire story, then put his head in his arms and tried to make his mind go numb. He felt personally attacked, personally targeted, because the birds hadn't done anything wrong except try to get some rest so they could keep going, and they got tortured and killed for it. And that was how he felt every day when he tried to get himself together to go to school, when he counseled himself to stay calm and not expect the worst, because hadn't they seemed for a while to be backing off? And then he would get there and they were waiting for him. And if they weren't waiting for him, they had left poisonous messages on his phone, to the point that he felt he carried, in his pocket, a small bomb.

There was another story in the newspaper. It pointed out that Montana's suicide rate was nearly the highest in the nation, and some expert said it was the fault of guns and alcohol and untreated depression. *Like if you didn't acquire a weapon, or drink alcohol, or let yourself get miserable, you'd live happily ever after. Like what about conditions outside yourself that might lead you to the conclusion that the world was a pit and a terror, and no place for anyone to want to live?* Clayton thought. *How about seven hundred acres of pure poison waiting to trap and kill innocent birds? What about being terrified to look at your phone messages because some of them would tell you you were already dead, even if*

you didn't know it, and where was your bodyguard? Or that
every girl in school believed you had an STD that was trans-
mitted by your putrid breath alone, and they'd be advised to
keep their distance? Or that a photo was going around of a
cock with huge dripping warts on it, and the message said it
was yours?

Every day a new surprise, to the point that when
the text ping went off now, he felt as if he'd been shot.
And what was there about going on with life, then, that
seemed so great? It was an exhausting and cruel business,
all of it, and now Raven was gone, on top of it all—could
she really be staying with some guy named Ralph?—and
he kept looking at his messages to see if she had checked
in, as promised, and there was nothing from her but
screaming silence.

If he casually took the gun out of his knapsack, and
just stood there in the hall with it when Josh and his posse
walked up, what then? Would they back off very, very
slowly, faces drained of color, all respectful murmurs,
and when he lifted the weapon a few inches, whimpers
and pleas? And then down goes the gun, and relief floods
their faces and then—whoops!—up it is again and they
are ready to grovel and apologize until they have no more
words in them.

Meanwhile: adult observers in the shadows and furtive skitterings, like rats in a basement, and whispered,
choked calls to 911 to make the next thing happen. And
would the next thing be the gun in his mouth and his decision to remove himself from the whole sordid setup and
their stupid pleas banging on his eardrums until everything was alarm and cymbal and clamor and end-stage

everything? No, better some dignity. Let them come in their jungle camo and automatics. Let them find him slowly swiveling, small smile on inevitable face, weapon ready for business, the off-screen clatter of terrified running, the sun a wound in the sky, the surging triumphal trumpets. Let them be the murderers.

Let Clayton Spooner lift off from the poisoned waters, the hissing of snakes, the faithless woman, the smashed home, the threat-chants, lift off to popping noises and overhead shadows of scrutinizing drones, lift off with a burning throat and a horizon that stretched in a silver line, magnetized and pulling, until he was across it and safely delivered to nothingness.

20

For two Mondays in a row, Rhonda had behaved in ways that worried Maki. Because her communicator sessions sometimes left her feeling exhausted, she tried to schedule them early in the workweek, after a weekend of rest and exercise. Mondays were typically high-energy and productive for her.

Maki arrived home, the first odd Monday, to find her finishing a conversation with a troubled cat whose human companions were trying to figure out why she had started yowling every night. As it turned out, Rhonda told Maki, she was warning her sleeping humans that a black bear had come down off the mountainside and passed through their yard, and that he intended trouble. The cat told Rhonda she'd watched the bear from her perch on a high window-sill, and that when he caught sight of her up there, he sat back on his haunches and did the most strange and chilling thing. He laughed. And then he reminded the cat, Trinket, that he could polish her off in one enthusiastic gulp and that he would have no problem inflicting serious wounds on any humans who tried to come to her rescue.

"Did she stay up there on the windowsill to be ver-bally abused?" Maki asked.

"She did not," Rhonda said. "She jumped down and went into the bedroom to make sure the humans were aware of an antagonistic animal walking around in their yard, having murder and revenge fantasies. Thus her yowling, which the humans think is about nothing. Dementia maybe. Deafness maybe. They say those things as if she isn't even in the room. But the bear could be back anytime, is Trinket's reasoning, so she does this warning ritual every night, and now the humans have about had it with her. The wife even jokes in a very unfunny way about sending her to the happy yowling grounds. I've tried to reassure her that she's done all that could be expected of her in terms of warning the humans, and that she should try very hard now to let them sleep. She's thinking about it."

Rhonda closed her eyes and shook her head. She looked pained and exhausted.

"You did what you could," Maki said. "Yes?"

Rhonda's mouth moved, but no words came out. A look of confusion swept her face.

"Rhonda?" Maki said, sharply.

She waved vaguely and shielded her eyes with her hand, as if he'd shone a flashlight on her.

She mumbled something, then cleared her throat and blinked. "What?" she said.

"What's wrong?" Maki asked.

"Wrong?"

"You stay out there with the critters too long," he said. "Sometimes I feel that you don't quite know your way back."

"Back?" she said, as if she was trying to place the meaning of the word.

"Yes," he said, scared and angry. "Stop it, please."

She searched his face. "I just feel spacey," she said. "And I have a headache. I think I'll take a shower, then maybe we can find something with a laugh track on TV."

"You hate laugh tracks," he said, tapping her lightly on the head.

"Very rarely, I like to watch them to remember how much I hate them," she said. "Find something truly awful, OK?"

Maki put the episode in a corner of his mind, but kept a sharp eye on her and was relieved to see, as the week progressed, that she was again the Rhonda who rose briskly and made her chai and joked with the creatures, even poor Roscoe, and fed them and kissed Maki and either sat down at her computer or drove out to the Humane Society for her six hours that paid almost nothing. On the weekend, she took several long walks, did no work, read, watched a movie, slept in.

She was reading *Fools Crow* by James Welch, a distant cousin on her mother's side. On Monday morning, she stayed in bed to reread the scenes in which Mik-api, the frail old Pikuni who tends to the tribe's sick, performs his healing ceremonies, sitting with the unresponsive person for many hours, singing, calling on the animal spirits. Her lips moved as she read. When Maki, on his way to work, appeared at the bedroom door, she motioned to him to sit for a moment on the side of the bed and read to him the last lines of the book. Winter was over. Spring rains had come to the Pikunis. The life-giving buffalo were out there in the dark.

"'Far from the fires of the camps, out on the rain-dark prairies, in the swales and washes, on the rolling hills, the rivers of great animals moved,'" Rhonda read, her voice almost a whisper. "'Their backs were dark with rain and the rain gathered and trickled down their shaggy heads. Some grazed, some slept. Some had begun to molt. Their dark horns glistened in the rain as they stood guard over the sleeping calves. The blackhorns had returned and, all around, it was as it should be.'"

When she put the book down, she clenched her eyes as if trying to block any tears. "Go," she said. "I have things to do." And so he did.

When he returned at the end of the day, she was studying a photo of a German shepherd whose head was cocked quizzically. Rhonda had dressed, but her hair was uncombed and she looked pale and worried.

Maki didn't want to know the dog's story. He had spent much of the day thinking about his interviews with Leo Uberti and Rydell Clovis, and he was depleted.

The fire had been deliberately set—he was sure of that now—and it had been set to be contained. There had been just enough fuel in the kitchen for it to burn itself out relatively rapidly. A meticulous calibration, actually. And of the two men who kept surfacing as suspects for Maki, the surprise was that Uberti was the stickler for detail. His place was a mess on the surface but there were those rabidly catalogued books and LPs; there was the coffee preparation that approached a laboratory procedure. And, of course, he had all the accelerants he could have wanted, right out there in plain sight: thinners, turpentines, paints, mineral spirits. Maybe he'd made a mixture that was a near-match for the smell of Coleman fuel. Or maybe he had obtained Coleman fuel somewhere else, then gotten rid of the container somehow.

Clovis, on the other hand, arranged his books haphazardly, and his bathroom, which of course Maki had visited at the end of his interview, was a warren of used towels and capless containers. To scare Herbie or warn him against blackmail, would he have been capable of setting a very precise fire, which he himself would then put out? Perhaps. Perhaps not.

At dinner, Rhonda took a long sniff of the gelatinous chicken soup he'd made and delicately spooned up enokis and chicken chunks from the bottom of the bowl. He stood above her like a solicitous waiter, trickling chopped chives through his fingertips, then moved to his own bowl and did the same. He sat down with a long sigh.

They ate in silence for a few minutes. Rhonda asked him if the Pheasant Run case looked to be on the home run. Her head was bent over her soup. Maki tipped her chin up so she had to look at him.

"Run?" he said.

"What?" she said.

"Did you hear what you said?"

She seemed for a moment to be listening to a replay in her head.

"Run," she said. "To home."

Rhonda tore off a chunk of baguette and dabbed at the dregs of the soup. She seemed confused and embarrassed.

"Home stretch," she said.

Maki decided to move on.

"Hanrahan has discovered that one of Wingate's previous enterprises got into tax trouble a few years ago because it wouldn't disclose the names and assets of its investors, who had incorporated as an entity called Sunset Inc. with business headquarters in the Cayman Islands," he said. "He says Sunset buys cheap properties and retools them into boutique memory-care facilities. In a couple of instances, they also made deals with quasi-government entities that needed the memory-care units to function as a front for other activities on the premises, like cyber-security facilities that needed to be very much out of sight."

"Who better than the memoryless to not ask questions?" Rhonda said. She was back in the room.

If it was someone like Sunset who had designs on Pheasant Run, and someone like Herbie crossed or threatened their agent, Longleap, they would likely want no muss, no fuss, Maki thought. Just pay him off or threaten him or maybe even run him off a road, make it look like an accident. It wasn't beyond the pale, he thought.

He held out his arms to Rhonda. She sat on his lap, an arm around his shoulders, her right temple pressed to his left. He could almost feel her in there, among his thoughts. The only sound in the room was a scritching in the lizard's cage.

"How long do you think it will take for Roscoe's tail to grow back?" Rhonda asked wistfully.

She got up and removed the cloth that covered the cage. The segments of the former tail jumped and shivered when she toed the enclosure, while the rest of Roscoe huddled in a corner, frozen.

"His enemies are supposed to be distracted by the

moving tail chunks while he—most of him anyway—slips away," she reminded Maki. "But he can't slip away, so I wonder what he thinks is going on."

"He's just trying to stay out of sight until he gets his chance to get the hell out of there," Maki said. "What does he think is going on? I'm not even going to hazard a guess. That's your department."

"It can't be enjoyable to see parts of yourself looking so ugly and desperate," Rhonda said. "Even from the wings."

The phrase reminded Maki that Hanrahan had suggested that the shadow developers might be waiting in the wings for events to play out at Pheasant Run. Longleap would be expected to watch and wait while things cooled down after the fire and Herbie's death. Then they might make another effort to empty the building while Sunset or something like it identified the "special-needs" purchasers who had, in the past, also included animal experimentation operations that didn't want to draw any attention to themselves.

He gave Rhonda the outlines of the conversation.

"The vulnerable!" she said. "Always the vulnerable. Scare old people out of their homes. Torture animals. Extort millions from the guilty relatives of the memoryless. Will these people ever stop? Money, money, nothing but money. Pretty soon we'll look up and see the flag waving in the breeze, and it will be nothing but a huge gold dollar sign."

She blinked rapidly and, to Maki's surprise, began to weep into her hands.

"Something is wrong," she wailed. "Something is off. The animals are upset; they are telling me they don't know why, but they are very upset. That cat on the roof talked to me again, and she said she is especially upset about me. She wouldn't give me specifics, but she was very concerned. She is sensing something huge, on the move, but doesn't know yet exactly what it is."

"Rhonda, please," Maki said, rubbing her neck with small, furious motions. "These thoughts are taking you nowhere. They're bringing you down. They're based on nothing."

Rhonda closed her eyes and removed his hand from her neck. "Nothing to you," she whispered. She tried and failed to smile, then shook her head with energy.

"That was good soup," she said briskly. "No surprise."

"Don't be angry at me," Maki pleaded.

"I'm not," she said. "I'm really not. I just need to lie down for a bit." She replaced the cloth over the lizard's cage. "I shall lie down for a bit and return transformed. Transformed, reset, recalibrated. And then we move on, into the dizzying future, into the who-knows-what."

21

The kid, Clayton, was sleeping on Cassie's couch. He'd arrived after school, and they'd spoken a little, and then he did what he'd done the last several times: he fell asleep.

He slept as if he were refueling, taking long, needy breaths. His body stretched the full length of the couch; his arms were flung over his head in a position of frozen exasperation. He'd removed his shoes, and his socks looked as if he'd worn them for weeks.

Except for the boy's breathing, the apartment, the building, were quiet. It was the late-afternoon hour before TV news and preparations for dinner, most of them minimal, as no one was that interested in putting together a meal anymore. They had made many thousands of meals in their lifetimes, the women especially, and had found that the appeal was gone when the food was only for yourself.

Cassie stood over the boy, studying him. His eyelashes quivered as he dreamed. His rib cage rose and fell. His hands were folded on his sternum, as if someone had arranged them that way. It was remarkable: something seemed to have been decided between them in the last week or so. He arrived, without notice, at the door. She let him in. They talked briefly. And then, at her bidding, he slept as he was sleeping now: dead to the world. This was the third time.

On the floor by the couch was his lumpy backpack. He always removed it in a careful sort of way, as if it were both heavy and fragile. And he never opened it in her presence. She touched it with the tip of her shoe. Whatever was inside was heavy.

He moaned a little in his sleep. It's all right, she wanted to say to him. There was a deep furrow between his eyes. He looked like the oldest fifteen-year-old in the world, and, not for the first time, she tried to think what she could say to him to restore him to his youth.

This, too, shall pass? Could she say that to him and be believed? Could she remind him of how much a life could change in the span of a day, weeks, a very few years? Anything she said along those lines presupposed in him a sense of context, of breadth; an acceptance of, a belief in, vicissitude. And she simply did not believe that he possessed such a thing. He felt consigned to ongoing desperation.

And what about you? Her advice, her perspective and wisdom, had turned into a question that pivoted and addressed her. And shamed her, now.

She walked slowly to the back room, to the closet, and lifted the cover of the old printer. The bottles were lined up like soldiers where the cartridge had once been. Her pills, her stash. And though she did not see them as the product, in any way, of an impulse, an unexamined impulse, they embarrassed her. For the first time, she looked at them and felt the heat climb up her face.

No, she thought. *No. You can't advise the boy against this when you are reserving the option for yourself.* You can't urge a kind of fortitude, or forbearance, that you aren't willing to enact for yourself.

In the living room, she once again assessed the boy, the depth of his unconsciousness, and she picked up the backpack and took it to the back room. She slid out the sweater and whatever was inside it and placed it on the bed. She opened the sweater and flinched. Very carefully, she lifted the gun out and held it in two hands. And she carried it that way to the closet, where she placed it on the floor, next to the printer, and covered it with a spare blanket.

Since Neil's death, she had used the room for a study. On the desk were several paperweights, one of them a heavy brass elephant that Marian had picked up at a street bazaar in Beirut. She placed the paperweight inside the sweater and returned them to the backpack. And, in her stocking feet now, she returned the pack to its place at the foot of the couch.

She found the mystery she was reading and stretched out on her single bed. The boy moaned again, and she began to drift, herself, toward sleep.

The voice was excited, inquiring, and she thought it was the residue of a dream until she fully woke and realized it was Clayton and he was speaking to someone on his phone.

"Where are you?" he asked. "Why didn't you call? Are you coming home?"

Then he laughed, a sound Cassie had never heard from him. It was adolescent and squeaky on the edges.

"Two hours?" he said, incredulous. "Cops? Real cops?" He listened.

"Awesome," he said. And then, more carefully, "Courtney said you wanted to hang there for a while. That you were cool. That there was a swimming pool and shit."

Cassie turned on the teapot and got her cup and saucer from the cupboard. The boy never wanted anything to eat or drink.

"Wild!" he said, and then, almost reverently, "Totally." His voice cracked on the word.

"I'll be there," he said.

He bent to retrieve his old sneakers from under the coffee table, then folded his arms on his knees and buried his head in them. His back moved as if he were gasping. Cassie made her tea.

He lifted his head and stood. Then he shook himself all over, head to toe, like a dog shaking off water.

"Oh," he said. "Oh, man."

He turned to Cassie and told her that his girlfriend, Raven, would be back from California in two hours or less. She was being escorted by some cops or the highway patrol, or some other kind of authorities, and they were bringing her home because she had been living in the house of a guy who had a reputation for dealing badly with girls he found on the street.

She would move back in with her mom and stepdad, it looked like, but they were going to have some major group counseling about inappropriate behavior and anger management. They'd had second thoughts about letting her make her bed and lie in it after they saw a documentary on TV about sex slave rings, and they had alerted the authorities, who found Raven and were returning her.

"You must feel relieved," Cassie said. She heard the sorrow in her voice and hoped he hadn't. "Maybe you'll stop by pretty soon and give me an update on everything, especially Raven." She knew he would be leaving her. Leaving her. She couldn't offer him the consolation, the company, the hope that Raven would bring by simply being present again in his life. Present a little. Present a lot. It might not matter.

In the laundry room tonight, Neil's handkerchiefs would fly through the humid heat and she would complete the ritual by ironing them and placing them in two white piles in his dresser. She would leaf through magazines while she waited for the laundry to dry, and there would not have been a fire, earlier in the day, to think about—all that threat and ruckus and, yes, excitement— and there would not be a wild-eyed boy bursting in on her, desperate to the point that she would make an outlandish promise of protection from scrutiny.

Something about him on that night had told her he would not survive an assumption of possible guilt, the leading questions, the probing, and so she'd made the boy and the fire disappear from the radar of the investigators, most especially Lander Maki.

And Maki had never pressed the issue, never questioned her version. These weeks later, she had decided that the reason was probably very simple: he knew who had set the fire, and why. And he wasn't, for some reason, willing or able to say.

———

Clayton picked up his backpack and prepared to leave. He was headed for the park across from the high school to wait for Raven. Whoever was bringing her home had agreed that she could talk a bit with an old friend before walking back into the cauldron of her family, where things were likely to get complicated and fractious pretty fast. They could have a quiet chat.

Clayton shifted the backpack to his other shoulder.

"I wonder if there will ever be another fire in this building," he said. "It seems so weird, that it even happened."

"Don't say things like that," she said. "Nobody needs another fire." But even as she said it, she knew that part of her was nothing but grateful that it had occurred.

After he'd left, she retrieved the gun, rubbed it all over with a cloth to remove any fingerprints, wrapped it in a scarf, and put it in her largest purse. She would take it to the river tomorrow, early, just after daylight. She would walk along the bridge. Just before she got to the spot where she had seen the man in the sleeping bag, she would lean on the railing, put the wrapped weapon at her feet, and casually, very casually, fix her eyes on the rising sun and kick it into the silver, moving water.

22

What had Leo Uberti said about seeing Viola Six when most of the Pheasant Run residents still slept and the fire was ten, fifteen minutes away from ignition? Maki leafed through his notebook. Yes, Uberti said he'd seen her "not long" after seven when she was "getting into the elevator." What he didn't say, and what Maki had neglected to ask, was where he had been at the time. Because the Six and Uberti apartments were near each other on the fourth floor, both within sight of the elevator, he realized that he'd pictured Uberti looking out his door, perhaps to check if the newspaper had arrived, when he caught sight of Viola entering the elevator.

Viola had a different version when she spoke with Maki after her return from California. Uberti, she said, had been getting off the elevator as she prepared to get on. He looked upset or ill, she said. He seemed distracted. He said he had been about to knock on her door and borrow some coffee, both of them being early birds.

Her son had driven Viola home from Santa Barbara, and Maki interviewed her the next day. He realized he had expected to find a wavery, flighty sort of woman given to extravagant speculations, theories and digressions.

But the residents who had encouraged that image got it wrong. Despite the trauma of being hauled off in her pajamas by the demented Herbie, and despite a fall that had landed her nearly comatose in the ICU before she came around, Viola struck him as steady, relieved, cogent, and somehow happy. As they spoke in her living room, she rose from time to time to adjust a photo, straighten a pillow, and her movements were sure and tender. It was as if the surviving of her ordeals had given her a new fuel.

Hanrahan had already taken her account of her time with Herbie, but Maki wanted to be clear on one point. Did Herbie seem genuinely surprised when he got word that Longleap had fired him?

"Yes," Viola said. "And then he just jabbered nonstop, saying all kinds of things about contracts and agreements and betrayal and leaving him out to dry in the wind or flap on the clothesline, something along those lines. All I could see in my mind's eye was a shark flopping around on a golf course. Did you hear about that?"

Maki said he hadn't, though the story sounded vaguely familiar.

"Fell out of the sky," Viola pronounced. "Landed on a putting green. That is the sum total of what I know."

Maki was in his thinking shed reviewing all the notes he'd assembled in the two weeks since the fire. The afternoon was bright, crisp on the edges, and a breeze pushed children's-book clouds across the wide sky and made the long dry grasses shiver and bend. Rhonda was inside the house, communicating and typing. They had been shy with each other all day, because the previous night in bed had left them racked and exultant. "Who are you?" Rhonda had whispered afterward, and Maki had felt amazed again that the ordinary could sometimes, so flagrantly, rip wide open and throw itself away.

He studied the most recent of his notes, made during this morning's breakfast visit with Hanrahan at Herbie's old haunt, the Den. They didn't have much luck adding to the sketchy profile of the late Herbie—the guy on duty remembered that he liked Polish sausages and kept to himself and sometimes seemed twitchy—but they hadn't really expected to.

Hanrahan had more interesting things to talk about, namely the fact that a Coleman stove and an almost-empty can of Coleman fuel had been found, along with two bald tires and a broken TV, in Herbie's storage unit in Pheasant Run's basement.

The autopsy had established that Herbie died by drowning and that he had dextroamphetamine in his system. Attempts to locate any next of kin had been futile so far, and Longleap's Wingate professed utter ignorance about the man. Beyond what Herbie had told the company about his background, Felix Wingate knew nothing, he said. Nada. "'These people come along and you trust that they are who they say they are, and sometimes your faith is simply misplaced,'" Hanrahan said in his mincing and pious Wingate voice.

Hanrahan's final nugget concerned Professor Rydell Clovis, who had seemed genuinely shocked, even horrified, when Hanrahan told him about Herbie's death. A few hours after their talk, Clovis texted Hanrahan that he'd pulled out of the search for a new director of ethics and the digital humanities, was putting his Pheasant Run properties up for sale, and planned to decamp to greener pastures where he wouldn't have to deal with "'fires, blackmail, kidnappings, criminals, murky university agendas, and deferred building maintenance,'" Hanrahan said, reading from his notes.

"What a wimp," Maki said. "He still could have stayed in town."

"I think the professor wants to put as much distance as he can between himself and both the university and Pheasant Run," Hanrahan said. "I mean, look: he might have almost made himself a party to some kind of arrangement that was going to make a dog's dinner of his blood pressure and mindfulness. That tracker would have bleated itself crazy."

Maki put aside his notes and stretched. He decided to take a long walk before dinner. A beef bourguignon was thawing in the refrigerator, and if he put it in a very low oven, it would be scenting the entire house when he returned.

He did that, then washed his face and put on his jacket. Sid had already taken a long walk with Rhonda and dozed, now, by the pellet stove, so Maki decided to leave him. Rhonda wore her intent listening look and typed as she gazed at a photograph of a beautiful gray cat with lemon-yellow eyes. Maki put a hand on her head and bent to kiss the back of her neck. She didn't turn, but reached for his hand and held it for a few moments, tightly. He kissed her neck again and left.

As he walked through the neighborhood park toward the university area, he tried to listen to whatever it was that tugged at him, demanding that he pay attention.

The discovery of the Coleman fuel made Herbie a definite suspect in the arson. He could have learned about setting a delayed-ignition blaze with a candle and balloon, giving him time to be far from the building when a fire broke out. But why set it at all? To further unsettle the building's residents and speed up the process of getting them to leave? And would he really have been so stupid as to put the fuel back where it would be linked to him? Wasn't it more likely that the actual arsonist picked a padlock and planted it there?

And why would Herbie bother terrorizing Viola Six in such a dramatic fashion? Could it have been one last lame-brained attempt to curry favor with the employer he had tried to blackmail? Maybe that was Herbie's version of logic.

There was something else, and he wanted to check it now.

When Maki had first met Leo Uberti, he had smelled something vegetal on him, something that reminded him of a house fire he'd investigated out by the fort. And when he examined Uberti's bathroom at the end of his interview with him, there had been those wet tennis shoes drying on the rim of the tub, their soles still saturated with sage.

Where would Uberti have been walking through sage? He couldn't picture it anywhere in town. What he was smelling was wild, uncultivated sage, a weed really, and it had been present in profusion near that burned house on the edge of town, next to the cemetery for the old fort. And Uberti had said he liked to visit the cemetery, because of its ungroomed quality, those interesting old slabs, and the way the nearby sheep reminded him of his childhood home in a village overlooking the Adriatic.

The late-afternoon sun warmed Maki's bare head as he walked slowly, across the bridge, to Pheasant Run. It was just after five. He texted Rhonda that he would be home by six.

As he approached the building, he saw Leo Uberti on his bicycle, rounding a corner to ride out of sight. *Not a good idea for the old guy to pick the going-home hour to join the traffic*, Maki thought.

Inside the building, he ducked under the yellow barrier and unlocked Herbie's apartment door. Most of the smoke smell had dissipated. The furniture and Herbie's personal items had been cleared out a few days after his body was found, but the cleaning company hadn't yet come to shampoo the rugs and do whatever else it needed to do.

Maki walked slowly through the carpeted, empty rooms. He slitted his eyes and summoned his nose. The hallway door opened on a short corridor. Through a door to the left was the kitchen. Straight ahead was the living room, with a short hall off it that led to the bedroom and bath. He started again at the hallway door, walked a few steps, and got down on his knees to sniff the carpet. He proceeded through the apartment in the same manner, finishing with the kitchen.

He stood and smiled. He'd learned what he had expected to learn. Only a very small area of the carpet that lay just beyond the hallway door smelled different from the rest. Its smell was absent in the living room, absent in the bedroom and the bedroom closet. The smell belonged to someone who had entered the apartment and turned immediately into the kitchen, and had never ventured into the rest of the place.

Leaving the unmistakable smell of sage.

He walked home in near-twilight. The solstice was just two weeks away, and then the days would begin to creep forward into greenness and light. A chill hit him, and he wished he'd worn his hat. The breeze had died down and the mountains were colored lavender and charcoal. Food smells came from several houses he passed, and the lights inside were soft and gold. The leaves of the maples had finally begun to let go, and he kicked at them like a kid as he walked briskly toward his little red house and Rhonda, down there at the end of the block.

In the distance he heard a sound, a thin wail, that he thought, at first, came from someone's TV. As he walked, it grew louder. It sounded pleading, mournful, unstinting. The lights in the little red house were not on. The sound was Sid.

Maki began to run.

February 23, 2020

23

Fourteen months later, and Maki still felt blindsided by the sight of Rhonda on her knees beside the couch, her upper body stretched onto it in supplication, Siddhartha frozen at her side, howling. Those headaches, those few short blip-outs, and the next day was her appointment to get it all checked out. But now, inside that beautiful curly-haired head, wreckage, a clot, and Rhonda gone from him forever.

Maki could scarcely remember the person he had felt himself to be before that discovery. He had lost the kind of life he had thought he was going to live out. He had been hollowed. He could no longer summon much interest in the puzzles of his profession. He had different eyes, and they felt very old.

He drove very slowly in the dark toward Pheasant Run, where he would briefly attend a gathering he dreaded in a muted sort of way. The residents had fashioned a tribute to Leo Uberti, who had been killed just a week after Rhonda's death when a florist's truck hit him on his bicycle near a downtown intersection. His estate had finally been settled, and Pheasant Run was the major beneficiary of a large life insurance payment, earmarked for the building's maintenance fund.

Maki didn't know why the residents wanted him there, except perhaps for his advice on fire-prevention upgrades, but he took it as a chance to put the place and its people behind him forever, linked as they were to Rhonda's evaporation.

He was accompanied by Sid, who pushed his head farther out the open passenger window as they approached Pheasant Run, then yawned hugely and shivered in an uninvested way.

Siddhartha, it occurred to Maki now, was the moral obverse of whatever entities might have hoped to acquire Pheasant Run on the cheap. After Herbie's death, Longleap Enterprises had relocated to someplace in the Sun Belt. And any interest the university might once have had seemed to flicker out with Clovis's abrupt departure. The Center for Ethics and the Digital Humanities was no longer on anyone's agenda, it seemed. The university had mentioned a financial reassessment.

Snow was falling now, in veils, falling and rising in the February night. Pheasant Run, just ahead, stood tall and bored and pale. The circular drive was lit, and human shapes moved behind the gauzy curtains of a big window on the ground floor.

Maki parked and lit another cigarette, then fished in the glove compartment for a meal-bone for Sid, who snapped it into his mouth and chewed with contemplative attention. When their small pleasures had been consumed, they both drew long breaths. Maki put Sid in the back seat atop a woolen poncho that smelled, still, of Rhonda.

He found that he couldn't move toward the building. The people inside were milling and clumping, and off to one side was something that looked like a long table topped with platters and bowls. There would be Crock-Pot meatballs, he guessed, and celery sticks and a sheet cake or two. He would be expected to greet and mingle. And then, he hoped, he could slip away and drive to the motel where he sometimes stayed when he couldn't bear to return in the empty night to his own small home.

His house was for sale, and Maki was investigating placements for the creatures—the mynah bird, the ancient turtle, the cat, and the glass snake. Sid he would keep because he sometimes couldn't imagine staying upright without the dog's steadiness. For more than a year, he had worked on automatic, going through the motions only. He had refused to talk further with Hanrahan about the Pheasant Run case, because he simply didn't care. Hanrahan ultimately told the residents that Herbie Bonebright, an unhinged loner, had regrettably been hired by Longleap without an adequate background check, and had very likely set the kitchen fire for reasons unknown.

He had completed the paperwork for his resignation as fire inspector, and had a meeting tomorrow with someone at the regional Forest Service office about openings that might be available for a seasonal fire lookout. He saw it clearly: A small wooden room on a mountaintop; good binoculars and a transmitting radio; empty, pine-smelling days and not another person except the supply guy with his pack mule, trudging upward on the first day of the month. Some books, just a few. Forested mountains sternly arranged between himself and the far curve of the earth. Bird sounds and chattery squirrels. A light and steady breeze rippling the treetops below. And below the trees, at the invisible bases of the mountains, on the valley floors littered with roads and houses, all the humans, going about their human business.

A fibrillating ache in his throat had intensified, but now he was sensing, also, the presence of a threat that had been sneaking around but hadn't, until now, fully announced itself.

The danger registered in the fine hairs of his ears. It wasn't the gluey pull of depression and loss, the familiar brute extraction of all feelings except itself. It wasn't his sense of banishment from all the humming little agendas and hopes of the healthy. It was, this new thing, some kind of unassailable information, which told him that the humming of the healthy was the equivalent of light from a long-dead star. It was flotsam, the detritus of something long and forever gone. Gone to him, at any rate. There was a trickle of terror in the idea, which he adamantly counteracted by conjuring the mundane. Had Sid gotten a drink of water before Maki put him in the car? Had he fed all the creatures at home? Had he made an appointment for the Volvo to get its oil changed?

He returned to the driver's seat and started the car, needing to mimic momentum, at least, before he was stuck indoors at the gathering. He was early anyway, so he could drive around for a few more minutes to try to uproot the tendrils of panic. He pointed the car down the empty street, gunning it a little. The bony branches of the tall maples arched overhead, creating a tunnel. Its floor was dusted with the light new snow and illuminated in vague, widely spaced circles by ineffectual streetlights. The dread stayed with him. He punched the wooden dashboard, hard, to banish it, then examined his knuckles and saw that he'd broken the skin, and, in the few moments that his eyes left the street, a large creature landed on the hood of his car, hooves aimed at the sky.

He slammed on the brakes and the Volvo lurched and sashayed as the animal flew off into the dark. He threw the car into park and ran to the unmoving thing. A deer, a doe, lay on her side and panted in a resigned way, like a spent marathoner. There was a long bloody scrape on her shoulder, but her legs looked unbroken. Her ears shivered. She raised her preposterous long eyelashes to look up at him. He touched her shoulder and she flinched.

The closest houses were dark; the street remained empty of moving vehicles. Somewhere a dog yipped metronomically. And then a woman in a long Cossack coat rounded a street corner and came to stand beside him. She wore glowing old-leather boots, and her straight black hair fell from beneath a beret. Her face was handsome, lightly lined. She said nothing, just sank into a graceful squat and placed the tips of her gloved fingers on the deer's neck as if feeling for a pulse. She closed her eyes.

Maki waited. Time elapsed. "What are you doing?" he finally asked.

"I'm trying to give her some energy," the woman said. "She needs energy for living, at this particular moment." Her voice was low and lovely. The trees had become walls and a roof. The smoky snow cavorted outside the fissures in those walls, and the space he and the woman occupied became extremely quiet. He could hear her light breathing, the rhythm and purpose of it.

The doe's right front hoof scraped at the scrim of snow. Some long moments passed. The woman hummed very softly, off-key. Maki felt a strange urge to sleep. The animal closed her eyes. Then she took a long shuddering breath, and in one fluid scramble was on her feet.

Maki backed away. The woman stood and stepped backward as well. The deer swayed her neck and head slowly, then flicked her tail and emitted a delicate, jagged sigh, the emissary of her rebounding breath. She took a few steps, scraped at the snow again. As if testing each movement, she slowly disappeared behind a dense black hedge.

They peered through the shrubbery and watched her gain momentum, lope across a large lawn, and leap a low fence on the other side.

"Oh, good," said the woman.

They faced each other, not knowing what to do or say next.

How long had it been since he hit the deer? Maki found it impossible to guess. He felt he'd stepped out of time altogether.

He extended his hand and she shook it. Then she gave him a slow, comradely pat on the forearm and set off down the sidewalk. He watched her turn the corner and go away.

He made his way shakily back to his car. His entire body buzzed. His big dog was asleep, his nose deep in the folds of Rhonda's poncho. Maki roused him and he clambered onto the curb, where he sniffed the air and gave two deep warning barks before climbing into the front seat. Maki drove slowly around the block and made for Pheasant Run. A block away, he yielded at an intersection for another car, resting his hand on Sid's haunch. Sid threw him a quick look and barked again. Not at the car. Not at scurrying danger. Not a warning this time, just pure canine eagerness for the next new thing.

And it was that bark, snatching at every pleasure to be retrieved from the wide dark beyond the headlights' reach, that Maki would later remember as the first small jolt of his long pivot in the direction, again, of *yes*, a *yes* that would persist in the face of all that was soon to come.

24

Inside Pheasant Run, there was a hum of voices coming from the large room off the modest lobby. There was a smell of Crock-Pot concoctions and sheet cakes. Sid lifted his head, nose quivering anxiously. Maki, too, felt bombarded by the complexity of the odors coming at him. Beyond the food, beyond that mélange of sauced beef and baked sugar and the cool vegetal presence of chopped carrots and celery for dipping, the human smells trickled forward in thready and intersecting vapors. Someone wore a cologne that had been Maki's grandmother's in the previous century. A woolen suit, somewhere behind him, had been retrieved from a closet containing mothballs. And the candles on the tables, he saw, were battery powered. The absent smell of pooling wax was palpable. This was a relatively recent turn in Maki's hyperosmia: he could smell, with acuity, what should have been there and wasn't. His olfactory sensitivity had become so intimately intertwined with memory that the smell of a remembered presence arrived in tandem with the smell of its absence.

Maki had changed his mind about leaving Sid in the car because a number of the building's residents knew and liked him. He did have to watch him, though, as his size and amiability made him something of a hazard for the bird-boned. Just yesterday the dog had leaned affectionately against a wizened octogenarian in the Albertsons parking lot, tipping him softly into the row of emptied carts. The man flailed but didn't fall, and appeared to shake it off. Then his adrenaline kicked in and he informed Maki, in a plaintive shout, that his dog was a walking death trap. Maki had a brief urge to respond that the man's age and frailty made him his own death trap, but he summoned a little empathy and apologized, while Sid fastidiously sniffed the man's shoes.

There were several dozen people in the room, most of them quite old and looking, in their dress clothes, like extras in a country-house drama. Several, however, had invited grandchildren or nieces and nephews, and the young ones were huddled in a corner giggling at something one of them had summoned on his phone.

Mavis Krepps, the president of the condominium owners' association, usually wore a sturdy knit pantsuit in a neutral color. Tonight she billowed forth in a long shiny skirt and a poet's blouse, her reading glasses dangling from thin rhinestone ropes. She greeted Maki in her deep lecturer's voice and begged him to shake the snow off his jacket before it melted through and soaked him to the bone.

"You're hurt!" she said when she saw the blood on his jacket sleeve.

He noticed for the first time an oblong splotch of the deer's blood.

"I'm late," he said. "I hit a deer and had to see if it was going to be all right. A doe. She had a big scrape on her shoulder and just lay there for a while, then sprang away."

"But you're all right, too, yes?" Mrs. Krepps asked.

For a long moment, Maki couldn't make himself say anything. He blinked back a ridiculous film of tears and nodded.

Mrs. Krepps grew brisk and urged him to eat, to mingle.

Sid ambled across the room and lay down at the feet of Viola Six and Cassie McMackin, who sat on a striped settee. Viola waved Maki over. She wanted to tell him about how she planned to incorporate her abduction by Herbie into a memoir she'd been working on for years. It would, she said, give her account the "fizz" she felt had been missing, and she'd already signed up for a local writers' conference to "try out" some excerpts on truly discerning readers.

Because of the dog at their feet, she couldn't rise to tell him more, so he reached over and shook her soft and bony hand, and that of Cassie as well. The room felt very hot.

Cassie smiled at Maki. Since the day he met her, Maki had felt in her presence something akin to infatuation. Though it had drastically receded in the wake of Rhonda's death, as all his feelings had in a dark rush, he could still remember it and approve of his discernment. She had the lovely facial structure and lit-up smile of a true beauty, though the beginnings of a dowager's hump and the arthritic nodules on her delicate long fingers confirmed that she was well into her eighties. But it was more, far more, than the way she looked. Avidity. That was all he had been able to come up with. Though he knew she was basically alone—that she'd lost both her only child and her husband—she seemed to have retained a remarkable level of interest in the peculiarities of human behavior, the human life span, the physical universe.

He and she had several long conversations immediately after the fire in Herbie's apartment, and a single long one just two weeks after Rhonda's death. Shattered, he had blamed himself for not recognizing the precursor ministrokes; for spending a full hour in Herbie's apartment before he walked slowly home that terrible day, lingering for a while by the river. He had come by to tell her he was finished with the investigation, satisfied that he'd taken it as far as it could go, and he'd appreciate it if she told the others. She listened, agreed to do that, and said nothing else. When she said goodbye, he felt he was leaving someone who knew something he never would about the secret of ongoingness.

At one end of the settee, a modest memorial had been assembled for Leo Uberti. There was a blurry photo of him, white hair springing from the bottom of his stocking cap, squinting into the sun. It leaned against a painting that rested in an easel.

"Beautiful, I think," said Cassie, as Maki studied the painting.

"What is it supposed to be?" he asked.

"I don't know," she said. "What it's supposed to be might be the least of it."

The painting foregrounded a window, fogged and seeping with rain. It was beautifully and precisely watery, so that the window seemed both alight and obscuring. Beyond it were the vague shapes of a white streetlight and a large tree with brown leaves. The composition directed the eye to the space between their tallnesses. In it floated three blurred images: a ship, a young woman's face, and a candle alight. Across the bottom was a line of tiny rough letters: "Don't tell me about time; it is all now."

Cassie told Maki that there had been much discussion in the building about what Leo meant to convey in the painting. Most of the residents knew the outlines of his experience on the Italian ship and his time interned on the edge of town. But who was the young woman? And why a burning candle?

Maki knew the answer to the last question, and he also knew, quite suddenly, that he was never going to share it with anyone at Pheasant Run. He had explained some of the technical details that suggested arson, but they never had to know that their gentle and courtly neighbor had been the one to set it. That could remain a mystery. The world was full of mysteries.

Leo's mistake in setting the fire was one that he couldn't have known he was making. He had worn shoes that carried on their bottoms a smell that was unique to him and that was not evident anywhere in Herbie's apartment except that short strip of carpet between the hallway door and the kitchen. Maki remembered the sound of Leo's voice when he mentioned Herbie, the restrained vehemence in it, and it seemed reasonable to conclude that the arsonist's motive was simply to get Herbie fired. Get him gone.

He had used Coleman fuel because it was an accelerant that would not have been immediately tied to a painter, the way turpentine and other thinners would. Maybe it was something he'd kept in his own storage unit, long after any camp-stove days. And he had placed the container in Herbie's storage unit as a kind of joke, Maki supposed. Certainly Leo seemed the kind of person who would know how to pick a lock.

Leo must have known that he was quite ill, and must have known as well that he could not go to a doctor for a diagnosis, not if he wanted to renew his term life insurance policy for the last time. And when he found out that Herbie was dead and that the condo association had voted unanimously to cancel all ties with Longleap and reject any buyout offer, he knew it was time to act. And so one day he unchained his old Schwinn and set out along the streets, knowing he wouldn't chain it up again. Maki felt quite sure about that.

He had specified in a recent handwritten, notarized will that proceeds from his estate—which turned out to be handsome—were to be applied to pressing maintenance issues at Pheasant Run, including fire-danger mitigation measures, and to structural improvements that would allow the building's residents to use a large grassy area behind the building.

The insurance company tried for months to fight the award, arguing that Leo had seemed to ride directly into the path of the flower truck, and that the case was a probable suicide, making any benefits moot. But a hardworking rookie investigator for the police discovered during a second interview with the truck driver that he hadn't slept for twenty hours at the time of the crash and had been texting his estranged boyfriend virtually nonstop, the last text coinciding almost to the minute with his unsuccessful swerve to avoid Leo.

The grassy space was the ceiling of Pheasant Run's underground parking garage, and structural engineers had long ago pronounced it not weight-worthy. No one was supposed to walk on it, much less place lawn furniture there or in any way use it as a public space. So it stared back at them, green and blank, when they looked out their windows or sat cramped on their tiny concrete balconies, a parody, a virtual vision, of a grassy park. All that was soon to change.

Now the basement area would be suitably buttressed, thanks to Leo Umberto's largesse. *He taketh away and he giveth*, Maki thought. *And that's the short and long of it.* Next to the photograph of Leo, someone had placed a potted yellow chrysanthemum with a miniature plastic bicycle stuck into the soil.

The wind had picked up—light snow had turned to a full blizzard—and the windows in the room rattled. February this year felt like a return to the real winter that had been so eerily in abeyance last year, and it was a relief. Maki was suddenly exhausted. He beckoned Sid to his side and began to make his apologies for leaving.

Across the room, someone at the door caught Mrs. Krepps's eye, and she buoyantly waved her inside. Maki blinked hard. The woman's hat and her long coat were heavily dusted with snow. She had clearly continued to walk after the deer disappeared. *A pale ghost*, Maki thought.

Mrs. Krepps introduced the woman in the long coat as Tessa Whetstone, the newest resident of Pheasant Run and "the very youngest." She was not subject to the over-sixty-five rule because she was caring for her great-aunt, Mrs. Rideout, in #115.

"We're so pleased she is here," Mrs. Krepps said, and invited Maki to stay just a little longer.

25

Perhaps a dozen people still occupied the room, which had taken on a low glow because the overhead fluorescents had been turned off in favor of table lamps alone. A few who were preparing to leave made final, slow passes to say good night, to take another look at the Leo shrine, to give Sid a pat on the head and their fellow tenants pats on their backs, a kiss on a cheek. A number of women had gathered around the food table to pick up the remains of the dishes they'd brought, and to make dinner plates for those in the building who had felt too old or weak or disinclined to leave their rooms.

One of them, Mrs. Rideout, had recently returned from a cruise that took her to picturesque ports along the coast of Mexico, and she had come down with a particularly concerning cough, and now, according to her niece Tessa, a fever.

There was a brief discussion about what to do if the recipients didn't answer the knocks at their doors because they were asleep or too deaf to hear them, and the consensus was that the bearers of the food, in those cases, would wrap it up and keep it in their own refrigerators overnight, to be offered again the next day.

Snow was falling in heavy waves, making the night beyond the large sheer-curtained windows silver and dark, in motion, indecipherable. Sprays of frozen moisture hit the window like fine gravel, and the wind moaned and huffed. Even those residents who drove cars would be changing their minds about going anywhere at all the next day, even to the nearby grocery for a few Lean Cuisines and a quart of milk. It was the sort of enveloping storm that had the effect of making it difficult to imagine easy locomotion on dry pathways, sun, the trill of a bird.

Cassie McMackin listened to the storm and tried to think about a summer day and herself in a lawn chair on the grassy green commons. About her would be her little mountain city in the light of June, the trees looking so drenched and pleased, the mountains vaulting toward the horizons. Yes, it might happen that she would be present. The thought gave her a small start, as it seemed to confirm that she had decided, absolutely, against a new date for a self-imposed exit.

At first, she had put it off because she wanted to find out what had happened to Viola Six and Herbie Bonebright. Then she had become curious about the cause of the fire, and the motive for it, and what the intimations of some larger potential crime would yield. And then she had come to know Lander Maki and Clayton Spooner, and it was only then that her pills, that stash in her printer, had come to seem silly, and worse.

So yes, she might be present when summer rolled around. And, equally likely, she might not. Because that was one of the quiet dramas of old age: ordinary-sounding expectations could not be treated as assumptions when you were in your eighties. Eleven residents had died since she moved into Pheasant Run, four of them somewhat precipitously, all of them well past their threescore and ten. "And if by reason of strength they be fourscore years, yet is their strength labor and sorrow; for it is soon cut off, and we fly away."

We fly away. She looked around her at the old lined faces, at the long table, soon to be clear of everything but its long white cloth.

Almost everyone had worn going-to-church clothes, pressed and decorous. She knew it would have taken some of them most of the day to get their clothes in order, get themselves clean if not showered, make a dish to bring and share, fasten a circle pin to a sweater. The world outside this world was cold, snowy, restless. But today it was well past the solstice, and the season would climb, now, toward thawing and light.

It's all borders, she thought. *All the way, all the time.*

Gone from the gathering now was Tessa Whetstone, the newest resident of Pheasant Run, who had talked for some time with Maki. They stood near the food table, and when Cassie helped herself to another sugar cookie, she caught shards of their conversation. It seemed to be about Maki's plans to quit his inspector's job and move to a fire lookout come summer. Tessa wanted details of the lookout—where it might be, how far it was from any other people, the attraction of a place that seemed the ultimate in solitude. Her voice was lovely, soothing. The questions were surrounded by a lot of room. Maki seemed to be weighing what she said, what she asked.

When she left to go to her great-aunt, worried about the new fever, Maki walked her to the elevator and Cassie watched them. They shook hands gravely. Tessa's hair, dark auburn in an old-fashioned twist, gleamed as she inclined her head.

Now, across the emptying room, Maki studied Leo's painting. He stood by himself, head tilted slightly to one side. He had acquired a stoop in the past year, as if he'd sustained a blow to his sternum. His hand rested on the head of his tall and patient dog.

He seemed to be listening to the painting in addition to seeing it. His head made minute adjustments as if to catch what was coming at him through the air. But when his nose twitched, minutely, Cassie saw that he was smelling, as well. Smelling now or remembering a smell.

From the first time she'd met him, she sensed (why, she wasn't sure) that he might be someone who shifted constantly between thought and memory, present and past, the past being incorporated always in a hybrid present that anticipated the future. Maybe it all stemmed from the conversation they'd had once about his fire-investigation methods, in which he had so memorably described the necessity of mentally reconstituting what the fire might have destroyed. Only when that very pragmatic act of the imagination had occurred could speculations begin about how the former presences had been removed. His olfactory gifts, he'd told her, were key to his successes.

She thought about the lonely male birds of Chernobyl

calling, calling for the absent females, responding so ardently to the before but unable to know how it had been taken away.

Leo's painting certainly encouraged a sense of blended time, or, more accurately perhaps, a sense that memory is as real as the present-time portals to it, in Leo's case that rain-smeared window, beyond which existed the streetlight, the tree, the ship, the face, the candle. Perhaps, for Maki, his young, gone wife remained as present to him as whatever, in the day at hand, could conjure her. She hoped that might be the case.

She wanted to walk over to him and place an arm around his waist, in solidarity. She wanted to rest her head against his shoulder, his chest, the way she had loved to rest against Neil. But, of course, that was inappropriate, would be misunderstood.

A few weeks earlier, walking under her umbrella in the almost-sleet rain, Cassie had passed a young couple who made her happy simply by their presence. The boy: thick red-brown hair combed forward to frame his face under a backward baseball cap. And that face: dark eyebrows, dark eyes, smooth-skinned with an olive cast, but, no, it wasn't so much the face itself (and his beautiful loping walk, smooth calves under long shorts) but his expression as he looked at the girl beside him (also slim and young and in some way physically perfect, their bodies still children's bodies, smooth and light and springy, but on the verge, on the very verge…).

Inexplicably, she wore gray mouse ears on a headband and painted-on mouse whiskers, done with a light touch, and she was a little taller than the boy and talked in an animated and happy fashion. And the boy? Lit up with interest and bliss and hope. Lit up.

She hadn't seen Clayton Spooner lately, but he stopped by every now and then, and he'd told her during his last visit that he was in "a better place." He and Raven had started a dog-walking business that was doing surprisingly well, and both of them had transferred to the alternative high school, where they hoped to focus on subjects that interested them, not people who judged them or tormented them in random fashions. Clayton thought he might become a "veteran," because of his newfound affinity for dogs, and Cassie didn't have the heart to correct him.

Never had either Cassie or Clayton mentioned her confiscation of the gun, though Cassie opened her apartment door one morning to find the brass elephant she'd put in his backpack to replace it.

All she wanted, finally, for Clayton Spooner was that his path forward take him far beyond the troubles that had dropped him into her life. Beyond any fists and phone threats and weeping mothers. Beyond the clashing drugs, the sleepy and terrified brain, the craving for vengeance and for attention, for love. Beyond, maybe, eventually, the fiercely inscribed bird-girl with the ancient kohl-rimmed eyes.

Cassie turned out the last table lamp and sat on the settee in the dark. Maki had been the last to leave. The snow had lightened to a granular haze, and she watched his car, low and running, at the curb. Exhaust vapors climbed lazily into the trees. Sid had his head out the open passenger window, and his breath, too, was visible in the frigid air. Maki smoked a cigarette and flicked it out his own open window. His headlights were on and they arrowed fuzzily into the dark. It all seemed to swirl and exhale, as if the car and its occupants might levitate or vanish.

Watching him, she felt she was witnessing a decision on his part. She guessed that it involved the fire lookout plan, and that he might be altering or abandoning it. Just a guess.

She closed her eyes and lifted a hand to let it drift. It came to rest in her lap. She was as vaporous as Maki and his big dog. *I sit here,* she thought, *on a winter's eve that caps a year of events no one could have divined: arson and abduction, premature death, a too-convenient accident, perhaps a murder. And beneath those shocks, a rising undercurrent of plain old venality, runaway greed, and a willingness to visit it upon those most easily damaged by it.*

And yet here we are, still, in our fair house. My old neighbors above my head are removing their good clothes and propping their aching feet. They are taking their pills, their countdown markers, finding sleep, or seeking it. Suspended in white air between sky and ground, they are rounding the last lap.

The table with its long white cloth glowed faintly in the dark room. Maki's car engaged and pulled away. Cassie listened to the whispered thoughts of all her neighbors, and, beyond the wall, the snow crystals colliding, the night animals murmuring. They sounded restless, agitated, prescient.

She heard the earth's battered but stalwart heartbeat shaking the branches of the winter trees, shaking them hard, as if the last leaves had reappeared and, once again, refused to fall.

ACKNOWLEDGMENTS

my thanks and appreciation go to:

Sarah Chalfant, my gifted and constant agent

Daniel Slager, who welcomed this book
and saw what it needed

Connie Poten, perceptive reader, dearest of friends

Lee Oglesby, Joanna Demkiewicz, Mary Austin Speaker,
Claire Laine, and the entire, exceptional
Milkweed community

Dana Boussard, for her haunting cover image
and her friendship of many years

Bob Rajala, fire expert (any factual errors are my own)

Carol Van Valkenburg, for her impressively researched
*An Alien Place: The Fort Missoula, Montana,
Detention Camp 1941-44*

April Bernard for the line about time
at the bottom of Leo's painting, borrowed from
the opening to her lovely poem "Wheeling"

Lois Welch for permission to use the passage
about the return of the blackhorns
from James Welch's *Fools Crow*

The faculty, students and staff of the Bennington
Writing Seminars, for support, inspiration
and enjoyment